DEATH COMES TO DURHAM

Also by Jeanne M. Dams from Severn House

The Dorothy Martin mysteries

A DARK AND STORMY NIGHT
THE EVIL THAT MEN DO
THE CORPSE OF ST JAMES'S
MURDER AT THE CASTLE
SHADOWS OF DEATH
DAY OF VENGEANCE
THE GENTLE ART OF MURDER
BLOOD WILL TELL
SMILE AND BE A VILLAIN
THE MISSING MASTERPIECE
CRISIS AT THE CATHEDRAL
A DAGGER BEFORE ME
DEATH IN THE GARDEN CITY

DEATH COMES TO DURHAM

Jeanne M. Dams

severn
House

This first world edition published 2020
in Great Britain and the USA by
SEVERN HOUSE PUBLISHERS LTD of
Eardley House, 4 Uxbridge Street, London W8 7SY.
Trade paperback edition first published
in Great Britain and the USA 2021 by
SEVERN HOUSE PUBLISHERS LTD.

British Library Cataloguing in Publication Data
A CIP catalogue record for this title is available from the British Library.

ISBN-13: 978-0-7278-8925-6 (cased)
ISBN-13: 978-1-78029-713-2 (trade paper)
ISBN-13: 978-1-4483-0434-9 (e-book)

All Severn House titles are printed on acid-free paper.

Severn House Publishers support the Forest Stewardship Council™ [FSC™],
the leading international forest certification organisation.
All our titles that are printed on FSC certified paper carry the FSC logo.

Typeset by Palimpsest Book Production Ltd.,
Falkirk, Stirlingshire, Scotland.
Printed and bound in Great Britain by
TJ International, Padstow, Cornwall.

AUTHOR'S NOTE

Nancy Reagan called it The Long Goodbye: the terrible and heartbreaking condition of dementia. It may not be, for the victim, the cruellest disease. We don't know what goes on in the minds and hearts of the afflicted. But for those who love them, it is surely devastating.

I have a dear friend named Sylvia, once brilliant, funny, and compassionate. She's gone now. Her body lives on, but her personality, her very self, has been taken over by the disease. My favourite cousin Dorothy (for whom my protagonist was named) never knew about the book I'd written in her honour, though she didn't die for some years after its publication. Sylvia and Dorothy were the inspiration for this story, and to Sylvia and her husband Ed (whom she no longer recognizes), this book is dedicated.

The city of Durham is much as I have described it, though I've exercised the authorial privilege of changing many details to suit my purposes, and inventing others. I hope I haven't named any of my unpleasant people or places after real people and places; if I have, it was totally unintended. In particular, those familiar with Durham University may recognize that the physical setting of the college I have named St Jude's is very similar to that of the real St John's. The reader is assured that St Jude's does not in any other way resemble St John's.

Finally, I owe to Susan Lowe a debt I can never repay. A resident of Durham and connected with Durham University, she not only arranged accommodation for me at the castle, but acted as my guide throughout my time there, took me to fascinating places I would never otherwise have known about, answered endless questions about tiny details, and even agreed to read the very raw manuscript and point out my mistakes. (Those that remain are, of course, due to my carelessness.) Thank you, Susan!

ONE

'Alan, I'm tired, and my feet hurt. And I need to find a loo.'

My husband, who had forged ahead, looked back and quirked an eyebrow. 'Ah. Tea, or a pint?'

I pulled off my hat and wiped my brow. 'Can you ask?'

It shouldn't have been hot. Durham is in the far north of England, nearly to the Scottish border. In late April the weather should have been cool and rainy. I'd packed with that in mind. Instead, the sun shone brightly and the temperature soared to the high sixties, which, in England, almost qualifies as a heatwave. (They use Celsius instead of Fahrenheit, but my American mind converts to what I still think of as the 'real' setting.)

We were wandering the streets of the ancient city (cobbled – see sore feet, above), because an old crony of Alan's had invited us for a visit. They'd known each other years ago when they both served in the police force in Cornwall. Alan had moved on, rising to the rank of chief constable in the county of Belleshire, which is where I met him one Christmas Eve. I was newly widowed and feeling very sorry for myself, a stranger in a strange land, wondering why on earth I'd moved from my lifelong home in Indiana to England. Alan, a widower, healed my mood rapidly, and we were married about a year later.

David Tregarth had remained in the village of Newlyn for a while, but had also risen in rank and moved to Exeter, where he'd retired after a distinguished career. When he'd lost his wife, family connections had sent him far away to Durham, an ancient cathedral city with a renowned university. When he'd written to Alan, he sounded a bit forlorn. 'Lonely,' Alan mused as we walked. 'Missing his home. The north is a long way from Cornwall, and not just geographically. Different terrain, different accent, different mindset. And he doesn't have enough to do. That granddaughter of his takes good care of him, maybe too good. He never has to lift a finger. That's not good for an active man his age.'

'Could he afford to live somewhere else?'

'I'd think so, even though housing here isn't cheap. He was always a thrifty, saving sort of chap. Here's a pub that looks pleasant.'

'I've never had David's sort of problems,' he continued after he'd brought me my pint. 'You've kept me from loneliness, and kept me busy.'

'We've both kept busy. Cheers.' I sipped, glad to sit and rest, and thought about our life together the past few years. A surprising amount of crime had come our way, as people in Sherebury and elsewhere had begun to trust us to solve some knotty problems. My penchant for detective fiction, and my natural nosiness, matched well with Alan's trained policing skills. Yes, we'd had plenty to occupy our time. And of course two autocratic cats and a large dog had also made their demands. 'I wonder how the animals are?'

'I thought you'd be thinking about them. Three days is about your limit before you start to worry, and we're over that. You know they're being thoroughly spoilt. Jane treats them like her own children.'

'Jane is a jewel. I don't know how she keeps up with her own dogs and our menagerie, at her age.' Our next-door neighbour Jane was certainly well into her eighties, though no one was ever so impertinent as to ask. We could guess, though, because she'd taught generations of Sherebury kids before finally retiring, and they still came to see her, with their children and grandchildren.

'If she ever slows down it'll be the death of her. She'll end up like David, twiddling her thumbs and fading away.'

'Well, he's shown no signs of fading away these past few days. Goodness, he's kept us on the run. I've seen more castles and churches than I knew existed. I'm actually glad to have a day to ourselves. If only there were fewer cobblestones and hills!'

Durham is a city built on hills. The heart of the city, the cathedral and the castle, is atop a hill, with a sharp curve of the River Wear on three sides. The castle in such a location was easily defensible against raids from the Scots, and is, in fact, the only Norman castle never to have been breached. This I had learned from reading tourist brochures, and given the number of ruined castles we had seen lately, I found the fact impressive.

The cathedral is also impressive, in a different way. I love cathedrals, and I think ours in Sherebury is the most beautiful in the world. It's late Gothic, my preferred style. But Durham, almost pure Norman, is remarkable. It, along with the castle, was completed in the early twelfth century, and has suffered little destruction over the ages. There is a purity and cohesiveness about it that many other ancient churches lack. 'I feel at home there,' I remarked, and Alan, for once, had not followed my train of thought. He raised his eyebrows. 'In the cathedral. It feels friendly. Maybe we could go to evensong later?'

'Sounds like a good idea to me. Meanwhile I'm getting peckish. Pub lunch?'

After lunch we repaired back to the castle for a nap. If that sounds odd, I should explain that after centuries serving as the residence of Durham's prince-bishops, the castle was purchased in the 1800s by the newly formed University of Durham to house its first college. Various parts of the extensive complex of buildings were modernized and adapted for use as student housing, and, when the students are on holiday, their housing becomes a B&B for visitors. So there we were, staying in a somewhat inconvenient room up a great many stairs, with ancient battlements directly outside our window, and eating our breakfasts in a breathtaking Great Hall with a three-story-high stained glass window. The Hilton was never like this.

By the time we woke, the weather, in tried-and-true English fashion, had changed dramatically. Clouds had rolled in, along with a gusty wind, and rain threatened at any moment. It was far too early for the five-fifteen evensong, but if we delayed we ran the risk of getting drenched.

'We could tour the cathedral,' I suggested half-heartedly.

'The last tour of the day just left. And we've already explored it rather thoroughly.'

'Drat. I wish we had our car and could go somewhere.' We had chosen to take the train to Durham, as parking was limited in the city, and driving on the peninsula, where castle and cathedral are situated, incurred a congestion fee which could mount up. So far David had driven us everywhere, but David was today paying a duty visit to a very old great-aunt at a nursing home outside the city. She didn't always know him, but he was scrupulous about seeing her regularly. He planned to take us to dinner when he got back, dinner at a lovely hotel.

I yawned. 'Maybe tea at the cathedral café?'

'I'm not very hungry. And in any case, they stopped serving at four.'

I looked at the bedside clock, sighed and got up to make us a pot of tea.

Alan's phone warbled as I was rinsing our cups out at the bathroom sink, and I could hear very little of his end of the conversation over the sound of running water.

I came out to find him sitting on the bed, frowning and running a hand down the back of his head, his habit when thinking hard. 'What's wrong?'

'We won't be having that fine dinner tonight. That was David on the phone. Something unfortunate has happened at the nursing home.'

'Oh, dear. One of the residents gone missing?'

'Far worse than that. One of the residents found dead. David couldn't say very much on the phone, but from what he carefully didn't say, I gather it looks like murder, and everyone's in a flat spin.'

I raised my eyes to heaven. 'Full cover-up mode? "We can't let this get out, we have a good reputation, it's probably just an accident, we can't call in the police, can't you deal with it, Mr Tregarth?" Right?'

'More or less. Somewhat more subtly expressed, I gather, but that's the gist. David isn't a bit happy about it, and I doubt he'll go along with their wishes, but he can hardly just leave them to their fate. Which means we're on our own for an evening meal. David did mention a Lebanese place about halfway down the street to the market square. He says it's quite good.'

'I'm not in the mood for Lebanese. What are the other options?'

'He didn't list any. I'm sure there are any number of small restaurants in the area, probably good and reasonably priced. The students would keep them going even if there were no other clientele. The trouble is we don't know where they are.'

'And I don't feel like wandering around in the rain looking for them. Look, it's getting on toward five. Why don't we meander over to evensong? Maybe we can ask someone there about a good place to eat.'

We very much enjoyed the service. An English cathedral choir, singing in the magnificent acoustic of ancient stone walls, is the nearest to heaven I expect to come for some years yet, and the words of the service are calming and soothing. But most of the attendees were tourists like us, and no one had any ideas about restaurants.

We stood and looked at each other as the church emptied. A verger was standing at the door, ready to lock up for the night. We had to make up our minds and go somewhere.

The rain had stopped, or had paused, at least. A little watery sunshine was making the wet paving stones glisten. I was glad to hold Alan's arm as we made our way back to the castle next door.

Alan grinned at me. 'Are you starving?'

'Not really, no. That was a very filling lunch we had.'

'Then why don't we just walk down to Tesco's and pick up some sandwiches or salads or something? If we had a micro-wave we could get a couple of ready meals, but we don't. I'm sure we can find sustenance in one form or another.'

The evening having turned pleasant, we enjoyed the walk, though the steep hills were challenging, with wet, slippery pavements and cobbles. We found quite enough portable food and brought it back to the courtyard of the castle, where we wiped the rain off a table and benches and sat down to enjoy our impromptu picnic.

We were polishing off a second glass of some cheap wine we'd found when Alan's phone rang again. *David*, he mouthed at me, and put the call on speaker.

David was full of apologies for his failure as host, and hoped we'd found a decent meal somewhere.

'Not your fault, and we managed splendidly,' Alan assured him.

'I do feel terribly negligent, but I'll make it up to you. The thing is . . . this is all turning madly complicated. I'd like to talk it all over with both of you, and I'd just as soon my family didn't hear. I could be there in about twenty minutes, if that would suit you?'

'Of course,' we both replied. 'We'll meet you at the entrance to our tower to let you in; there's a coded lock. You sound really worried, David,' I added. 'Are you all right?'

'Yes and no. I'm considerably distressed. You see . . .' He paused for a moment. 'The . . . er . . . matter we discussed did turn out to be the crime we mentioned. And the principal suspect, at least for now, is Great-aunt Amanda.'

TWO

Our room wasn't really big enough for three, but we made do, Alan sitting on the bed and David and I on the chairs at the minute table. David had brought a bottle of Alan's favourite whisky, Glenfiddich, and I had the remains of the bottle of wine; we rinsed out our tooth glasses and one coffee cup and passed around the small packet of crisps we had left over from our supper. Raising his glass in a silent toast, David began.

'I'll try to make this coherent, but there are so many strands to the story, I hardly know where to begin.'

'Try the news format,' I suggested. 'Who, what, when, where, why.'

'The who part is easy. The victim is Blake Armstrong, a man in his mid-sixties. I didn't ask his exact age; that's not important just now. He was a semi-retired doctor in private practice in Durham, specializing in geriatrics. He had admitted himself to the nursing home a week or so ago, claiming exhaustion and the need for a complete rest.'

Alan raised his eyebrows. '"Claiming"?'

'Truthfully, so far as I know, but I thought I heard a hint of scepticism in the director's voice when he said that. But Dr Armstrong is – was – a wealthy man, and sent several of his patients to the home, so they accepted what he said.'

Alan nodded a 'go on'.

'He was a popular resident, mingling well with the others, even those who, like Aunt Amanda, have limited cognitive skills.'

'Ah, yes, Aunt Amanda.' Alan leaned forward, listening intently.

'Great-aunt, actually, but I usually call her Aunt. My grand-mother's sister, and nearly a hundred. You know my mother hailed from these parts, but no one of her mother's generation is still living, save Amanda, who was the youngest of her

family, actually not much older than my mother. She was once
a lively, funny person, and she's still sweet, even though she's
almost completely gaga. Many victims of dementia get crabby
and impossible to live with as their disease gradually destroys
their brain. Not Amanda. She's always very glad to see me,
always welcoming, even though I know she hasn't the slightest
idea who I am. We can't have much of a conversation
anymore, as her memory won't hold from one sentence to the
next. She never married, so I'm really the only one left. She
asks me about the family, and I tell her comforting lies, and
the next moment she asks the same question, and I answer.'

His voice broke and he sipped at his drink.

'Oh, David, that's so hard! I do think Alzheimer's is one
of the cruellest of diseases, taking away those we love a little
at a time while their bodies sometimes live on for a long time.
I remember a cousin of mine, back in Indiana . . .' I rambled
on for long enough for David to regain his composure.

'Yes, well.' He put down his glass. 'That's Aunt Amanda.
She had become a friend of Dr Armstrong. She was heart-
broken, for a moment or two, to hear of his death.'

'Yes, now we're coming to it.' Alan sounded like a
policeman. 'What can you tell us about his death?'

'Very little. No one knows exactly when it happened. He
was discovered mid-afternoon and had been dead long enough
for rigor to begin in the hands and fingers.'

'And that means – how long?' I asked.

Alan and David exchanged a grim smile. 'Dorothy, love,
rigor is one of the most variable of post-mortem changes.
Anything can affect it: room temperature, medications the
victim has been taking, the means of death – dozens of things.
That's why the police always try not to introduce it in court
as evidence. If one medical man says one thing as prosecution
witness, the doctor hired by the defence will say something
quite different. But at a rough guess, perhaps three to four
hours, wouldn't you say, David?'

'About that. But as you say . . .' He lifted his arms in a
large shrug. 'Useless for all practical purposes. It would be
nice if we could use time of death to eliminate possible
suspects, but we can't. It would be hard even if we could pin

down the time to the minute.' He sighed and leaned back in his chair. 'You have to understand the sort of home this is. It's small, for one thing, and is not run according to rigid rules. There are only about a dozen residents, and they're not held to any set schedule. No herding from one place to another. Meals are served individually, when the resident wants to eat, within reasonable limits. There is a dining room, and anyone who wants can eat there, but they can also eat in their rooms if they prefer, alone or with a friend, as they like.'

I frowned. 'Activities? Meds? There must surely be some plan for the day.'

'There are many things to keep residents' minds busy, but on their own schedules. There are plenty of games available for those who wish to play, and a fine library for those who wish to read. Television, of course. Some of the residents have been active gardeners; a plot of fertile soil has been set aside for those who still wish to potter about in a garden, and tools of every sort are available. As for medications, of course they must be given at regular intervals, but again, flexibility is allowed. The home doesn't accept patients who require close and careful nursing. There are other institutions for that. The Milton Home is designed for elderly people with very few medical problems, but with varying degrees of dementia. It's meant to be a place where they can live out their lives safely and peacefully in as homelike an atmosphere as possible.'

'So long,' I sniped, 'as they have plenty of money.'

Alan frowned at me, but David gave me a rueful smile. 'Yes, it is extremely expensive. The families of the residents expect the very best treatment for their relations. That's why this murder is such a huge disaster, and not just for the victim.'

'But how on earth does your aunt figure in all this? She sounds like a sweet lady, not at all the murderous type. And the dead man was a friend.'

'You may well ask, Dorothy. They have lighted on her for two reasons, neither very creditable. She was, as you say, a good friend of the victim. And before you say that makes her even less likely, you need to know that they had a bad quarrel yesterday. No one seems to have heard enough to know what it was about, but she was visiting in his room, and he was heard shouting at her. She left sobbing, and cried for some time in one of the common rooms before a nurse could persuade her back to her own room. That incident has left the management with the impression that she had a grudge against him.'

'And what does Aunt Amanda say about that?' There was an odd edge to Alan's voice.

'As I think you've guessed, Alan, she has no memory of the episode. When the man's name is mentioned, she smiles and gets up to go and see him. When she's told she can't because he's dead, she is hearing it for the first time. Every time. It's . . . heartbreaking.' David had to clear his throat and look away for a moment.

'May God preserve me from ever losing my mind!' I said fervently. 'I'd rather lose my limbs, my eyesight, anything, so long as my mind still functions.'

'I agree,' said Alan, reaching for my hand. 'Unfortunately, it isn't our choice to make. In many ways I'm glad my Helen died young, before either of us had to go through that ordeal. But David, you said there was another reason why the bigwigs are trying to blame Amanda.'

'This one is even worse, as cold-blooded as a motive can be. Of all the residents, Amanda has slid the furthest down the damnable slope of Alzheimer's. She is the least able to defend herself. It's easy to make her the scapegoat.'

'That's – that's unforgiveable!' I thumped my glass down on the table. 'And besides, surely someone in her condition could never be convicted of a crime? Why, she couldn't even testify in court!'

'Yes, you're right, of course. She would be deemed incapable of standing trial. Probably, lacking any admissible evidence to decide that matter either way, the case would be dismissed. Aunt Amanda would be condemned in the court of public opinion and allowed to go on peacefully living as she has been, without her good friend.'

'And all the other residents, the ones who still have memories anyway, would treat her like a pariah. Some happy, peaceful atmosphere!' I glared at David.

'Dorothy, love, don't shoot the messenger.' Alan turned to his friend. 'I gather you think there's some way we could help with all this.'

'You're on holiday, and I hate to ask. But you've both worked on some worrisome problems in the past. This one will, I fear, never get to an official investigation. Do you suppose you could delve into it a bit, unofficially? I – I'm fond of Aunt Amanda, and even though she'll never know she's under a cloud, I can't quite leave it at that.'

'Not to mention the little question of justice.' I was still furious. 'Somebody killed that man, and it wasn't Aunt Amanda. The guilty person deserves to be identified.'

'Dorothy,' said Alan patiently, 'you don't *know* it wasn't Amanda. You're on her side, as you're always on the side of the underdog, but there's actually no evidence either way.'

'You're looking at it like a policeman. I'm looking at it like a human being, and one who isn't young herself. If there's a chance that old lady is going to be railroaded, I intend to head that train in another direction.'

The two men looked at each other, united in their system of male logic.

'And Alan Nesbitt, don't put on that face! I will not have you humouring me like a silly child. I'm as entitled to my opinion as you are. And David, you have even less reason to dismiss my reasoning. You don't think Amanda is guilty, either.'

'No. I don't. There's no proof, except for what I know about her character, and that's a good deal. No, I don't think she could have done such a thing. But I don't know how we're going to prove it. The Milton people aren't going to cooperate willingly. They've decided that matter is solved and can be neatly swept under the rug.'

'Well, we're not going to let them get by with that! David, let us sleep on it, and first thing in the morning we're going to map out a plan of action.'

Alan raised his hands in surrender. 'When my wife makes up her mind to do something, I've learned not to stand in her way. She's not always right, but often enough that I've learned to respect her will. Right after breakfast tomorrow, then.'

'Good. I'll pick you up at the top of Owengate – that's the one leading down to the market square – and take you out to the home. Is half past nine too early? I hope by then our heads will be clearer. Good night, and I thank you more than I can say.'

THREE

D avid had explained that he couldn't drive on the peninsula from ten in the morning till four in the afternoon without incurring the congestion charge, which had to be paid the same day. 'And if one forgets, the fee mounts to fifty pounds, which is a great nuisance.' And he was not allowed to drive into the cathedral or castle precincts at all; those areas were closed to all but buses, taxis, and delivery vehicles.

Which meant we rose rather early, went down to the Great Hall for our excellent breakfast, and took the short walk to our meeting place. 'At least it's not raining,' I commented. 'I understand why they have to restrict traffic, but this bit of walking everywhere would get a little old in the rain.'

'The price of living in a medieval city,' said Alan with a grin. 'The antiquity you so love, my dear.'

'Yes, well. It's lovely, but I'm glad Sherebury is somewhat more convenient.'

'We don't have an encircling river to contend with. Ah, here's David.'

We hopped in as smartly as we could; traffic behind David's car was building. Plainly drivers took advantage of the morning and evening free times. He headed down a street so steep, and so clogged with pedestrians, that I had to close my eyes until Alan nudged me and murmured 'Better now'.

And then we were out of the city and into lovely open countryside, with lush fields of bright green wheat and even brighter yellow rapeseed. Where the earth was somewhat less fertile, farmers had let it go to pastureland where sheep grazed steadily. The lambs were growing up a bit, not quite as lively as a few weeks ago, but still adorable.

I sighed contentedly. 'I do love the English countryside. Of course, all the rain that I complain about is the reason it's so lush and beautiful.'

'Mmm,' said David, passing a large lorry. 'Dorothy, I hate to spoil the beautiful view for you, but I'd like to tell you a little more about the situation at the Milton Home.'

'Of course. That's why we're here.'

'Well, first of all, you know it's an expensive and rather exclusive institution. I actually hate to use that word, because they do try to run it more like an actual home. None of the staff wear uniforms, and they've somehow managed to keep the place free of disagreeable odours. I imagine a fair number of the residents are incontinent, so I give them great credit for that accomplishment. I've told you there are few regulations. The residents are allowed, and encouraged, to go where they wish, and all are mobile; those who can't walk have scooters, and doorways are wide, floors smooth.'

'What about stairs?' I asked. 'If it's an old house . . .'

'It's a large and beautiful Georgian manor house with a modern wing at the back. All the residents' rooms are on the ground floor. The kitchen and larder are secured by a keypad lock. The first floor is used for offices, storage, that sort of thing. There are lifts for the convenience of the staff, but they are kept locked so that no resident can stray upstairs. The stairs themselves are shut off by metal gates, very lovely wrought-iron ones, again with keypad locks.'

'You've said many of the residents have dementia. What keeps them from wandering away? My mother, in her late years, had to be watched every minute for fear she would disappear.' I shook my head, remembering. 'She hated it.'

'That is of course a genuine difficulty. The exit doors cannot be kept locked, for fear of fire. They've dealt with the problem rather neatly. There's a lovely garden, and sunrooms, and porches, many places where the residents can go to enjoy the out-of-doors. All of them, of course, are sealed off from the rest of the world. The actual entry doors to the house itself have been reduced to two, the gracious front entry and the staff door at the back, and both of those open into foyers accessible only when a code is entered on a keypad. So you see, the security is very good.'

'Yes, in terms of residents getting out. What about people getting in?'

'There are no restrictions on visitors; they may come in as they wish. It's all part of the effort to make the atmosphere as home-like as possible. They are asked to sign in when they come, and when they leave, though very few remember to do that last. The staff know those of us who visit regularly. It's – you must understand – it's a pleasant place. The residents are treated like family, and indeed become like family to the staff. This terrible thing mustn't be allowed to ruin that!'

I could understand and sympathize with that point of view. His dearly loved Aunt Amanda had found a haven for her last days on this earth, and he quailed at the idea of that peace being disturbed. All the same . . . 'David, a man is dead. Murdered. That can't be ignored.'

'No.' He was silent for the rest of the journey.

The house, when we approached it, looked entirely serene. As David had said, it was a substantial house in Georgian style, solid, beautiful in an austere way. The addition he had mentioned was tucked away at the back, invisible from the drive. A few cars sat in the car park, again discreetly screened from the bulk of the house. No police cars were in evidence.

I looked at Alan and raised my eyes to heaven. He shook his head and helped me out of the car.

We went up the gracious, shallow steps to the impressive front door and went inside. No locked door, no one to stop us. When we got to the second door, however, and went into the foyer, a guardian was in evidence, ready to challenge any incomers.

When she saw David, she relaxed.

'Oh, Mr Tregarth! Your aunt will be very glad to see you. She's been a little upset this morning. Her friend . . .' The young woman made an ambiguous gesture.

'Yes,' said David, utterly noncommittal. 'I've brought some visitors to see her. Is she in her room, do you know?'

'I think so. She didn't go in for family breakfast.'

'Family?' I queried when we had moved on into the main part of the house.

'They try to treat everyone as family,' David replied. 'I think, myself, that it's sometimes a little forced, but on the whole it's better than the nameless, faceless institutional approach.'

Great-aunt Amanda's room was the first one in the addition, just off the spacious sun porch that was part of the original house. Once the dining room, I guessed, and it seemed to serve that function still at mealtimes. Small tables were scattered about, all decorated with tasteful flower arrangements. A couple of elderly men were sitting in easy chairs, reading the paper or snoozing behind its shelter. We didn't need David's finger-to-lips to keep us silent.

David had said Amanda was close to a hundred, so I was surprised to see a woman with the soft pink face of a baby. She was dozing in her wheelchair by a window that looked out on a lovely garden, full of roses at this time of year. Knick-knacks stood here and there, bits of lovely china, a photo or two, a pretty little cushion on the loveseat: mementoes of a life that was past.

Amanda was small, with wrinkled neck and arms, but her face was virtually unlined. Her silver hair was beautifully cut and arranged, and she was dressed with care in what looked like a cashmere sweater set and tweed skirt.

'Wool at this time of year?' I whispered.

'The elderly are often cold, love. Our time will come.'

Our whispers, soft as they were, wakened the lady. She opened her eyes and sat up straighter in her chair. 'Good morning,' she said in a surprisingly deep voice. 'Are you going to take me for a ride? It's a beautiful day, and I promised the children we'd go to the seaside today.'

I looked at David for guidance. 'Maybe a little later, Aunt Amanda. Today I thought we'd go out into the garden. These are my friends Dorothy and Alan, come to pay you a visit.'

'How nice! Do you live here?'

'No,' said Alan, 'we live in Shrerebury, in Belleshire.'

'Never heard of it,' said Amanda decisively. 'I want to go to the seaside. When are we leaving?'

David was used to coping. 'We'll have a little time in the garden first, I think. I've been driving for quite a while this morning and I'd like a little rest.'

'Don't you live here? I know I've seen you here before.'

He let that one go unanswered. 'Will you be warm enough outside, Aunt Amanda?'

'You're very sweet, dear. Are you my son?' She smiled lovingly at him.

'You're like a mother to me, darling. Here we go.'

He wheeled her deftly down the hallway to the end, where an automatic door opened for them onto a cement pathway through the garden. There was a spot under trees, beside a small pool where fish frolicked among the lily pads. David parked her there and asked, 'Would you like a cup of tea, Aunt Amanda?'

'No, it's very warm. I think I want something cold. I know! I'd love a gin and tonic. With ice and lime, please.'

I looked at the lovely old clock on the back wall of the building. It read ten-fifteen.

'Coming right up, then, dear.'

'Oh, you don't have to fetch it. Blake will get it for me. Where is Blake? He said he would meet me here. Blake is my best friend, you know.' She smiled impartially at all of us, three people she didn't know, and then frowned. 'Blake should be here. Why isn't Blake here?'

'He can't come right now, Aunt Amanda. I'll get your drink.'

Her face had begun to melt. 'No! I want Blake! Where's Blake?'

I stepped in, hoping a different voice would calm her. 'I believe someone said Blake isn't feeling well today. I'm sure you'll see him later.' And that wasn't even a lie. Amanda wouldn't see her friend this side of the great divide, but I firmly believed they would meet eventually.

It didn't work. Tears started to roll down those pink cheeks. 'Something's wrong. Why won't anyone tell me what's wrong? Where's Blake?'

It was Alan's turn. 'Blake won't be coming, Amanda. He died suddenly yesterday. I'm so very sorry.'

The tears became sobs. An attendant materialized. 'I'll take her in, Mr Tregarth,' he said quietly. 'The doctor prescribed a mild sedative for her. It's hard for her, because she can't remember what's happened from one moment to the next, so it's always a fresh sorrow. She'll need some time to let him vanish from her memory, but it will happen. She won't always be grieving.'

We watched while the aide wheeled her away, murmuring soft consolations.

'I can't decide,' Alan finally said, 'whether the inevitable loss of her memory of Armstrong is a mercy or a great pity. Grieving is painful, but in the end it's a part of dealing with death.'

'In this case it's a mercy, I think,' said David. 'She's essentially a happy, cheerful person. When the memory of this awful thing goes away, she'll be happy and cheerful again.'

'Oh, David, you hope so, but she's in her late nineties!' I shook my head. 'How much longer will she have even the limited mind she has now?'

The man shrugged. 'Don't know. Nobody knows. The man who was killed claimed he had some ways of slowing the degeneration, but I for one was sceptical.'

'You knew him, then?'

'Knew of him. He was well-known for his work with the elderly, and very popular in some circles.'

'You sound less than wildly enthusiastic.'

'Oh, I knew nothing to his discredit. I've been living in Durham only a few months, you know, and it takes a long time to blend fully with the people here. So many of them are connected with either the cathedral or the university, and those are tightly-knit groups.'

'Unfriendly? I had the impression Durham was a very friendly place.'

'It is, it is. No, I've met with no rejection – quite the reverse. It's just that it takes quite a long while to be admitted to the grapevine, so I've heard only a few fleeting rumours here and there.'

'Rumours about the doctor?'

'Hints that he might have been a little too close to some of his patients.'

I tried not to be shocked. 'Unwelcome advances? At their age?'

'Oh, no. Money. This is all unproven, mind you. But I told

you the man was wealthy, and there's some talk that a good deal of his money was left him by his adoring patients.'

Alan heaved a sigh. 'Undue influence.'

'That's the idea. But it's just an idea, and what I've just told you is slanderous.'

We hadn't noticed the gathering clouds until a chilly wind began to blow, and the garden began to clear rapidly. 'Right. Let's go in and have some lunch, and work out what we ought to do next.'

FOUR

David had, it turned out, already ordered our lunches. 'They're always happy to accommodate guests, given enough notice. I think you'll find the food surprisingly good.'

It was, in fact, excellent. The kitchen had prepared salads, in anticipation of another hot day, but had soup ready, just in case. We had both, and I accepted a serving of sticky toffee pudding, just this once.

We'd eaten in a private room, normally set aside for family conferences. As we settled to our coffee, Alan began asking questions.

'For a start, how did the man die? You haven't said.'

'He was smothered with a pillow. We found the pillow tucked into the cupboard in his room, with marks of his teeth on the torn case, and saliva.'

'Wouldn't that have required a good deal of strength?' I queried. 'Well beyond the ability of Aunt Amanda, I'd think.'

'It depends. If Armstrong was asleep at the time of the attack, or if he was sedated, it would have been easy.'

Alan groaned in frustration. 'And since they're dithering about calling in the police, valuable evidence of that sort is being lost every moment. What, by the way, have they done with the body?'

'Cold storage. They do have a small morgue here, of course. I insisted that they not put him in the hands of a mortuary, not yet.'

'David, when are you going to insist they notify the authorities? It will have to be done, and the sooner the better.'

'Don't you think I've told them that? They keep saying they will, just as soon as I've come up with some answers. What they mean is when I've found proof that Amanda killed him.'

'Which you're not going to do, since she didn't.'

Both men frowned at me.

'I don't care what you think, you two with your policeman minds. That poor woman never killed anyone.' I folded my arms across my chest and glared at them.

'We don't think she did either,' said Alan wearily. 'But there's no proof, either way.'

'All the more reason to get the police here. What we need is forensic work, and you both know it. And if you're not going to force the authorities here to call them, I'll do it myself.' I pulled out my phone. 'This has gone on long enough.'

David laid a hand on my arm. 'You're quite right. I've realized that. I'd have done it immediately, but with Aunt Amanda's possible involvement I lost sight of . . . well. I'm going right now to threaten Mr Williams – that's the director's name, by the way – with the loss of the home's licence if he doesn't report it at once. I'll leave it to him to explain why he didn't do so yesterday. Excuse me.'

'Meanwhile,' I said when David had left the room, 'is there anything more we can do here?'

'Not a great deal,' said Alan. 'The entire staff, and all the residents, will have to be questioned as to their whereabouts. But until the time of death can be determined, those inquiries are virtually futile. Not to mention the fact that some of the residents may not remember where they were and what they were doing ten minutes ago, let alone for an undetermined period of time yesterday.'

'*And* the fact that the residents must be treated carefully, gently. The staff won't be able to say much about where the residents were, either, given the flexible nature of this place. I must say it would be easier if one could say that Mr Doe and Mrs Roe were, of course, in their rooms, or in the dining room, or playing bingo, at such-and-such a time.'

'Indeed.'

We sat silent until David returned.

'They're not best pleased, but they have reluctantly agreed. The director was on the phone as I left his office. It's infuriating that it will now be almost impossible to determine a time of death, even approximately.'

'Not to mention evidence of any possible sedative. So many

of these drugs dissipate quickly, as we learned to our sorrow
in our working lives.'

'And of course,' I added, 'no one on the staff will admit to
have given him anything of the sort.'

'No.'

Silence again.

'You know,' I began, 'we're down to the variable you cops
like least. Anyone could have had the opportunity. The means
was readily to hand. So we're left with . . .'

'Motive.' Alan sighed. 'Who wanted him dead? I knew
you'd get there sooner or later, Dorothy.'

'Well, what else is there? I know it's almost impossible to
convict anyone on the basis of motive, but once you have a
motive pinned down and know who you're looking for, building
a case against that person is a whole lot easier. Am I right, or
am I right?'

Alan suddenly grinned. 'You're right, my love. Much as I
hate to admit it. That means this is where your much-admired
penchant for asking nosy questions comes into play. Where
are you going to start?'

'That's the hard part. I don't know a soul in Durham except
you, David. And your granddaughter. And Aunt Amanda, but
she can't tell me anything.'

'Then I think you need to start making friends with the
staff,' said David. 'You have a gift with people, and these are
good, friendly people.'

'They may not be so friendly when I start asking them
sensitive questions. However, I'll give it a shot. I'll start with
the lower echelons. The bigwigs will all be busy with you and
the police, to begin with. David, where's the kitchen?'

He told me, and added, 'It's behind a locked door, remember.'

'I'll manage somehow.'

A very young man was coming out of the kitchen door as
I approached; his courtesy overrode his training about the door,
and he politely held it open for me.

I thought it would be easy to talk to the kitchen staff, and
so it proved. Mid-afternoon was a slow time, with lunch over
and tidied up and tea goodies already prepared. I could honestly
praise the food, which made for a cordial beginning.

'I must admit,' I said to a young woman who was somewhat languidly chopping vegetables, 'that I was surprised to find institutional food so delicious. You all do a great job.'

'Well, it makes it easier,' said the young woman, 'that we're not dealing with hundreds of meals. I worked in a hospital before, and that was a real challenge. All sorts of special diets, not to mention patients in all stages of illness. Here no one is terribly ill, though of course they're all headed in the one direction. Our goal is to make the journey as pleasant and easy as possible.'

'Isn't that a bit depressing?'

'Not really.' She fingered the small cross pinned to her lapel. 'We're all of us on that same journey, aren't we? The dear old souls here will just reach their destination sooner than most of us. And a quiet, easy death is far from the worst thing that can happen to anyone.'

'You're quite right, of course.' Though at your age the matter is far less urgent than for some of us, I thought but did not say. 'I've heard, though, that one of your residents was pushed along that journey, not at all peacefully. Yesterday, wasn't it?'

Her face closed. 'We're not supposed to talk about that.'

'Oh, how thoughtless of me! Of course you won't want to dwell on the poor old soul's misfortune.'

'No, it isn't that.' She looked around nervously and lowered her voice. 'I wasn't actually all that fond of Mr Armstrong. Most of the old ladies loved him, but a lot of the staff thought he was creepy. I made sure I was never alone in a room with him.'

'Oh, dear! That sort, was he?'

'Well, he never . . . but I'm not supposed to talk about the residents. Especially not to— Are you with the police, ma'am?'

'Oh, no, just a visitor. I came to meet Amanda – I don't know her last name, I'm afraid. She's the great-aunt of my husband's dear friend.' That seemed to put her at an impossible distance from me, and while I was trying to find a way to rephrase, the young woman settled the matter.

'I see. Not really anyone you'd really care about meeting, especially since she won't remember you five minutes later.

And her great-nephew is Mr Tregarth, isn't he? A policeman, or was. Excuse me. If I'm late getting these cut, the chef will have something to say.' She turned her back and began to wield the knife with some vigour.

So much for the kitchen. Drat. Now I couldn't approach any of the other staff there, at least not today. The word would get around in seconds, the word that I was trouble. At least I had learned one thing: the staff, at least some of them, hadn't liked the doctor. Was he in fact a sexual predator, or did he simply create unease? 'Creepy', the young woman had said. Useful information, but vague.

Well, the other staff, then. It would take a little longer for them to be alerted. How could I get into conversation with the caregivers?

I drifted into the sun porch, but no one was sitting there. The clouds had brought rain with them, and the view was grey and gloomy.

Let's see. Afternoon. A time, as I knew all too well, when older people were apt to take naps. I wondered if there was a common room for the staff to use when they weren't urgently needed.

I remembered that David had said the offices were on the first floor (second, to my American mind) and that both the elevators and the stairs were locked off to keep the residents from wandering. The common room was probably up there, too. How was I to find it?

I'd just have to ask. Surely someone would be about.

But no one was. This was truly a dead time.

Oh, dear. I wished I hadn't thought of that particular phrase. At last I heard voices coming from the front part of the house, and headed toward them. Probably the police, along with David and Alan and Mr Williams, the director.

I didn't especially want to run into them just now, but I did want to get upstairs while most of the residents were resting and I could talk to the caregivers. But how? Drat it, they'd made this place secure, all right. Too blasted secure for my purposes right now.

Ah. My phone. I belong to a generation that isn't accustomed to instant communication, and I often forget about my mobile.

But it might just come in handy. I took it out of my pocket and called Alan.

He answered instantly; we have special rings for each other.

'Alan, don't say anything if you can help it, but I need the elevator code – lift, I mean. I have to go upstairs to talk to some of the staff and I want to get there before the police do. Do you suppose David has it?'

'I'll ask,' he murmured, and came back on the line instantly. 'No, but he'll ask the receptionist to call you.'

Which she did in only a moment, and I had found the elevator and keyed my way in just before I heard the voices enter the lobby. The police were on the move.

I found the common room instantly. There were indeed a number of people relaxing with cups of tea or coffee, and of course they were talking about the murder. None of them wore uniform, so I couldn't easily work out who was who. Conversation stopped when I entered the room. 'May I help you?' asked one young man, in the tone that so clearly says 'go away', the first unfriendly attitude I'd met here. Well, not counting the frightened kitchen worker.

'I'm sorry to intrude. I know I don't belong here. My name's Dorothy Martin, and I'm visiting with David Tregarth, who came to see his Aunt Amanda. I expect you all know him.'

The temperature thawed a degree or two. 'I came up here to get away from the police, if you want to know. I can't really tell them anything about what happened to Dr Armstrong, and since I don't believe poor Amanda had anything to do with it, I wanted to hide for a little while. I'll try not to be a nuisance.'

That eased the atmosphere, too. 'We don't think Amanda could have done it, either, Mrs Martin. She's a sweet person, and she doesn't have the strength.'

'I heard she had a quarrel with Dr Armstrong.'

'Oh, that was nothing. He shouted at her, and it upset her dreadfully at the time, but she'd forgotten all about it half an hour later. You have to understand, Mrs Martin, she is literally incapable, at her stage of dementia, of holding a grudge.'

'She seemed like a really pleasant woman, when I met her this morning. Of course, it's a little hard to tell, given the state of her mind.'

'She *is* a pleasant person. Never complains about anything, never makes demands, just happy and cheerful all day long. Anyone will tell you; we all love her.'

'Isn't that somewhat unusual for victims of dementia? I've heard stories – well, I've known a few people myself – whose personalities changed completely as the disease took greater and greater hold. Some became grouchy, petulant, even given sometimes to violent outbursts of temper.'

Several of the people in the room nodded in agreement. 'But not Amanda,' said the woman who'd been doing most of the talking. 'She's gone downhill rapidly in the past few weeks, and she doesn't recognize many people now, but she's unfailingly charming to everyone.'

'Especially to that Dr Armstrong,' said another woman, rather waspishly. 'I never could see the attraction there.'

'Oh, Velma, come now! He flattered her, made much of her, just as he did to all his old ladies. He had to do it every time he saw her, of course, because all she would remember was that he was a person she felt comfortable with.'

'And his name. She remembers his name.' I told them about the pathetic episode this morning when she had to be told yet again that he was dead. 'That's one reason I'm sure she had no part in his death. She wasn't faking her distress. But what do you all think about the man's death?'

'Who did it, you mean?' Another woman, youngish, very attractive. 'Oh, we all know Mr Tregarth is a retired policeman, and we can guess why you're here, Mrs Martin. Your husband used to be with the police too, didn't he?'

I was too astonished to frame an instant reply. My interrogator laughed. 'There's no mystery about it. One of the aides here is from down south, near Sherebury. She knows all about you and your husband and all the detecting you've done. When Mr Tregarth first decided to invite you two for a visit, he happened to mention it to Judith, and she spread the word. I'm Dharani, by the way.'

'Oh, dear. I . . . that is, I'd hoped to make a few discreet inquiries – sometimes people will talk to me when they won't to the police. I'm not really a detective at all, you know, just . . . Oh, I suppose you could call me a Paul Pry,

except I prefer to think I'm a person who's interested in
other people and cares about them, and . . .' I ran down.

'Yes, we know. Judith has told us. All done with kindness.'
Velma's waspishness was still slightly in evidence. 'You don't
have to justify yourself to us. We won't stand in your way.
Speaking for myself, I haven't the slightest idea who did in
the old . . . gentleman, but I'm not especially sorry he's gone.
He was upsetting the place, and he didn't belong here anyway.
If you ask me, he was hiding from something. Emotional
exhaustion, my foot! He was no more ill than I am, and I'm
strong as an ox.'

'I had already gotten the impression that the staff weren't
terribly fond of him,' I said cautiously.

'No,' replied Dharani. 'And as long as we're unbuttoning,
you might as well know that we weren't the only ones. His
sweet old lady patients adored him, but their families weren't
always so pleased. Oh, he was good to them, and treated their
maladies properly, but their kids seemed to think that he
charged a good deal for very little. Many of them didn't have
much wrong with them except loneliness and hypochondria,
but he was in private practice and could charge what the traffic
would bear.'

'Now, Dhar,' said one of the men. 'That's rumour and
speculation, and we shouldn't be spreading that sort of thing.'

Dharani tossed her head of handsome black hair. 'With the
police nosing into everything, it will come out anyway. Akbar,
you know this place isn't run along conventional lines. Strict
professionalism takes a back seat to loving care for the residents. Anyway, I'm neither a nurse nor a doctor, so I don't
have some set of rules to live by, except the rules of decency
and empathy. And for the sake of decency, and the sake of
our residents, I want this mess cleared up as soon as possible.
If that means speaking out of turn, then get out of my way!'

I had recovered my composure. 'Well, now that my cover
is well and truly blown, I want to ask the silly question that
the police will certainly ask: did any of you see anyone going
in or out of Dr Armstrong's room at the relevant time?'

'Ah, but what time is that? No one seems to know. Did
anyone serve him breakfast that morning?'

Dharani's question hung in the air. No one spoke until a young man, an aide I would guess, spoke up. 'He didn't usually eat in his room. He liked being with the others in the sun porch.'

'Right,' I said. 'So did anyone notice him there that morning? That would at least establish that he was alive then.'

But no one had. 'You've been told about our free-for-all scheduling?' asked Velma.

'Yes. I thought it must make things more difficult for you all, never knowing where anyone would be at any given time.'

'It does. Or it would, except that we have only a few old dears to look after, and plenty of staff, so it all goes relatively smoothly.'

'I've heard,' I said hesitantly, 'that people suffering from dementia sometimes do better in a carefully-structured environment.'

That raised a babble of comment. Everyone in the room, it seemed, had a point of view. It was a plump, middle-aged woman who prevailed.

'That was what I was always taught,' she said, 'and I've been nursing quite a while. But after working here, I have to say: better for whom? It's true that some patients function at a higher level, for a longer time, when they're rigidly controlled. But are they happier? And isn't their happiness and well-being our goal? I find that our residents are quite content with the regime here, encouraged to do what they want when they want.'

'That's true for some, Alice, but not for all. You can't lump people together in a category called "demented" and expect them all to be alike.'

'That's true, but—'

'Don't you think—'

'Excuse me.'

The director had walked in unnoticed. 'Ladies, gentlemen, representatives of the police are here and would like to speak with each of you, individually. And I believe some of our residents are awake and in need of your attention.'

With startled cries and glances at watches, the gathering broke up, checking with the police officers at the door, presumably making appointments. I was left with Mr Williams, David, and Alan, everyone looking as disgruntled as I felt.

'Anything?' asked Alan.

I shook my head. 'Not much.'

'Then we might as well repair to someplace more comfortable, where we can talk more freely and see if we can work out some plan of action.'

'I suppose,' said the director grudgingly, 'that it was really necessary to bring the authorities into this.'

David just looked at him. 'A case of murder? Yes, it was necessary. We'll stay in touch.'

FIVE

'I can't believe that man thought he could write off a case of murder as a minor disruption.'

David drained his glass and set it down with a thump. We'd found that, with the students out of town, yesterday's friendly pub was still quiet and an ideal place for a conference.

'Well, David, we promised we'd help, in the hopes of getting it all worked out quickly. But I'm not sure that's going to be possible. Alan, I'd like the other half, please.'

He got refills for all of us, and a few packets of crisps, and we settled down to it.

I began. 'I may as well say right up front that I made almost no headway. There was a woman in the kitchen who might have been forthcoming, but I was too direct in my approach, and I scared her off. She did tell me that none of the staff cared much for Dr Armstrong, and the caregivers in the staff room said the same. They also, or some of them anyway, thought his reason for being here was somewhat suspect. At least one of them thought he was hiding from someone or something. They know about the rumours of "undue influence", by the way, and implied that some families of his patients weren't very happy with him.'

'Nothing definitive, then,' David said with a sigh.

'No smoking gun. I'm sorry. It begins to look as though almost anyone in the place could have done it. And I'm loath to say it, but I'm not sure you'll find any willing witnesses, if that's the case. They all adore Amanda, and they know he made her unhappy that one time, and I don't see them putting themselves out to be cooperative.'

'An inside job, you think?' Alan frowned. 'But why? Simple dislike isn't enough to drive someone to murder.'

'Aha! Motive! I knew you'd admit it in the end. I said it before. You already know the means, and anybody could have had the opportunity. Anybody in the building, that is. That tight security system would make it very difficult for someone from outside to actually get in, find his room, smother him, and get out again, without being noticed. They couldn't, in this case, even use the simple disguise of a white lab coat, because—'

'Because nobody in the place wears a uniform.'

'And another thing. The free-and-easy way the place is run would make it easy for any staff member to go to anyone's room at any time. There'd be no busybody to say that So-and-so was supposed to be looking after Mrs Whosis just then. I'm sure the police are asking the staff that sort of thing, even as we speak, but I think it's futile. There are far more staff than patients, and no time clocks to punch, so to speak. As for the residents, they don't have much to do except watch what's going on, but how reliable are they as witnesses?'

'Not very, most of them,' said David sadly. 'I was waylaid the other day by one sweet old woman who wanted to tell me all about her recent trip to the Taj Mahal. Her caregiver said later that she hadn't been away from the Milton Home since she moved in some years ago, and had certainly never in her life been farther from England than Boulogne.'

'Dorothy, you're not thinking a *resident* could have done this?' Alan sounded shocked.

'I don't think it's likely, but you of all people shouldn't be shocked by the idea. We're getting to an age, all three of us, when we understand what young people don't always know: the passions of the old can run just as strong and deep as those of the young. And some of us have become very adept at hiding our feelings. Oh, it's possible all right. In fact, the more I think about it, the more I like it.'

David was the one to look horrified this time.

'I don't mean that the way it sounds, David. Of course, I don't *like* the idea that one of the residents might be a murderer. It's frightening, and of course you're worried about Aunt Amanda. But as a hypothesis, it has its points.' I thought for a long moment, sipping my beer. 'Consider this: a man has an old grudge against Armstrong. Or a woman, but I'm suggesting a man, partly because men are said to have been less impressed by his charm. All right. Said man with a grudge comes to a point in his life when caring for himself becomes burdensome. He has plenty of money and few serious health conditions beyond the normal irritations common to old age. So he moves into the Milton in expectation of a slow, idyllic decline. For a while his expectations are fulfilled. He has a pleasant home, plenty to keep him busy if he wants, long stretches of idleness when that's what he prefers, excellent food. What more could a man want?

'But one day a serpent comes hissing into his paradise. He comes across Blake Armstrong in the sun porch, where he (the man with the grudge) has come to sit and enjoy the view. There sits the man he detests, basking in the very chair he has marked out as his own.'

'Wait, I'm confused. Who has marked out?'

'The man with the grudge. We can call him X, if you want. Anyway, there's Armstrong in the chair X thinks of as his very own, apparently dozing peacefully. X can hardly believe it. His newly won peace is utterly destroyed. His anger, long damped, breaks out with new force. He talks a bit to the staff, tries to find out why the man is here and how long he's going to stay, but he – X – is cagey about it. He doesn't want to reveal his fury to anyone.'

'What is it that he's furious about? What has Armstrong done?'

'I have no idea. It doesn't matter. It might have been something quite trivial that X has built up into an irremediable evil. It's what it has done to X's mind that matters. He tries to hold onto the hope that the man will soon leave, as the staff have implied.

'But one day there is some incident. Again, it doesn't much matter what, but it touches a match to the fuse, the very short fuse, of X's obsession. Armstrong must go. X lays his plans. He complains to the staff that he hasn't been sleeping well, which is the simple truth. He saves up the sedatives he is given until he thinks he has enough, finds an opportunity to put them in Armstrong's tea or coffee or whatever, goes in when Armstrong is sound asleep, picks up a pillow, and voilà.' I dusted my hands and sat back to await their reactions.

'It's plausible,' said Alan at last. 'Given the way the home is organized, it's possible. Of course, it's all a fairy tale, spun from air.'

'Spun from many, many years of dealing with people,' I retorted. 'If you have a better hypothesis, tell us.'

Alan groaned. 'We're policemen, Dorothy. We don't want fairy tales, we want facts. Good, solid, verifiable facts. Show me any facts that bolster up your little fable, and I'll consider it more seriously.'

'You know, though,' said David thoughtfully, 'it might be possible to check on a few of her ideas. The staff at the home are very observant, very alert to any changes in their charges. If someone changed his— You're still positing a man?'

'Strength,' I said briefly. 'Even under sedation, Armstrong would have fought back. In fact, we know he did. The torn pillowcase.'

'Ah, yes. Very well, if someone changed his behaviour shortly after Armstrong came into residence, the staff will know. That would give us a place to begin nosing around, Alan. Look into his background, see if there was any trouble with Armstrong, that sort of thing. It would still be hypothetical, but it would begin to look more like a lead.'

Alan sighed. 'I'd be a lot happier about the whole thing if we had a really solid time of death.'

'And you know quite well we're not going to get one.' David shook his head in frustration. 'It's hard enough when a body is discovered immediately and the forensics people get to work at once. After all the time that's been wasted, we'll be lucky if the coroner agrees that the man's dead!'

I glanced at Alan; we silently agreed not to remind David that he had collaborated in the time-wasting. 'At least they can tell us what drugs, if any, were in his system. If they find any kind of sedative, something that wasn't prescribed for him, that would be a definite pointer.'

'We'll hope, then, that he *was* given something, and that it's detectable with the usual tests, and that it's rare and easily traceable to X.'

I frequently remind my dear husband of the old adage about sarcasm being the tool of the devil. I decided not to say it this time.

David took us out to dinner, not at the fancy hotel he had promised earlier. We were none of us feeling festive, so a modest meal at a modest little place near the Market Square served us nicely. Then we walked back to the castle, the rain having abated to a drizzle. We asked David to come up for coffee.

'No, no, it's very kind of you, but Susan worries if I'm out too late.' He sighed. 'She's a dear girl, but . . .' And he was off to his granddaughter's house.

'How long do you think he's going to be content to go on living with her?' I asked as we climbed the many steps to our room. 'I know she spoils him dreadfully, but doesn't he miss his freedom?'

'He's said as much to me, from time to time. But he was very lonely in Exeter after his wife died.'

'Yes, but he could live in Durham, near his family, without actually living *with* them. Unless money is a problem. As you've said, housing here is probably pretty expensive; it's a big tourist town, and of course there's the university.'

'I don't get the impression David's hurting. We don't discuss it, of course.'

Of course not. That's not the kind of thing men say to each other, especially English men. Women aren't as squeamish about money. I made a mental note to have a little talk with the granddaughter at the next opportunity.

'What's on the docket for tomorrow?' I asked as we climbed wearily into bed.

'Don't know. I'm sure David will call as soon as he knows anything. Meanwhile, how about a tour of the castle? And/or the cathedral? They're both well worth seeing in more detail than we've yet had time for.'

'Mmm. Sounds good. Especially' – I yawned widely – 'if it goes on raining.'

'Go to sleep, love.' Alan gave me a quick peck on the cheek and turned out the light.

Sometime in the night I woke to the rush of rain against our window. I got up to lower it, and go to the bathroom, and went back to sleep with the cosy lullaby of falling water.

*   *   *

We woke early, having gone to bed early, and looked out on a depressing sort of day. The cobbled courtyard shone with water. The sky was a uniform grey with no blue to be seen anywhere. 'I should have appreciated the hot sun while it lasted,' I said with a sigh as I made coffee. Instant is not our favourite, but when it's the only form of caffeine available, we're not picky. 'Definitely a tour day, unless David calls early.'

He called Alan just as we were heading down for breakfast. 'Nothing to report,' Alan said, pocketing his phone. 'By afternoon, he hopes. Meanwhile he suggested a tour of the castle or the cathedral.'

I laughed. 'Great minds. Which one first, would you say?'

'If we hurry through our breakfast we can take in morning prayer and then tour the cathedral. Then we can rest our feet for a while and find out when the castle tours are scheduled.'

I didn't mind rushing through breakfast. The food provided for castle guests was very good, and plentiful, but I was getting tired of an endless succession of bacon and eggs and hash browns. At home we often prefer cereal or toast and fruit. This morning I sliced a banana into a bowl of what I've learned to call muesli (granola, to my Hoosier mind), gulped a quick second cup of coffee, and was headed down the steps into the courtyard as the bells for morning prayer began to ring. I'd forgotten my walking stick, helpful on slick cobbles, but Alan's arm was strong and steady, and we made it with a minute or two to spare.

The congregation was sparse, mostly cathedral volunteers, I guessed, but the peace and calm were just what we needed after a stressful yesterday. The tour of the building was the same. Our guide was well-versed in Norman architecture, of which I knew little, and he pointed out features I would never have noticed: the elaborate detailing of the arches, the decorative carving on the massive piers that support the vast weight of the roof. The decorations were, our guide said, carved into the individual stones that made up the piers, not added when the huge columns were assembled. If I'd had any idea that twelfth-century stonemasons were primitive craftsmen, I was disabused of the notion. Their tools might have been extremely primitive by modern standards, but there was nothing wrong with the artistic eye or the net effect. They knew exactly what they were doing and how to do it, these men who had been laid to their well-earned rest centuries before any European even thought of going to what we now call America, much less construct any magnificent building. And now, after hundreds, thousands of buildings erected since have crumbled to dust, Durham Cathedral stands, essentially unchanged since its completion in 1133.

I listened politely as the guide explained that the cathedral was the shrine of St Cuthbert (of whom I had never heard) and the most-visited shrine in England until the martyrdom of Thomas à Becket at Canterbury led to his popular shrine in the thirteenth century. Becket's shrine was long ago destroyed; Cuthbert's is still in Durham. I didn't go to see it; several more stairs were involved, and I'd about had it with stairs. Alan and I did stop for a moment of reverence before the tomb of Bede. Yes, 'the Venerable Bede', the first English historian.

Our last stop in the cathedral was the café in the undercroft, where we could sit (oh blessed relief) and enjoy coffee and a sandwich, and relaxation. Somewhat to Alan's surprise, I resisted the temptations of the cathedral shop just across the foyer. I knew if I once set foot in there I'd spend far too much money. Later, when we were about to go home. We did stop to look and marvel at the scale model of the cathedral, some twelve feet long, built of Lego bricks, stained glass windows, landscaping, and all. It might have been cutesy and repellent, but it wasn't; it was an amazing achievement, and we were glad we'd seen it.

'Castle tour next?'

'Not until I've had a nap. I want to see the castle and hear about its history. Just not right now.'

We hadn't heard from David, so we walked back to our room (through the rain that had returned with renewed enthusiasm) and rested until tour time.

SIX

The rain had sobbed and sniffled its way into a sulky drizzle by the time we assembled in the lobby of the university library to begin our tour. Our guide was a pleasant young man with a good loud voice, who introduced himself as Timothy, and apologized that we would begin outside in the courtyard. 'We won't be there long, so you shouldn't get too wet. Perhaps those with umbrellas can share with the others? Right, then, off we go.'

Alan and I hadn't bothered with our brollies in such a light rain, and our jackets had hoods. We stayed well away from the potentially eye-poking implements carried by others, and kept close to the guide, who herded us to the centre of the courtyard after showing off the remarkable carving of the gatehouse archway.

'Right, now I'm going to give you a quiz, just a brief one, one question. What would you say is the oldest part of the castle?'

Nearly everyone pointed to the impressive circular keep, high on its motte, or hill. Timothy chuckled with delight. 'Ah, I get them every time. In fact, the keep is the newest building in view.' Startled gasps from the group. 'Yes, I know it looks ancient, but it is in fact of nineteenth-century construction, or rather reconstruction. When the university took over the buildings from the Bishop of Durham in 1827, the keep was in such bad shape that it had to be completely rebuilt. However, the original plans were still extant, so it retained its medieval look. You don't get failing marks for your mistake!'

He went on to explain that, although the cathedral is built on bedrock, the castle's foundations are much less secure, nor is the stone of which it is built very suitable for the purpose, having the propensity to weather badly. 'Thus, although there are still bits of the original twelfth-century buildings, a very great deal of repair and reconstruction has been necessary over the centuries. I'll point out both ancient and more modern as we go. Right, then, we can get out of the rain now.'

'Can we see the keep?'

'Unfortunately not. It is used entirely for student housing and is off-limits to the public. Sorry. Inside, though, it looks pretty much like any place where students live, slightly scruffy and untidy!'

As we went inside, Timothy came over to me and spoke softly. 'Will you be all right on the stairs, ma'am? There are a good many of them, I'm afraid.'

I was carrying my stick, mostly for use on the slippery cobbles of the courtyard. 'Thank you for asking, but I'll be fine. A bit slow, maybe, but fine.'

He cocked his head. 'Are you American, then? Or Canadian?'

I laughed. 'My accent confuses people, I know. I'm American-born, but my husband is English, I've lived in England for a long time, and I carry a British passport. When I go back to Indiana, everyone thinks I sound English.'

Our guide grinned. 'Citizen of the world, eh?' His expression told me he knew it was a cliché, and I grinned back before he returned to his spiel for the tour.

He was good, no doubt about that. He knew the history of the castle inside and out, but didn't bury us in facts, only enough that we could appreciate what we were seeing. He told us the legend of the ghost, the Grey Lady, who is supposed to walk the gorgeous, and famous, Black Staircase. He pointed out incredible bits of carving here and there, amazingly preserved virtually intact for all these years, but reserved his greatest enthusiasm for the Norman Chapel, a tiny room below grade level and the oldest part of the castle, dating from 1080 or so. 'It's been pulled about over the years,' he said, 'but never destructively, and now it serves its original purpose. Tunstal's Chapel, up above, is more impressive, and it's where people like to have weddings, but this one . . . well, for me, this is still a place of worship, and still has that feel.' He grew silent, as did our small group. There was something about the atmosphere of the place, something perhaps exuding from the very ancient stone pillars or the small paving stones. Prayers had ascended from this place for well over nine hundred years. Surely some sense of them remained.

We ended our tour in the Great Hall, our breakfast room, and stayed to talk to our guide after the rest of the party had left. 'You are very knowledgeable about the history of this amazing place,' I said admiringly. 'Are you by any chance a student here, maybe reading history?'

'I am a student, yes, but reading theology. I brushed up on the history in order to do the tours properly. It doesn't pay a lot, but every little bit helps.'

I groaned. 'Oh, the eternal problem of how to pay for education! Eons ago, when I went to college, my parents were able to pay for it, and they were far from wealthy. Nowadays students graduate with such a terrible burden of debt, and then if they can't get good jobs, they're buried under that mountain for years. If you ask me, it's a scandal.'

'It's not as bad here as in the States, but yes, it is a burden for those who aren't wealthy,' he said, again with that disarming grin. 'Most of us have at least two jobs to try to make ends meet.' He looked at his phone. 'Speaking of which . . .'

'Off you go, then,' said Alan, reaching out to shake his hand.

Timothy gave a startled look at the money left in his palm. 'Thanks, sir, but we're not supposed to—'

Alan looked around the room. 'Unless I'm missing something, there isn't another soul around to see. Perhaps your conscience as a theology student won't let you accept it, but I'd be greatly obliged if you would. A bright and eager young man shouldn't have to worry about where his next meal is coming from.'

'Well, thank you very much indeed! And the next time you and your lady want a meal, you might try the Court Inn. Anyone will tell you where it is. It's where I have to go right this minute or I'll be late for my shift!'

'Two jobs, at least,' I commented as we wandered out of the Great Hall and back up to our room. 'While working on a degree in theology, which can't be a snap.'

'And more work at the end of it, before he can be ordained. That lad knows what he wants, and he's going after it with everything he has. I only hope he's making enough money not to end up with impossible debt when he's attained his goal.'

'You think he intends to be a priest, then? Or to teach theology?'

'From the heartfelt way he spoke about the old chapel, I'd say a priest. It isn't too often these days that you find young people who speak about religious matters with conviction. I wish him well, but I fear for him in today's economic climate.'

'I'm glad he accepted your tip. How much did you give him?'

'A couple of twenties, and my card just in case. I wonder what's happening with David. I expected a call by now.' Alan pulled out his phone and called David. 'Voicemail. He's probably busy at the home, or else in his car. What would you like to do while we wait?'

'First, have a cup of tea. Then if we still haven't heard from him, I'd like to explore the area a little. The rain has stopped, or paused, anyway, and we haven't seen much of the river. It's so important to the town, I'd like to get a feel for it.'

David finally called while I was tidying up the tea things. Alan put him on the speaker. 'Sorry to abandon you for such a long time. I've been trying to put together some information. It isn't easy, since I have no official status here. The local police are courteous, but distant.'

'And not only are you retired, you're a foreigner.'

'Yes, there's that, too.'

I gave Alan a puzzled look, but he ignored me.

'And have you reached any conclusions? Is there by any chance a "man with a grudge", as Dorothy put it, who might have acted as she imagined?'

David's laugh didn't sound amused. 'Well, yes and no. There certainly was such a person, a man who had lived at the home for about a year and was visibly displeased when Armstrong arrived. He never said much, but the staff noticed that he avoided Armstrong to the point of snubbing him, and wouldn't talk about him.'

'Oh, he sounds perfect. Was he taking sedatives? Could he have slipped some into the man's tea or whatever?'

'Again, yes and no. He was prescribed a mild sedative when the staff observed his agitation, and he certainly could have saved up enough to give Armstrong a significant dose—'

'Oh, forgot to ask,' Alan interrupted. 'Had Armstrong in fact taken something that would have knocked him out, or at least made him a bit groggy?'

'Yes, they found enough traces, even after such a long time, that they think it quite possible he was deliberately drugged. Unfortunately Robinson is out of the running as a suspect.'

'But why? Surely—'

'Because, Dorothy, the man suffered a massive heart attack about a week ago. He was taken to hospital and died there three days before Armstrong was killed.'

'Darn it, it was such a *good* idea!'

'It was. It was most inconsiderate of the man to die.'

I sighed. 'I was even beginning to picture him in my mind – a small man, stooped and grey, the sort who does hold grudges and seek revenge. Not a very nice person at all. And probably he wasn't like that at all, and now he's past defending himself.'

'Or carrying out his revenge, if that is in fact what he had in mind.'

'Oh, well. We'll come up with something else. The one fact we have is that the man is dead, indisputably murdered. There's that to cling to. Oh, by the way, what did you mean by calling David a foreigner? I thought he was English.'

Alan laughed. 'Certainly he's English, but from the West Country. There are regional differences in England, my love, just as well-defined as your American ones, though the territories concerned are much smaller. The way people speak, the foods they eat, their political preferences, all are distinctive, just as different as, say, Georgia is from New York. A Cornishman like David is in many ways more foreign here in Durham than you are. You yourself have observed the northern accent here.'

'And sometimes have a hard time understanding it. David sometimes sounds a bit odd, too.'

'So you see. He's a "foreigner" here, someone who's

different, not quite "one of us" – and therefore not taken quite
seriously. Perhaps, even, not quite to be trusted.'

'Why don't they treat us that way? We don't talk the way
they do, either.'

'Ah. You, of course, still sound slightly American, and
Americans are largely tolerated as well-meaning, if somewhat
ignorant.' He grinned at my indignation. 'And you've not dealt
yet with the police here. As for me, I lost my Cornish accent
years ago and speak in a bland way redolent of nowhere in
particular. But I, too, will be treated by the local authorities
with deference and courtesy, but a good deal of reserve. Think
a New York policeman dealing with a Georgia sheriff, and
you'll get the idea.'

We were walking by the river on a lovely path we'd discovered, just down the hill from the college buildings. I had been
told that Durham University operated, like its venerable
Oxbridge cousins, on the college system. The oldest of them,
University College, was housed in the castle, but there were
several others scattered nearby. I had given up, with my
American background, on understanding fully the relationship
between college and university. I think it's like cricket: if
you're not English, you'll never get it.

Anyway, the river walk was close to the castle and University
College, but actually belonged to the city of Durham. The
walk meandered through a wooded area, at this time of year
burgeoning with trees and undergrowth in countless shades of
green, as well as a few daffodils and bluebells. In the peaceful
setting we'd dropped the subject of crime and police investigation. 'The plants have loved the rain.'

'The river, too. Look, it's very high.'

The paved path ran close to the river's edge, but there was
a small area of uncultivated greenery in between. Or at least
there was meant to be. With the river very high, in some places
the water came right up to the path, even lapping over by a
few inches.

'That could be dangerous,' I said. 'I don't see any lights
along the path. On a dark night someone could miss their
footing and fall in the river.'

'You ain't just whistlin' Dixie, lady,' said a voice from

behind us. I was so startled by the accent and the idiom that I nearly fell into the river myself.

'Heard your voice and figgered you might be American,' went on the man, catching up with us and holding out a hand. 'Sam Burns, from Dallas.'

Somewhat stunned, Alan and I introduced ourselves.

'I'm here on sabbatical from SMU, and havin' a whale of a time. Not much like home, is it? But what you were sayin', ma'am, about this path bein' dangerous, is nothin' but God's truth. I've only been here since September, and in that time at least one student has fallen in and drowned hisself.'

'No! Really?'

'Really. 'Course, I won't say he wasn't a little lit up. Students are the same everywhere, I guess. They like their beer. But what I say is, they oughta put up a wall or somethin'. 'T'aint safe the way it is.'

The wind was picking up; the leaves overhead shook their burden of water down on us. The sky began to look ominous, as well. It was time to say goodbye to our new friend and head back to shelter.

We made it just before the heavens opened. By the time we had laboured up the stairs to our room, we could barely see the outside world through the rain.

'Stair rods,' said Alan gloomily.

'Axe heads and hammer handles, my father used to say. That kind never lasts very long, or at least it never did back in Indiana.'

'I can't predict what it does up here in the north,' Alan groused. 'Especially now that weather patterns have shifted so much. And do you realize, love, that it's dinnertime? And our next meal is somewhere out in that deluge, and I forgot to arrange for an ark.'

SEVEN

'Oh.' I had not, in fact, considered that detail. I looked at our tea tray. Not a single biscuit left; we'd eaten them all with our tea, and they wouldn't be replenished until our room was serviced the next morning. We sat and looked at each other glumly. Someone's stomach rumbled.

Alan's phone rang.

I could make little of his end of the conversation, which consisted of half-finished remarks. He rang off with a quizzical expression. 'That little fool just spent every cent I gave him on a meal for us from the place where he works. He called to ask our room number and make sure we were here. I gave him the key code.'

'Timothy? He'll drown!'

'That's what I tried to tell him. He wouldn't let me finish a sentence, just said it rains a lot here and he's used to it, but he thought we might not want to go out, and he hoped we like burgers.'

'Well, he's studying theology, and he seems to have taken it to heart. This is certainly the act of a Good Samaritan.'

In a very few minutes there was a knock at the door. Alan opened it on a dripping young man. His anorak and hood were streaming with water; his jeans and trainers were sodden; but his face, also dripping, wore a broad smile. He held out a large and well-used plastic bag.

'Good job I always carry a Tesco bag with me. I may look like a drowned rat, but the food's nice and dry, and still warm, I hope.'

'You walked through this downpour?'

'Biked. Just as wet, but quicker.'

We hustled him into the room, had him take off his anorak and shoes and socks, and gave him towels. 'I wish we could offer you a hot bath and a change of clothes, but we have only a shower, and you'd swim in Alan's slacks, or even mine.'

'Not to worry. I'm tough!' He opened the bag. 'I brought some for myself as well. They're all alike; I hope they're okay. And there's chips and salad and slaw and onion rings. And I brought a bottle of wine, just plonk.'

'You are an angel straight from heaven,' I said devoutly.

'And,' said Alan severely, 'a very wicked young man to spend on us what I meant for your needs.'

Timothy ducked his head. 'I got paid today. And I get a discount. And I thought about you, maybe caught by the storm, and here I was with all this food around me and my shift nearly over. Not to worry,' he said again.

Meanwhile we were letting perfectly good hamburgers, which smelled scrumptious, cool off. I laid out tissues on the bed for placemats and fetched plastic glasses and coffee cups for the wine while Alan opened it with the corkscrew on my Swiss Army knife, and we set to.

For the first few minutes we were all so hungry there was no conversation not related to food, but when my appetite had diminished from a roar to a whimper, I wiped my mouth, swallowed some wine (okay, plonk, but perfectly acceptable), and said, 'Now I want to know something about you. For a start, whatever possessed you to pursue a degree in theology? Forgive me, but you're obviously not wealthy, and you must know that such a degree and a couple of pounds will buy you a cup of nice coffee.'

He smiled, but his voice when he answered was serious. 'Yes, of course I know it doesn't make a lot of sense financially. I'm trying to get by without taking out a lot in loans, because . . . well, I don't like the idea of getting into debt. The thing is . . . well, you used the word "possessed". I suppose that's what it amounts to. I'm being called to the priesthood. I'm not sure why. I mean, I'm nothing special as a chap, but I know this is what I'm meant to do.'

There was just a trace of defiance in his tone, a little 'Call me crazy if you want to'. But not much. Timothy knew quite well that a claim of a vocation is an oddity in the twenty-first century, and he didn't know us well enough to be sure of our reaction, but he wasn't going to back down.

'If you feel that way, and the fear of poverty hasn't deterred you, then I salute you,' said Alan, raising his coffee-cup of wine in a toast. 'You've managed to cobble together adequate funding?'

Timothy sighed. 'Not quite, actually. There's the loan, and I had hoped for a small scholarship. And then there are the two jobs, though they don't pay much. I was promised . . . well, when I first started down this path, I thought I would have another resource, but it didn't work out, so I'm quite a bit short, really. I may have to stand out for a year or try to find yet another job.' He took a healthy swig of wine. 'Now I want to know more about you. How did you come to leave your home, Mrs Nesbitt, and settle in England?'

'It's Mrs Martin, actually. I kept my own name when Alan and I married. But I'm more comfortable with Dorothy, if you don't mind. And how I got here is a long story, but I've always been an Anglophile, and when I was widowed some years ago I moved to Sherebury and met Alan, and there we were.'

'The abridged version. I see. I'm speculating that you might have been a teacher at some time of your life.'

I blinked. 'Goodness, does it show? I hope I don't come across as one of those bossy, always-right women that are such nuisances!'

'Certainly not,' said Alan before Timothy could reply. 'Not always right. Only ninety-seven per cent of the time.'

'Now, now,' said Timothy. 'No bickering in front of the children. I don't find you a nuisance, Mrs . . . Dorothy, but you do have an air of authority. I can see you being a very effective teacher. And you, sir, have that same authority, but perhaps not academic?'

'Should you ever decide against the priesthood, young man, you'd be a shining star in the police force, seeing through people as clearly as you do. That was my profession, so you got it in one. Authority, but not academic. I'm also good at asking intrusive questions, and I'm not going to let you drag a red herring across our path. Before you changed the subject, you started to say you were promised additional funding for your education. I'm not too keen on unfulfilled promises. Was this a scholarship of some sort, or grant, or . . .?'

Timothy could easily have found a nice way to say that was

none of our business. It might have been Alan's 'air of authority' or the kindness in his voice, but Timothy hesitated, grimaced, and then replied. 'It's just such a trite old story. You'll find a thousand variations of it in any library. A woman I called my aunt had a good deal of money and had promised to leave it to me when she died. She was very ill, and suffering, so I thought it wasn't too frightful to wish her a speedy end.'

'You're not going to tell us she was murdered!' I said in horror.

'One moment, Dorothy. You say that you called her your aunt. She was not really an aunt?'

'No, she was my mother's best friend. She never married, so my sister and I became almost like her family. She took us on holidays, always remembered Christmas and our birthdays, that sort of thing. She was a dear, and we loved her. When my parents were killed in a car smash a couple of years ago, she was as devastated as we were. That was when she promised she'd look after me and see I got the education I wanted.'

'What about your sister?' I put in.

'She's three years older than I am, and she married young. She's very pretty,' he said with the dispassionate judgement of a brother who can't quite see the attraction. 'She and her husband live in London. He works for a Labour MP and she works from home for a publishing house. Even with two young kids, they're doing all right. Aunt Sue knew they didn't need her help, and she knew I did, and she knew she was dying. So she told me not to worry.'

'And then she let you down! What a despicable thing to do! What made her change her mind?'

'Well, that's rather the thing, you see. Her doctor moved away and she changed to another one some of her friends had recommended. He was supposed to be very good with the elderly, and since Aunt Sue had plenty of money, she could afford a private doctor.'

I had a nasty feeling I knew where this was going.

'Go on,' said Alan in a grim voice.

'She loved him – thought he was wonderful. She said she felt so much better. She thought he was going to save her life, and in gratitude she changed her will. That's all. She died about a month later, and he came in for all the money. All of it.'

'And his name,' Alan said with a deep sigh, 'was Blake Armstrong.'

Timothy's mouth dropped. 'How did you know?'

'Dorothy and I have become involved with another matter concerning Dr Armstrong. Do you have a little time, or do you need to get back to your job, or your studies?'

'I should be studying, but it's not term time, and the night is yet young. What's the story?'

I opened my mouth, but Alan silenced me with a look. 'Timothy,' he said, 'a friend asked us to go to the nursing home where Dr Armstrong was staying. The man is dead.'

We were both watching his face, and if the news didn't come as a complete surprise to the young man, I'll retire to Bedlam.

'But – nursing home? He was ill? I knew nothing about any of this!'

'Is there some reason why you should have known? Have you been in contact with him?'

Alan sounded a bit sharp. Timothy gave him a wary look. 'I thought my solicitor would have told me. I've asked him to contest the will, alleging undue influence. I suppose that's moot, now. I had hoped—'

'I don't imagine you can afford to pay a lawyer.' My heart was aching for him.

'He's doing it – he was doing it pro bono. He said there had been a lot of talk about him – Armstrong – but that he'd always been careful before. The little old ladies who left him their fortunes had been alone in the world, with no family to protest. He must have been somewhat surprised to learn about me. I wonder if that was what shocked him into the heart attack, or whatever put him in the nursing home.'

'He was said to be suffering from nervous exhaustion.' I couldn't keep the sneer out of my voice. 'Of course, as a doctor himself, he didn't need a referral to the Milton Home.'

'Oh, is that where he is – was? I've heard that's a posh place for the rich to spend their declining years, not just for sick people.'

Alan nodded. 'In fact, not principally for the sick. The residents don't need skilled nursing care, just a staff to look after their needs and of course to deal with memory issues.'

Timothy frowned. 'And do they boot them out when they get really old and have serious health problems?'

Alan and I looked at each other. 'I don't know,' I said. 'I didn't think to ask.'

'But,' said Timothy slowly, 'if Dr Armstrong wasn't really ill – nervous exhaustion, you said—'

'He said,' I corrected. 'The staff didn't seem too sure about it.'

'Anyway, nothing critical. Then what did he die of?'

Alan sighed. There was no getting around it. 'He died,' he said precisely, 'of having a pillow held over his face until he stopped breathing. He was in fact murdered.'

EIGHT

'**M**urdered.' The boy's voice was flat. I've heard more passion expressed about toothpaste. Bad reaction.

There was some Glenfiddich left in the bottle. Alan rinsed out his coffee cup and poured a small tot. 'Drink that.'

Timothy took the cup politely and drank. And choked. Eyes streaming, he pulled out his handkerchief and wiped his face. 'What *is* that stuff?'

Alan grinned. 'Some of the finest whisky God ever made. I gather you don't routinely drink spirits.'

'A little gin now and again. With tonic. That stuff is pure fire!'

I chuckled. 'The aboriginal people in America, the ones we inaccurately called Indians, used to call whisky firewater. But it's a gross insult to a fine product like Glenfiddich. I'm not much for scotch; I prefer bourbon. But even I can tell that "stuff", as you call it, is a very superior potable. Try sipping it, instead of knocking it back.'

'Well, I didn't know, did I?' he said, and took a cautious sip. 'Hmm.' He took another, and Alan reached out a hand for the cup.

'I've no thought to getting you drunk, young man, and when you're not used to it, whisky can pack a mean punch. It's excellent for medicinal purposes, however. You seem now to be present and accounted for.'

'I was a bit gobsmacked, wasn't I? Sorry about that, but it isn't every day that someone you know gets murdered. I still can't come to terms with the word. Or the idea.'

'You knew him, then?' I asked before Alan could. I was afraid he couldn't keep the policeman out of his voice.

'I only met him once. That was enough. And before you get around to asking, no, my feelings for him were not exactly what you might expect from someone reading theology. All Christian teaching to the contrary, I hated and resented him, and if I'd had a chance I might have enjoyed kicking him downstairs. But I did not, repeat *not*, murder him.'

'I never thought you did,' said Alan calmly. 'I'd be a poor policeman indeed if I couldn't see that the news came as a complete surprise to you. Nor can I see that you had anything to gain by his death; rather the opposite, indeed.'

'Right. As long as he was alive there was some chance my lawyer might get some sort of settlement. Look, I want you both to understand that I'm not a litigious sort of person. In fact, it's rather against my principles. That sounds rich, doesn't it, coming from someone who just talked about kicking a man downstairs?'

'Sounds very human. I'm not much for lawsuits, myself, and neither is Alan. They're so often prompted by sheer greed, on the part of the lawyers as well as the clients. But in this case, I think you were certainly justified. What a pity it's all for naught.'

'It might not be,' said Alan, running a hand along his chin. 'I'm no expert on the law, but surely it might be possible to sue his estate. It might depend on who his beneficiaries were. I don't know. If that lawyer of yours is still willing to work gratis, you might ask him about the possibility.'

Timothy thought about that for a long moment. 'But if I do that, it would give me a motive for his murder, wouldn't it?'

We talked about that for a long time after Timothy took himself out into the rain. It had slackened off a little, but he would still be very wet when he got back to his no-doubt bleak room.

'At least he has a little liquid warmth inside him,' Alan commented as I looked out the window to watch his splashing progress.

I turned away as he reached the gatehouse and moved out of sight. 'I feel so sorry for him,' I mourned. 'The poor kid's between a rock and a hard place. He's afraid to press ahead about the inheritance, because it will put him in the spotlight as someone who could benefit from that dreadful man's death. But if he does nothing, he just drifts deeper into debt and might have to take out more loans or even leave the university. And he's bright and committed.'

'And "called". If that's truly the case, he must continue. I hate to think of more loans, even though, as he says, the system here is far less punitive than in America. Presumably Tim will be given the means, somehow, if we really believe that God looks after his own.'

'I do believe that – in the long run. But look at all the saints who were tortured for their faith, or killed. I don't think we were ever promised life was going to be easy for anyone, no matter how saintly. Alan, isn't there anything we can do?'

'We could afford to pay his fees for a term or two, but not beyond that. And he wouldn't take it, in any case. You saw how reluctant he was to take a tip, and then he turned around and spent it on us. He's hell bent on making his own way.'

'I'm not sure that's the right expression, but I see what you mean. So we stand by and watch a promising priest fall by the wayside?'

'No. We do our level best to find out who really killed Dr Armstrong, so Timothy can, we hope, eventually get his rightful inheritance.'

'And how, O guru, do we do that? Seems to me we're at a dead end.'

'We're tired and discouraged. By morning we'll have ideas. We always do. Let's tidy up the mess and get to bed.'

'Because,' I trilled a few bars of the famous theme song, '"Tomorrow is another day".'

'Right. 'Night, Scarlett.'

The morning dawned clear and serene, having forgotten its bad temper of the day before. I felt sunshiny myself. 'I've had an idea,' I announced, as soon as I'd imbibed the requisite dose of caffeine.

'And are you going to share the secret? More coffee?'

'No, I'll wait till we get downstairs. Their coffee is much better than this stuff. I'll wait on coffee, I mean, not my idea. Though it has nothing to do with solving the murder.'

Alan just looked at me.

'All right, all right. What I thought was, since Timothy is

having a hard time making ends meet, what if we could find a way to lower his housing costs? He isn't living here in the castle, which means he's on his own somewhere, and it's bound to be costing more than he can afford.'

'And how . . . oh.'

We shared a look. 'Exactly. David needs to get out of his granddaughter's house, but he'd be lonely living alone. We think he has enough money to get a reasonably nice flat, or even a house. If he finds one with two bedrooms, why shouldn't he let Timothy use one at a nominal rent, or maybe no rent at all in exchange for some household chores? It would be a great solution for both of them, and it wouldn't feel to Timothy like the charity he's so loath to receive.'

'Hmm. Might work, if we put it to them the right way. You do realize we don't have an address or phone number for Timothy. Not even a surname.'

I waved away that difficulty. 'He's a student here. We can find it. And I'm starving. Let's get some breakfast and then go over to the library. Someone there will know who our guide was yesterday.'

The best-laid plans, as Burns reminds us in more interesting language, don't always work out. We were just finishing our meal when Alan's phone rang. He listened for a moment, then rang off and turned to me. 'We need to hurry a bit, love. David's picking us up in a few minutes at the same place, the top of Owengate.'

'But it's after ten. I thought he said he couldn't drive there at this time of day. Yes, OK, I'm coming!'

Alan led the way out of the Great Hall at a rapid pace. 'Something urgent, he said. No explanation. Apparently he's willing to face the charge this time. Let's hope he pays it in time, so it doesn't cost him a fortune. We have other uses in mind for his money!'

David explained when we got out of Durham traffic and out on the open road. 'There's been a development. A witness has turned up at the Milton with a story that might be important. I managed to persuade the management there that it would be a good idea for you two to hear it.'

'A witness to the murder?'

'No. But it might matter, all the same. It's a bit complicated, so I won't try to summarize. Better you hear it from her own lips.'

'Her? The witness is a woman?' Alan sounded surprised enough that I was reminded of his deeply buried bias about women. It doesn't often surface, bless him.

'A girl. A young woman, I suppose I should say. She's a student at the university, St Mary's College.'

And he would say no more.

Today no swarm of police was in evidence. There was one car in the Milton car park that was so very unobtrusive that I figured it had to belong to the police who, unlike those in the country of my birth, often prefer subtlety. I raised an eyebrow at David, he nodded.

We didn't need to announce ourselves to the receptionist or sign in; she was expecting us and took us to the director's office. He stood when we entered, as did the man in the suit, and a very pretty young woman. Three empty chairs took up most of the space in the room.

Mr Williams indicated the other man. 'This is Detective Inspector Harris. Mr Harris, David Tregarth, who recently moved to Durham from Exeter, where he was a senior police officer.' They shook hands. 'Alan Nesbitt lives in Sherebury, where he was chief constable until his retirement, and his wife Dorothy Martin is from America originally.' We nodded and smiled. 'They're here visiting with Mr Tregarth. And this young woman is Eileen Walsh, a student at St Mary's, who has some information that might be very important. Shall we all sit down? Miss Walsh, the floor is yours.'

She sat composedly, showing no signs of embarrassment or unease. The morning sun coming through a window set her strawberry-blond hair on fire and turned her pale, smooth skin almost translucent. When she spoke, the hint of a lilt confirmed her Irish origins.

'I am a student, as Mr Williams said, studying a course in biosciences.' She nodded to the director. 'My special interest is botany. I enjoy walking along the river, simply because it's beautiful and peaceful, but also because of the variety of plant species at different times of the year. They're very lovely;

some of them are unknown to me from my home, and I love learning more about them. I walk usually in the morning, but occasionally at night after a difficult day. I'm always very careful at night, as the path is not well-lit in places, and because the rowdies are often out then and I've no wish to get mixed up with them.'

She took a breath. 'I'm sure you know, Mr Harris, that the louts sometimes fall into the river when it's high and they've taken too much beer. Once or twice some young idiot has drowned.'

It was almost 'eejit' but not quite. She must have lived in England for some time.

'About a month ago,' she went on, 'I was out walking, rather late, and I witnessed one of those drownings.'

'And you reported it?' That was Mr Harris.

'Of course. I called emergency services and told them I'd seen someone fall in the river. I was on the upper path by then, not near enough to see exactly what happened, but it was a quiet night. I heard a cry and a splash, and looked down to see someone struggling in the river. Or not quite that. It was too dark to see details, but a light on the other shore showed the water being disturbed, splashing about and so on. I phoned 999 and then ran down to see if I could help, but I tripped on a long streamer of ivy across the path, and by the time I got back to my feet and down to the river, the rescue squad was there. They're very quick, you know.' She swallowed, and the director poured her a glass of water, which she sipped with a nod of thanks.

'It was really rather horrid. When I finally reached the scene, the boy had disappeared. The rescue team had to drag for him, and of course he was dead by the time they finally pulled his body out. You know all about this, of course, Mr Harris. It would be in the police reports.' She sipped a little more water. 'What you don't know is that there was someone else at the scene.'

David and Alan sat up, their attention at high alert.

'Who, Miss Walsh?' said Harris. 'Why did you not report this at the time?'

'I forgot all about it. I caught only a glimpse of the man,

and he was farther from the river than I, almost at the end of the upper path. It would have taken him even longer to get down to the river. I remember I was a bit resentful at the time, seeing he was moving even farther away, but then I fell and in all the ensuing distress I forgot.'

'Miss Walsh, what made you remember?'

Alan sounded as if he thought she had some ulterior motive for coming forward, though for the life of me I couldn't imagine what.

'I was talking with a friend, Tim Hayes. I think you know him. He's a Castle student.'

Alan and I nodded, now completely at sea. Timothy might have been involved in unpleasant ways with Blake Armstrong, but what could he have to do with the drowning of a drunken student?

'He told me that Blake Armstrong was dead. Murdered, he said. Is this true?'

'It is.' Harris was tight-lipped.

'Then I knew I must tell you everything I had seen, the night the man drowned. Because the man I saw moving away from a drowning man was Blake Armstrong.'

NINE

The silence sat in the room for several seconds while we tried to make sense of this. Then David cleared his throat. 'And you believe that Armstrong might have had something to do with the man's death?'

'No.' The girl was quite definite about it. 'That wouldn't have been possible. He was too far away from the river. Look, if I can have some paper I'll show you.'

She drew a rough sketch and showed it to David. 'See, here's the river, with the path beside it. The lower path, that is. But here, up the bank a bit, is the upper path. There are stairs to get from one to the other. You know them?'

David nodded, and so did I. I remembered seeing that there was a way up from the riverside path at several intervals.

'All right. When I heard the splash I was about here.' She marked a place on the upper path. 'I had just come up, and I was about to go back to my room. I saw the splashing in the river and looked around, I don't know why. I suppose I wanted to see if there was anyone besides me to help, but I saw only this man, right here.' Another mark on the sketch. 'That's where the path ends, with stairs up to the pavement and the college buildings. The man there was turning to go up the stairs. As I think back on it, he wasn't moving fast, or panting as if he'd been running. He could not have been on the lower path only a few seconds before.'

'Then why do you think he was running away?'

'He wasn't running. I've just said that. He just "passed by on the other side". I don't know why he wasn't going down to try to help. Maybe he didn't hear the splash, or the cries. Was he deaf, do you know?'

'We observed no hearing loss while he was staying with us,' said the director.

'Then I don't know. I have no answer for you. The man's

dead. P'raps he was one of those "don't want to get involved" cowards. I don't know.'

'Miss Walsh,' said Alan, 'one thing puzzles me.'

'Please call me Eileen,' she interjected. 'Everyone else does. I feel daft being "Miss Walsh" in this company.'

'In the company of those old enough to be your parents, or grandparents.' Alan smiled. 'Very well, Eileen. You've said you saw this man only fleetingly, at a time when you were considerably distressed and distracted. Yet you're certain of his identity. How can you be so sure?'

She raised her eyes to the ceiling. 'I knew someone would ask that sooner or later. I am certain for several reasons. One is that there is a light just there, to light the stairs I imagine. When he turned to go up, it shone full on his face, and I recognized him at once.'

'You knew him, then?' I asked.

'Not to say know. I had met him once. That was quite enough.'

She was echoing Timothy. We waited.

'He was a doctor. His speciality was geriatrics, and he treated old women. Old women with money.' Her lip curled. 'He didn't suffer by it. He died a very wealthy man.'

'And you met him how?' I persisted gently.

'You've probably worked that out,' she said, addressing Alan and me. 'Tim went to see him after his auntie died. You know the story.'

Alan explained to the others. 'Timothy Hayes had a courtesy aunt, an old friend of his parents. She had made a will in Timothy's favour, leaving him her considerable estate. Dr Armstrong treated the lady, and before she died she altered her will, making the doctor her sole beneficiary.'

Eileen took up the tale. 'So Tim went to talk to him, try to make him see how unfair it was. I went with him. He was odious. Smarmy, oh so charming. He quite understood, but he had inherited lawfully under a proven testamentary instrument, and he could hardly try to overturn it, now could he, and had Tim any idea how much contesting a will could cost, and so on. I tried to keep my temper, but Tim lost his. He's going to be a priest, and a good one, but he can tolerate only so much before he goes spare. We were escorted from the good doctor's office, none too gently.

'So you see why I would remember him quite clearly.'

'Yes.' Mr Harris cleared his throat. 'What I still don't understand is why you thought it necessary to bring this to our attention. You have said that Dr Armstrong could not have been near the unfortunate young man who drowned. What importance, then, does his presence in the vicinity have for you?'

If the inspector meant by his formal turn of speech to intimidate the young Irishwoman, he underestimated her. She drew herself up and looked him straight in the eye. 'He was there. He did nothing to help. I find that despicable. But that is not the only reason I think you might be interested.' She picked up her sketch. 'I told you I could not see clearly what was happening at the river. Trees and underbrush were in the way. But Armstrong was here, up where he would have had a clear line of sight. The trees are not high enough to restrict his view from that point. I think he saw exactly what happened. Suppose the poor laddie was pushed, and suppose Armstrong saw it. Why did he not come forward?'

'She hates him. Hated him. She wants to involve him in this unrelated death.'

David, Alan and I were sitting in what had become our favourite pub, with sandwiches and beer, hashing over what we had just heard.

'David, the man's dead, for Pete's sake. What possible harm could she do him now? Granted he was a first-class sleaze. She said over and over that he could have had nothing to do with the kid's death. What was his name, by the way? He deserves that dignity.'

'I don't remember, Dorothy, but I can look it up. His death didn't raise a lot of ripples, I'm afraid. It happens all too often. The students *will* drink too much, and there's not much to prevent their falling in. Oh, some safety features have been introduced, but the possibility is still there. Most of the time their mates pull them out and they're not much the worse, but a few have drowned.'

'We met a man on the river path,' I commented, 'who thought there ought to be a wall, or a fence, or some sort of barrier.'

'It's been suggested, but the general feeling is that it would spoil the beauty of the path, and walkers simply need to be more careful.'

'Hmm. Drunks are not generally noted for their caution.'

'We're straying from the point,' said Alan, ever the policeman. 'David, why do *you* think she told us this rather odd story?'

David shrugged, but I had an idea. 'She thinks he might have seen something, something important. Suppose she's right. Suppose someone did push in the poor kid, and Armstrong saw it. He said nothing to the police, but suppose he told someone else? It would certainly be worth checking that out, don't you think?'

David raised his hands in the classic gesture of futility. 'Worth it, perhaps, but not at all easy to do. How would you suggest that we find, among the entire population of Durham, one person in whom Armstrong might have confided? Police resources are limited, you know—'

I groaned and held up a hand. 'Spare me. I can recite that lecture by heart. Too few personnel, too little money, et cetera, et cetera.'

Alan frowned. 'It's all too true, Dorothy. The public expect miracles from their police, but lose interest when it comes to supporting them.'

'I know all that, and yes, it's shameful, but David is exaggerating the problem here. We're not talking about a huge group of people, certainly not the entire population. We're talking about Armstrong's friends and colleagues, the people he spent time with. It couldn't be too hard to track them down and ask a simple question.'

David and Alan both shook their heads. 'That could be done, certainly would be done if this were a case of murder,' said Alan patiently. 'It's the sort of plodding routine that solves most cases, in the end. But it takes a good deal of time and a good many men and women, and there's simply no justification for such a search in order to track down an entirely mythical confidante, simply to satisfy our curiosity.'

I wasn't going to give up easily. 'But this *is* a case of murder. The murder of one Dr Armstrong. It was odd, his turning away from a drowning man, and I believe any odd things connected with a murdered man deserve an investigation.'

Both men smiled and shrugged. Don't distress the lady. Don't argue with her. Change the subject. She'll be off on some other tangent soon.

Alan should have known me better than that.

Before we left the pub I asked David for the phone number of the Milton Home and the name of the director, which I'd forgotten.

'It's one of those forgettable names. Billings? Wilton? Willard? Something like that. Why?'

'I think I may have left my wallet in his office. Not that there's much in it, but I don't want to lose my credit cards. I'd just as soon speak directly to him. I don't want my loss known to everybody in the place. I'm sure they're honest, but . . .' I yawned elaborately. 'Goodness, I do believe it's nap time. Oh, and David, don't forget to pay your congestion fee before it bankrupts you.'

Alan looked at me suspiciously but said nothing. And when we got back to our room in the castle, I waited until Alan was in the bathroom and then pulled out my phone.

It took longer than I had hoped to get connected – the man's name turned out to be Williams – but I got through to him just as Alan emerged. Drat! Well, no help for it.

'Mr Williams, this is Dorothy Martin. I wanted to talk a bit further with Miss Walsh, and I wondered if you had her phone number. Yes . . . yes . . . got it. Thank you very much.'

'So that's what you're up to,' said Alan. 'I wondered. Lost credit cards, indeed!'

'You were both so smug about Eileen's story. I intend to follow it up. If the police don't want to waste their time on a "mythical confidante", I don't in the least mind wasting mine. You always say I'm good at talking to people.'

'The best of British luck, my dear. I'm sorry if I sounded smug. I simply don't have quite as much faith in Eileen's intuition as you seem to do.'

'She's Irish, Alan, even if she's lived in England long enough to lose most of the accent and idiom. That Irish heritage counts for something, and don't you laugh. Her people have been credited with "the sight", time out of mind. I find a little extra perception in Eileen quite credible, and I intend to follow her lead.'

'And how do you propose to do that? I remind you that we do not have a car in Durham.'

'We have our feet, which is the way most people seem to get around here. And I'm sure there are buses. Eileen will know, and I'm going to call her right now.'

I reached her with no trouble, reminded her of who I was, and then told her of my conversation with the two men. 'I'm afraid they're inclined to dismiss the incident as irrelevant, but I am not.'

I could hear the smile in her voice. 'You're a woman. We understand some things men do not, poor things.'

I heard a male chuckle in the background and thought I knew who was with her. 'And you're Irish, which makes you aware of even more. Look, I've had an idea that I'd like to talk over with you and Timothy. Could we take the two of you out to dinner tonight?'

She didn't even need to ask him. 'That would be very kind of you, thank you. Not a posh place, if you don't mind.' She didn't say, but I suspected Timothy's clothes might not run to 'posh'.

'We know very little of the city. Suppose you name the place, and tell us how to get there, and we can meet you.'

'No, no, we'll come and get you. Too easy to get lost in Durham if you don't know your way. You're in the castle, yes? Right. We'll meet you in the courtyard at – what time?'

We settled on a time and ended the call.

'Am I to come along to this conference,' asked Alan with mock humility, 'or as a doubting Thomas am I beyond the pale?'

'Of course you're coming. Who do you think is going to pay the bill?'

I found I was ready for that nap I'd used as an excuse earlier. When I woke, and prodded Alan awake, I made us a pot of tea to get our brains functioning again, and then it was time to meet the kids.

They took us to the restaurant where he worked, and it turned out to be quite nice, if not utterly 'posh'. The menu was extensive and interesting, and we opted this time for Italian specialities, a risotto for me and lasagne for Alan, hoping our guests would also go for a square meal. Eileen had a very nice figure, but Timothy was far too thin. I cast curses toward the greedy doctor who had deprived this young man of his rightful inheritance.

I looked up at Alan when we had eaten our fill, but he shook his head. 'It's your agenda. I'm just along to pay the bill, remember?'

'About that,' Timothy began, but I overrode him.

'We invited you out to dinner. It's our treat. No argument will be accepted. In other words, shut up, Timothy. We have other things to talk about.'

'Okay, if you insist. But please call me Tim. All my friends call me Tim.'

Pleased to be numbered among his friends, I smiled, then looked around and lowered my voice. We were in a quiet corner, and what I was going to say wasn't particularly private, but it pays to be careful. 'Eileen, I told you, and I've no doubt you told Tim, about the conversation earlier with David – Mr Tregarth – and Alan. We discussed your story about seeing Dr Armstrong moving away from a drowning man, and why you thought we should know about it.'

'I thought he might have seen something important. I said that, but no one seemed to take it seriously.'

'Well, that was what I wanted to talk to you about. Suppose he did see something important. Suppose he saw that someone pushed that poor guy into the river. He didn't tell the police, for whatever insane reason, but suppose he told someone else.'

I paused. Eileen and Tim looked at each other, eyebrows raised.

'Because,' I went on, 'if he did talk to someone else, the police need to get hold of that someone, to find out what he said. At least I think they do. Alan and David think that kind of investigation would take too many scarce man-hours. The student's death was accepted as accident; asking questions at this stage would stir up matters, and in any case it has nothing to do with Armstrong's death, which is the one under investigation.'

I picked up my wine glass and found it empty. Alan picked up the bottle, doled out a little more, and gestured at the other two, who shook their heads.

'All right. I disagree with the two men. My point of view is that anything odd in the background of a murder victim deserves at least a glance. And that's why I wanted to talk to you two. Neither of you knew Armstrong well. Both of you detested him. But do you know anyone who knew him, anyone he might have talked to about the drowning?'

They considered. 'I suppose he must have had friends,' said Tim hesitantly. Eileen snorted. 'I never heard of any, though,' he went on. 'He had a nurse-receptionist, of course. She might know something about his friends. And there were his patients.'

'He wouldn't have talked to them,' said Eileen. 'He was scum, a . . . well, there are very few words fit for this company. But he cultivated a professional manner. He wouldn't have spoken to patients about anything but their symptoms, along with lashings of sympathy and hope.'

Tim nodded in agreement.

'Hmm. Well, then we're left with his friends, if any. Did he have a family? Wife, children?'

Both of them shook their head. 'I don't think so,' said Tim. 'I know he lived alone. He must have had a housekeeper or something.'

'Ah,' said Alan, getting interested in spite of himself. 'Where did he live? Neighbours can be chatty.'

'I don't know,' said Tim, 'but my solicitor would have his address.'

'And his name?'

Alan nodded at me, and I obediently got out the little notebook I always carry and wrote down the name and phone number Tim read from his phone. 'And while we're at it, Tim, what's the address of his office? Armstrong's, I mean. Or his surgery, or whatever you call it here. The place where he had his practice.'

'I don't know the address, but I can show it to you. Or again, my solicitor will know. Why?'

'Because if the office hasn't been closed, and the receptionist is still there, she might be a very useful source of information. She might be useful wherever she is, but without a name, she'd be very hard to find. I'll take you up on that offer to show me where the practice was. Tomorrow.' I glanced out the window at the darkening sky. 'It's going to rain again, and anyway it's too late now. No one would be there.'

'Mrs Martin,' Eileen began.

'Dorothy.'

'Dorothy – why are you going to all this trouble? It's the business of the police, and if they've decided to do nothing about it, that's no responsibility of yours.'

Alan tilted his head to one side, awaiting my response.

'I hadn't thought about it,' I said honestly. 'Partly, I guess, it's that something in me can't abide an unsolved puzzle. I'm a bit like a rat terrier in that respect; I have to find out where that elusive little devil of a fact is hiding. But it's also that I have grown to like both of you, and I hate to see you suffering under this cloud of suspicion. Oh, you both know it's there. So far Tim is the only person at all connected with this business who is known to have a serious grudge against Armstrong, and in a case like this where almost anyone could have done the murder, the police must take a very close look at someone who hated the victim.'

'I did. I confess that I did. I'm meant to love my enemies. I'm under commandment to love my enemies. I couldn't love Armstrong, to my everlasting shame. But I didn't kill him.'

'Of course you didn't. But as long as we don't know who did, you'll be under some suspicion. That must be cleared. Not just for your sake, but for the sake of justice itself.'

My voice had risen a bit, and the waiter, coming to present the bill, applauded softly. I choked on my wine and was glad my red face could be attributed to that. I don't often climb on a soap box, praise be!

TEN

Immediately after breakfast the next day, Alan called David to see what plans he had for the day. 'Nothing much,' he reported to me after he ended the call. 'He's going to see his aunt this afternoon, just for a visit. He hasn't talked to her for a day or two, and he wants to make sure she's okay after the trauma. I told him we were going to try to track down Dr Armstrong's acquaintances.'

'And what did he say to that?'

Alan grinned. 'Enthusiasm great enough to be obviously insincere. Courteous in the extreme.'

'He'll see, when we get something useful. Meanwhile it keeps us busy and out of his hair. Now, do we need raincoats or not?'

Alan studied the sky and shrugged. 'At home I might be able to hazard a guess. I don't know weather patterns here. I'd say, take them and brollies, just in case.'

We got mildly lost a time or two trying to find the office Eileen and Tim had pointed out to us the night before, but got there in the end.

A sign on the door read 'Closed', and the door was locked. A blind was pulled down in front of the glass portion of the door.

I made a disgusted noise. 'Okay, what now?'

Alan moved to the side of the door to squint into the narrow gap between shade and glass. 'I think the lights are on. Presumably the sign simply means the practice is closed. Try knocking.'

I hammered on the door, first on the wood and then on the glass, which made a louder din. When there was no response, I persisted.

Eventually a very angry woman opened the door a crack. 'I assume you can read. The office is closed. Permanently.'

'Yes, we do know that,' said Alan, neatly inserting his

umbrella into the small opening. 'We came to talk to you, actually, if you can spare us a few minutes of your valuable time.'

I have sometimes said that Alan is a genuine person, not 'charming' in the oily sense. But he can employ considerable charm when necessary. The woman opened the door a little wider and her tone moderated. A bit.

'I'm sure I don't mean to be rude, but I really am very busy. Have we ever met?'

She knew they hadn't, but at least it was better than 'I don't know you. Go away.'

'No. I'm certain I'd have remembered.' The warmth he gave that remark almost destroyed my composure. He was in splendid form. 'You are the assistant to the late Dr Armstrong, are you not?'

'Yes. Mildred Frome.'

'Then let me introduce myself. My name is Alan Nesbitt. I live in Sherebury, and my wife Dorothy and I are visiting an old friend, David Tregarth. We were colleagues for a time, years ago in Cornwall. Now we're both retired, he has moved to Durham, and he invited us to come for a visit. He and I both served in the police force at one time, and David asked us to help him look into the matter of Dr Armstrong's death. We hope you might be of some help.'

A few drops of rain fell, and a freshening wind promised more.

'Oh, well, come in, then. I don't know how I can help. I've told everything I know to the police, and it wasn't much. But that's no reason for the two of you to get wet, and it's going to pour in a minute.'

She was right about that. We had barely got inside before the rain came down like Niagara. The wind carried a lot of it into the foyer before Alan could get the door shut.

'Goodness,' I said, 'what a mess we've made. If there's a mop somewhere, I'll clean it up for you.'

If Alan's deliberate charm had appealed to the woman's ego, my housewifely offer did away with the rest of her resistance. 'Oh, don't bother,' she said. 'The cleaners still come round twice a week, and tonight's one of their nights.'

'The practice isn't still open, is it?' Alan asked as if he really wanted to know.

'Oh, no. Nobody could fill Dr Armstrong's shoes. Such a tragedy, his death. No, but his patients come round, poor things. It's only been a few days, and they can't quite believe it. I think they want me to tell them it isn't true.'

'Or maybe they find some comfort just in being here,' I said with hypocritical sympathy.

'You know, I think they do. We can sit and cry together. That doesn't get my work done, but I feel I'm helping in my small way.' She sniffled and reached for a tissue. 'But you didn't come here to listen to my troubles. Ask anything you want, though I don't know that I have any answers.'

I thought I'd let Alan handle this one.

'Actually, we were hoping you might be able to tell us about Dr Armstrong's friends. His colleagues, perhaps?'

She sniffed. 'Not them. Jealous of him, the lot of them. He was the best geriatrician in town, and they all knew it.'

I ventured a comment. 'I imagine there are a good many elderly people in Durham. I don't know why, but somehow English cathedral cities seem to have a large ageing population.'

She looked at me more closely than she had bothered to do earlier. 'You're not English, are you? Something about your accent . . .'

'Not English by birth, no. I've lived in Sherebury for many years now, but I lived most of my life in America. The state of Indiana, if you know where that is.'

She shook her head. 'A cousin of mine knows someone who lives there. I'd never heard of it before she talked about him. In any case, you're quite right about cathedral cities, at least this one. It may be something about the influence of the church, but people here do tend to live a long time. And that's not always a blessing, believe me. I've seen some sad cases: minds gone, bodies good for another ten years.'

I shuddered. 'I've always prayed that my mind would be the last to go, but of course there's little we can do to assure that.'

Alan took control of the conversation again. 'Right. But if

his friends were not found among other doctors, who was he close to?'

Mildred hesitated. 'He kept himself very much to himself. He was extremely busy, of course; his patient load was enormous. And then – I don't think he found people here very congenial. He came from London, you know, and he was used to a much more cosmopolitan, intellectual atmosphere.'

Translation: he was a snob with virtually no friends. I could almost feel sorry for the woman: trying to defend her boss, whom she had obviously worshipped, now that he could no longer defend himself.

'A pity,' said Alan. 'We had hoped to talk with someone in whom he might have confided. We know very little about his life immediately before he went into the home, and often a man's background provides some hints about his death. Why did he go to the home, by the way?'

'He was . . . was tired. He had some worries about his heart, and he thought it was time for a complete rest.'

'I see. His cardiologist recommended the home?'

'No.' She paused. 'He had no need for a referral. He was familiar with the home, as he had referred many of his patients there when they were no longer able to live alone. And he had no personal doctor here in Durham. He was perfectly capable of assessing his own health and treating any problems.'

A man who acts as his own lawyer has a fool for a client, says the old adage. I thought the same might be true for a doctor.

Alan sighed and shook his head. 'Ah, well, it was worth a try. We know that he saw a young man drown in the river not long before he went to the home—'

'How did you know that?' asked Mildred sharply. 'He didn't tell anyone about—' And then she shut her mouth firmly.

'I hardly know.' Alan sounded genuinely uncertain. 'A cathedral city is a great place for the grapevine, as we know from our own experience at home. But you're saying he told you about it?'

'He . . . I . . . he mentioned it. He was of course very upset.' She took a deep breath. 'He did his best to help the boy, but there was nothing he could do.'

'What a pity,' said Alan again. 'This happened when, do you remember?'

'Of course I remember! I'd hardly forget something that distressing! It was the day before he went to the home. In fact, I believe it was what led to his break – that is, to his collapse. It was just too much, on top of his exhausting schedule. And now, if there's nothing else . . .' She gestured to her desk, which was indeed full of ledgers and other papers demanding her attention.

We accepted our dismissal, apologized once more for taking up her time, offered condolences on her loss, and went back out into the teeming rain.

'Not one of the world's talented liars,' I remarked as we sat over plates of pasta in a little Italian restaurant. We were the only customers in the place; it was very early for lunch, but we had no wish to splash back to our room and then go out again.

Alan looked meaningfully around the empty room. Our waiter had delivered our meal and disappeared, but could no doubt hear our every word from the kitchen. 'Not everyone is as gifted as you, my love.'

'You say such sweet things.' I nodded to show I had taken his point about discretion, and would watch my words. 'So what do you think?'

'The same as you. A certain amount of gold amidst the dross. A great deal of tarradiddle.'

'At the end, don't you think? Before that it was probably truth.'

'Considerably sugar-coated. Speaking of which, I'm minded to throw caution to the winds and have something sweet. What about you?'

The speed with which our waiter appeared verified our suspicions about his excellent hearing. I hoped we had been obscure enough to leave his curiosity unsatisfied.

We dawdled over our tiramisu, hoping to wait out the rain, and had some espresso (thereby putting paid to our afternoon nap), but at last there was no help for it. The restaurant was filling up and they wanted our table, so we struggled into our still-wet rain gear and waded home.

We stripped to the skin. I longed to wallow in a hot tub, but student housing didn't run to such luxuries; a shower had to do. When we were warm and dressed again, I made us a pot of tea, and we sat drinking it and debriefing.

'All right, he wasn't a popular man,' I began. 'Mildred was telling the truth about that. She interpreted it as jealousy. I'm more inclined to think it was reaction to an unpleasant personality. He was a predatory egotist.'

'A greedy predatory egotist. All his patients had a certain amount of money, since he was in private practice. I wonder if one reason he consulted no other doctor, even about his own health, was that he didn't want anyone looking into his methods.'

'Alan, I was thinking exactly the same thing! I also wonder how many of those little old ladies who died and left him all their worldly goods might have lived if someone else had been treating them.'

'No way to know, at this point. There are dozens of ways a doctor can speed a sufferer on her way and leave no traces. The wrong medicine, the wrong dosage, an incorrect diagnosis – anything. And if you treat only geriatric patients, no one is very surprised when many of them die.'

'Their families—'

'Ah, but you remember that Tim's solicitor said his victims had no families. Presumably the ones with families either survived or did not make a will in Armstrong's favour. Apparently there was no talk of his killing his patients, only rumours that he was profiting a bit too regularly from their deaths.'

'Hmm.' I picked up my cup, took a sip, and put it down again. Cold. 'I'm inclined to think that means he was honest in his medicine. If there had been the slightest hint of the irregular, someone would have jumped on it.'

'Almost certainly. You know, I think his unpopularity must have been almost universal, except amongst his patients. Mildred would never have admitted it if she'd had a hope we wouldn't find out anyway.'

'Yes, she worshipped at his shrine. Like virtually every other woman close to him. Not at the home, though. The staff saw through him. That's interesting, actually. I wonder why he didn't mesmerize them as well.'

'You're not thinking, Dorothy. He made no effort to be charming with them because he had nothing to gain. They weren't his adoring patients, ready to turn over all their worldly goods. They were just servants, there to see to his comfort and fulfil his every wish. Of course he reverted to type with them.'

I made a face. 'Remind me why we want to find out who removed this viper from the face of the earth.'

Alan shook his head. 'It's a good thing tomorrow's Sunday. Your values need a wash and a brush-up. But the point is not just "Thou shalt do no murder". Don't forget that every single person who was in that nursing home that day is under suspicion until the killer can be found.'

'Okay, okay. Am I allowed to be happy he's gone?'

'Good can come of evil. That's part of our belief system too. And I don't know if you've noticed, heart of my heart, but the rain has stopped and the sun's out and I think it's time for a walk.'

ELEVEN

The cobblestones were slippery, but my sneakers got a good grip, and Alan's arm was steady. Without thinking about it much, we headed for the river walk.

When we reached the bottom of the first stairs, the beginning of the upper-level walk, I stopped and looked out toward the river. The drop down from our level was steep, so even though the trees and bushes were in full leaf, they didn't obstruct the view.

'Look, Alan. There's a clear view, all the way down to the bridge. And you can hear the river rushing along. Armstrong could certainly have heard the splash of someone falling in.'

'Or being pushed. Of course, the river is high just now with all the rain, and noisy. If there was background noise then, a jet overhead, or a siren—'

'But we know he heard and/or saw the boy fall in. Eileen saw him react, and anyway he told Mildred. He lied about going down to help, though. Alan, you can move faster than I can. How long do you think it would take you to get down to the river from here, going as fast as possible?'

He looked at the path and distant steps. 'Longer today, with all the wet footing, than on a dry day. Shall I give it a try?'

'Carefully! And wait till I find the stopwatch on this stupid thing.'

I remember when a phone made and received phone calls. Period. Now I think they could send a rocket to the moon – if you could find the right buttons. I finally located the stopwatch, poised a finger over it, and said 'Go!'

My husband is a big man, built along the lines of the late beloved Alistair Cooke, whom Alan resembles to a marked degree. When he was serving in the police, even though his last years were purely administrative, he was as fit as a man half his age, and even in his retirement he has stayed in good shape. As I kept my eye on the stopwatch, he moved away from me at a pace I couldn't even hope to achieve, catching hold of bushes here and there to avoid a slip. He disappeared from me as he headed down the steps to the lower level of the path, and I heard a crash of shrubbery that brought my heart to my mouth, but he reappeared at the edge of the river and called up to me. 'How did I do?'

I stopped the counter. 'Roughly four-and-a-half minutes. Was that a fall I heard?' From this distance it looked like he had collected quite a lot of leaves and mud.

'Slid into a bush. No harm done. Can you make it down, or shall I come up for you?'

'I have my stick; I can make it.'

It took me quite a lot longer, but at least I slid into no bushes and was much cleaner than he when I reached him. 'All right. If it was a dry day, and he was at least as fit as you, he could have done it faster. That's if this is the right place, the place where the poor guy went in.'

'He was younger, at any rate.' Alan's breathing still hadn't quite slowed to normal; he sounded annoyed at the slow-down imposed by age. 'He almost certainly could have got down in time to at least try to help.'

'Yes. And the question is: why didn't he?'

There was a bench just a few feet away. It was wet, but we were both wet anyway from brushing against the shrubbery. We sat. 'You're making the assumption,' said Alan, 'that Eileen is telling the truth and Armstrong was lying to his office help.'

'Yes. And you are assuming the same. Can't fool me. And besides our personal inclination, there's the fact that the man reported nothing to the police. I repeat, then, why did a doctor, a man in the business of saving lives, not even try to save this one?'

'Get out your notebook and we'll make a list.'

'I didn't bring my purse. But wait a minute.' I rummaged in the multiple pockets of my rain jacket and found a napkin and, for a wonder, a pen. With my phone serving as hard surface, I could make do. 'OK, shoot. But we'll have to keep our ideas short.'

'Right. My first notion is he was in a hurry. Late for something, perhaps.'

'We can check with Mildred. I'm sure she kept his calendar.'
I wrote down *Late?* and then chewed my pen in thought. 'That
would mean he was running *toward* something. But people
also run *away*. And they usually do it out of fear. What could
he have been afraid of?'

'Afraid of being pulled into the water and drowning himself.
Afraid of being unable to save the chap.'

'That last would be a terrible blow to his ego, of course.
Dr Armstrong the superman, can't even pull someone out of
the river.' I wrote down *Drowning* and then *Incompetence.*

'Or we could adopt Eileen's hypothesis.' Alan thought for
a moment. 'If the poor fellow was pushed, and Armstrong
saw it, he ran from fear of a murderer.'

The very thought terrified me. A breeze had sprung up, but
it wasn't a chill that made me shiver. 'And Eileen was there,
too. And she did run down to try to help! What if the murderer
had seen her? She could have—'

'Easy, love. We're dealing with a hypothetical situation here.
If there was a murderer, if someone saw him, if, if, if. Do we
know the time of the drowning? The time of day, that is?'

I searched my memory. 'Eileen said "rather late". I don't
know what that means, though.'

'I was wondering about the vision question. How dark was
it? How clearly could anyone have seen? And I'm trying to
work out the geography. Were there streetlamps anywhere that
could have got in someone's eye or dazzled away their night
vision? And of course all this matters only if the man was
pushed.'

'And there's no way to know that, at this late date.' I sighed
and put the napkin back in my pocket. 'Alan, we need a
miracle.'

The cathedral bells began to chime for evensong just then,
and we both laughed.

Alan called David as we wandered back to the castle after
evensong. 'Any news at your end?'

He listened for a moment and then turned to me. 'He wants
to take us to dinner tonight, and wonders if you'd enjoy the
posh place he mentioned before.'

'Tell him I'd like that very much.'

'He'll pick us up at the usual place at seven,' said Alan.

'Good. That'll give me time to bathe and change into something worthy of the elegant surroundings.'

When we got to the Hotel Indigo, I was glad I'd taken the trouble to put on a dress. I usually travel with one presentable outfit, just in case, and I would have felt very uncomfortable in jeans in the marble and stained-glass surroundings. 'It once housed the Durham County Council,' David told us as we were escorted into the lofty domed dining room, 'and when they moved out the university bought it and used it for some time. The hotel, I'm told, spent a fortune converting it, and the results show off the effort and expense.'

The food was just as impressive as the surroundings, and we paid it full justice by leaving the discussion of crime and mystery until we had finished our meal. David, very animated, talked at some length about the history of the building, of the room we were seated in – 'the old Senate chamber' – the university use of the building, the renowned chef, and so on. I wondered how he, a very recent resident of the city, knew all this, but kept still. I was too busy enjoying the food and my surroundings to care, really.

When I had eaten the last bite of my treacle tart, David summoned the waiter for the bill, and said, 'Shall we repair to the bar for something pleasant to round off the evening?'

'I couldn't eat one more thing,' I protested. 'Not a peanut. Not an olive. Zero.'

'But I'm sure you could manage a small cognac,' he insisted.

'I could, at any rate,' said Alan, so off we went to the bar, which was at least as intimidatingly elegant as the rest of the place.

'All right, old friend,' said Alan when we'd toasted our host, 'you've wined and dined us, and we're extremely grateful, but it's time to start this meeting. You hinted that there were things you needed to tell us.'

The cheerful bonhomie was wiped off David's face as if by a switch. 'I hadn't wanted to tell you, but I must. First, I want to apologize. I should never have involved you in this, a family matter. I had wanted you to enjoy Durham, and instead I've thrust you into an unpleasant and possibly dangerous situation. I'll never forgive myself. I had no idea it would turn into such a—'

'David.' I interrupted him and put my hand on his arm. 'Alan and I have not been "thrust into" anything. We could have said no and gone home. We have stayed here, and stuck with the investigation, because you needed help. And I know Alan feels the same way I do; we're not giving up until there's a resolution. Now tell us what's upset you.'

'There's been another attack. And this time there's very little doubt that it was Aunt Amanda who was responsible.'

TWELVE

We were back in our room at the castle. 'I think,' Alan had said with deliberation, 'that we should discuss this in private.' So we abandoned our drinks and David drove us as near home as we could get.

Alan appropriated a chair from the Great Hall and took it up to our room. That pretty well filled the available space, but at least we could all sit in some comfort. I made decaf for everyone, and we settled, cups in hand, to hear David's story.

'They called me this afternoon. It was a woman who was attacked this time, a resident who's at least as far gone as Aunt Amanda. She wasn't killed. Apparently she was able to struggle and cry out. She knocked the lamp off her bedside table, and the crash brought a staff member in a hurry. By that time the woman was sobbing and panting for breath.'

'And she accused Amanda.' My heart was so heavy I could hardly speak.

'She accused no one. She wasn't even able to tell us what had happened. By now she's probably forgotten most of it. She certainly would not be able to testify in court, or even dictate a deposition.'

'But why are they trying to pin it on Amanda?' Now I was angry.

'The pillow was hers.'

'Was from her room. That doesn't mean—'

'No. It was her own, a special, small, soft pillow with handmade lace trim.' I nodded, remembering the pretty thing. 'She brought it from home because it's very special to her. A favourite niece made it; she remembers that, for some reason. She never uses it, but it always sits on the little sofa in her room. Now it's stained with lipstick, and the lace is torn, and she's very upset.' He shook his head. 'Every time she sees it she cries and wonders how that could have happened.'

'But surely they'll have taken it away as evidence?' Alan frowned.

David threw up his hands. 'Evidence of what? No one saw the incident. The victim can't tell us about it. Amanda can't tell us about it. No one was seriously hurt. Yes, the pillow was found in Mrs Carly's room – she's the victim – and it didn't walk there by itself. But there's no question of prosecution.'

We waited. 'But?' asked Alan after a fraught silence.

'But they're booting her out. They told me, just before I talked to you, Alan, that I have a week to find her another place to live.'

I thought of that sweet old lady, living happily in a world of her own, surrounded by her few cherished keepsakes, cared for by people who were kind and who understood about her muddled mind. I thought of her being uprooted, confused and miserable, and I had to wipe away a tear. 'That must not happen,' I said in an unsteady voice. 'We mustn't let that happen!' That came out better. Anger was replacing sorrow. I have always found anger, righteous anger, to be a wonderfully energizing emotion.

'We can't stop it, Dorothy. Their minds are made up.'

'Then we have to unmake them. Who's "they", anyway?'

'Williams and the board of trustees. They have a legitimate concern. I accept that. They can't have the residents going in fear of their lives. The whole point of the Milton Home is to provide a safe and serene and comfortable haven where the elderly can live out their lives in peace.'

'And for the owners to make a great deal of money while they're at it,' I growled. 'If word gets out that there's a maniac about the place, actually living there among them, families are going to take their grannies and aunties out of there so fast they'll trample anyone in their way. And there goes all that lovely lolly.' David and Alan both opened their mouths, but I held up a hand. 'Okay, I'm not saying they don't provide value for money. They do. The residents get the loving care their families are paying for. The staff are, I think, genuinely devoted to the old dears. But the bottom line is always the first consideration of any business, and this is a business, no matter how compassionate. Of course, they'll throw Aunt

Amanda under the bus without a second thought. But we're going to stop them!'

'How?' asked David, in utter defeat.

'We're going to find out who the real criminal is and vindicate Amanda once and for all.'

'How?' This time it was Alan asking, and sounding as if he really wanted to know.

'I don't know yet. And I've had too much wine and cognac to think clearly tonight. But first thing in the morning we're on it. David, how early can you be here? We'll wangle some way for you to join us for breakfast and have a council of war.'

I had forgotten, the night before, that we would wake to Sunday, but the bells reminded me. They weren't as loud as at home, where they were almost over our heads, but they woke us and got us moving. We had thought about attending the early service, since we love the old *Book of Common Prayer*, but our meeting with David seemed to take priority. There was very little time to accomplish a Herculean task. We'd get our plans made and go to church later. 'Because,' said Alan in his pre-coffee grumpiness, 'it's certainly going to need divine intervention.'

David told us he'd eaten breakfast before he came, but he was glad of a cup of coffee in the room before we went down to our splendid dining hall, and he patiently sat with us while we indulged in far more calories and cholesterol than we ever had at home.

'Has anyone had any brilliant inspirations since last night?' I asked brightly.

Silence. David sighed heavily. 'I'm sorry, Dorothy, but I haven't had any productive ideas at all.'

Alan shook his head. I was determined to keep up an optimistic façade. 'Well, never mind. Our minds will work better after we've finished eating. You know you always blame low blood sugar when I go all muzzy. And morning in church won't hurt, either. Will you come with us, David?'

He shook his head. 'I'm going back out to see Aunt Amanda. I suppose I ought to be looking for another haven for her, but . . .' He spread his hands in despair.

'Never mind. She won't have to move. You'll see.'
I had the feeling they both knew I was whistling in the dark.

The service at the cathedral was, of course, lovely. Our first
Sunday in Durham, David had taken us to a small parish
church, so this was our first experience with the magnificence
of Durham Cathedral worship. The organ was being repaired,
but they had a small portable one that produced an amazing
sound, and the choir was wonderful. We were accustomed to
terrific music at our home church in Sherebury, of course, and
had come to expect it at any English cathedral. What I had
not expected in this mammoth and world-famous church was
the sense of family, of a parish church. I had already experi-
enced the sense of belonging here. Now I felt a part of the
fabric of the church. This place was plainly still a place of
worship, no matter how many tourists thronged its impressive
aisles. Like the tiny Norman chapel at the castle, this church
had preserved its reason for being. I stopped gaping at the
architecture and settled myself to listen to the lessons.

On this Sunday not long after Easter, the scriptures focussed
on love. 'Greater love hath no man . . . The good shepherd
lays down his life for his sheep . . .' The choir sang one of
my favourite anthems, John Ireland's lovely setting of the text
from the Song of Solomon, 'Many waters cannot quench love,
neither can floods drown it . . .'

Floods. Drown. Suddenly my mind flew from the church
down to the riverbank. I was watching a young man drown,
and an older man doing nothing to save him. Water. Drown.

Alan had to nudge me to pass the collection plate along. I
followed the rest of the service, sat and stood and knelt at the
right times, made the responses, but only the very top layer
of my brain was engaged. The rest was furiously thinking.

As soon as the service was over I grabbed Alan's arm and
hurried him out, passing the Venerable Bede's tomb without
a second thought.

When we hit the cobblestones he made me stop. 'We're
neither of us young enough to hurry on this surface. And why
are you acting like you're fleeing a fire?'

'I've got to call David! I've had an idea!' And I wouldn't

say another word till we were back in our room with David on the phone.

'David, we have to meet. I'm sorry to pull you away from poor Amanda, but we can't go out there without a car, so you'll have to come to us. Will you come to the castle, or shall we meet you some place for lunch?'

The small restaurant was crowded with families seeking Sunday lunch. In our secluded corner, we could talk, if we kept it down.

'All right, here's my idea. Alan, you said it was going to take divine inspiration, and certainly it came to me in church, for what that's worth. I don't know how brilliant it is, but it at least takes us in a new direction.' I took a deep breath. 'David, I want you to find out as much as you can about the man who drowned. Now, before you both roll your eyes and say again that you think I'm going off on tangents, just listen to what I have to say. Dr Armstrong was there the day of the accident – if that's what it was. He behaved oddly, not even trying to help, and he lied about it later to his office assistant or nurse or whatever her title was. Something about that drowning is peculiar, and a peculiar thing involving a man who is murdered a few days later is worth looking into. And we've hit dead ends everywhere else.'

I took a deep breath. 'Investigating a crime in a setting where most of the possible witnesses can't remember what happened five minutes ago is pretty challenging, I admit, but we must do what we can. No, scratch that. We must do everything necessary to identify the criminal.'

'You are a fighter, aren't you, Dorothy?' David looked at me with a new respect.

'I never thought of myself that way, but in a good cause, yes, I guess I am. I'm stubborn, anyway. Maybe that's sometimes a good thing.'

'Very well,' said Alan. 'I don't say I agree with everything you've said, but I do agree that this is an avenue worth pursuing. David, you have contacts with the police. If you can get us a name and other particulars, we can then decide how to pursue the chap's background.'

'And it will be our pursuit,' said David with a sigh. 'The police aren't going to be interested, or willing to commit resources to the task.'

'But that's what we do best,' I said, trying to sound cheerful. 'Rushing in where angels, or in this case the police, fear to tread. David, I hate to hurry you, but we haven't much time. Do you suppose you could get anything out of them on a Sunday?'

That at least brought a smile to the faces of the two men. 'The police don't take Sundays off, Dorothy. Yes, I'll go to the station. Someone will talk to me, if only to get me out of their hair. But we can take time to enjoy our lunch first.'

I suppose it was good. The chunk of roast lamb was huge; so was the Yorkshire pudding. There were enough vegetables to make a meal for a vegan. I later regretted ploughing through it without tasting a thing.

Alan looked at my plate when it was empty, and then at me. 'You certainly enjoyed that.'

I looked down and realized my plate was empty except for a few smears of gravy. 'Oh. Yes.'

'Anyone want dessert?' David offered. 'They do wonderful crumbles here.'

I tried not to show my impatience. 'No, thank you.'

Alan, of course, caught it. 'She's champing at the bit, David. Shall I go with you to the police station?'

I don't know how I survived the next couple of hours. I couldn't settle to anything. I lay down to try for a nap, but the squirrel in my mind refused to stop running around its wheel, posing the same questions over and over. Why didn't Armstrong go to the rescue? Did someone deliberately drown the young man? What did this have to do with Armstrong's death? Why is someone still raising havoc at the nursing home? Who killed Armstrong and why?

I had nodded off into a nightmare when Alan opened the door and startled me awake, still in the grip of horrors. I must have cried out, because Alan was at my side in a moment.

'What is it, love?'

I shook my head to clear it. 'I don't know. I guess I was dreaming. Something awful, but I don't remember what.'

'Coffee,' he prescribed.

While the water boiled, I got up and washed my face to complete the return to consciousness. We sat down to our cups of instant.

'All right, did you learn anything?'

'The officers were very accommodating, actually. It was a slow day, with most of the students away. They come back at the end of next week, so the petty crimes will pick up then.'

'Alan! You're accusing the students of being troublemakers!'

'And so they are, by virtue of being young. Have you forgotten what university students are like, you who spent many, many years in a college town in the States?'

'But they were American kids. And it was a long time ago.'

'Adolescents are much the same the world over, my dear. A mixed bag. All the way from serious, dedicated students to confirmed hell-raisers, and all shades in between. Much as I'd like to claim that the English variety are better behaved than the general run, it simply isn't true. And it seems as though the drowning victim was much like any student. Not particularly troublesome, but occasionally reprimanded for drunken behaviour. Nothing too bad, just noisy and quarrelsome.'

'Hmm. Go on.'

He spread his hands. 'That's it. Oh, a name, Nathan Elliot. From Birmingham.'

'Good grief, Alan, that's totally useless. We need to know what he was like, who his friends were, all that! A Brummie who sometimes drank too much – that doesn't lead anywhere!'

'My dearest love, we're talking about police records. That was absolutely all they had at the station, besides his college here. He was a student at St Jude's, but he didn't live in their housing.'

'Studying what?'

'That wasn't in the record. Now, before you fly apart, David is even as we speak working on the St Jude's end. It isn't as easy as it would be in term time, but David's lived here long enough to make a few contacts. He'll come up with some people who knew young Elliot.'

'But it will take ages, and Alan, we have less than a week!' I put down my coffee cup, stood up, and put my shoes back on. 'I'm going to call Tim and Eileen. They're the only students we know. Maybe one of them knew the boy.'

'Surely they would have told us if she did. His death must have been a tragedy for the whole university.'

'Oh. You're right.' I sat back down again. 'Why wouldn't they have told us? Well, never mind. I'm going to call her anyway.'

I was lucky. Eileen answered right away, and she was with Tim. Well, no big surprise there.

'Hi, Eileen. What are you up to?'

'Hi, Dorothy. Nothing much. It's such a nice day, we were going to go out on the river with some sandwiches, but Tim says he has to study. Term starts up again next week.'

'Oh, dear. I was hoping to talk to you both.'

'About . . .?'

'Of course. I want to know lots more about the boy who drowned, and I hoped, since he was a student, that one of you might have known him.'

'Uh, no. You see, Dorothy,' she said in the gentle tone one uses to children or the subnormal, 'the university has nearly 17,000 students, and most of our friends are either in one of our colleges or in our discipline. The chap who died – I forget his name – well, he wasn't in my college or Tim's, and I have no idea what he was studying. So neither of us had any contact. Sorry.'

'Oh, dear, I was hoping . . . Look, could I come and see you? Even if Tim can't come along? Something has happened, and it's really important. I'll meet you anywhere you like.'

'No, I'll come to you. Meet you in the courtyard in fifteen minutes.'

I didn't invite Alan to come along. Somehow I thought this conversation would work better as just girls together.

THIRTEEN

The hot, sunny weather had returned. I hadn't brought a
sun hat with me. Who thought I'd need one in the north
of England in April? So I suggested we walk down by
the river in the welcome shade. We found a convenient bench,
and I told her the latest development at the home.

'But that's frightful! That poor old woman! And she's done
nothing.'

'No. That's why we must find the killer, and right away!
And the only idea I have right now is that somehow that
drowning is linked to Armstrong's death. And the only way
that I can see to find out about the drowning at this late date
is to find out about the victim. Now. The police told Alan he
was a student at St Jude's, but that he didn't live there. How
are we going to track down people who knew him?'

'Well. I know a girl at Jude's. She's a first year student in
natural sciences, and is in some of my lectures. Pleasant person.
We're not special friends, but friendly.' She gave me a quizzical look, and I nodded to show I understood. 'Now, Jude's
is one of the smallest colleges, which means all the students
probably know each other, even the ones who live out of
college. And a death would bring them together. I can try to
talk to her, if you like. She probably lives in college, but as
it isn't term time she might not be around.' She paused for
thought. 'I'll tell you what. If you're up for a bit of a walk,
we'll go over there and see what we can dig up. It's not really
far, just past the cathedral.'

We toiled up the steps back to street level. Well, I toiled;
Eileen politely let me set the pace, when she could have run
up them double-time. My chief memory of Durham, I thought
as I stopped at the top to pant, was going to be of steps. And
cobblestones, and steep grades. 'A city built on a hill cannot
be hidden' according to the apostle, but it sure can have a lot
of hidden corners to lead one up and down and around. When

it's been there for a thousand years or so, and is now trying to cope with modern traffic, getting anywhere becomes a challenge. And awfully hard on the feet.

We passed the cathedral and walked briefly down the rather steep Dun Cow Lane. (I will never cease to be entertained by English street names. So much more imaginative than Maple and Oak and Fifth.) Then we turned right into one of the narrowest streets I've ever seen. There was little vehicular traffic and what pedestrians there were walked in the street for preference. I could see why. The narrow pavement (*sidewalk*, to my American mind set) was made of stones that had probably once been flat and even but were now tilted at odd angles, and mostly toward the street. If I stumbled I knew I'd land in the street, probably just as a delivery van came along.

It wasn't really far to St Jude's College. I was by now not astonished to see a small, attractive flight of steps up to the door. I did wonder what students with mobility problems did, but that was an issue for another time.

Once inside, we were in a foyer that could have belonged to any attractive house. A decorative stairway curved up; I smiled to myself, but wondered again how on earth anyone with disabilities might manage.

Eileen gave a name to the man at the reception desk, who knew the answer immediately.

'Sarah Hoskins. Yes, she does live here, and stayed in residence during the vac. I don't know if she's in at the moment. Do you have her phone number?'

'No, I don't think I do. We sometimes study together, but usually in a group. Could you call her for me?'

'Well . . . we don't usually – but just this once.'

I had the feeling my elderly presence made us look ultra-respectable. Either that, or the porter didn't have enough to do in this slack time.

'Tell her Eileen Walsh, from botany lectures.'

The porter murmured something into his mobile and turned back to us. 'She'll be right down.'

The young woman who greeted us in a few moments was pleasant looking, though not in any way beautiful. On a Sunday afternoon in vacation time she wore the ubiquitous jeans, with a colourful top that had seen better days. Her hair was tied back carelessly with a nondescript scarf. 'How nice to see you, Eileen. A pleasant surprise.'

'Sarah, this is my friend Dorothy Martin. She and her husband are visiting Durham and staying in the castle, where they met Tim.'

Sarah nodded. She knew about Tim.

Eileen continued. 'Dorothy is looking into the recent drowning. She'd like to know more about Nathan Elliot. I thought you might have known him.'

Sarah frowned. 'We can't talk here. Come with me.'

She led us to a small lounge down a corridor. 'Now, Mrs Martin, what's this all about?'

She was perfectly polite, but plainly wanted a direct answer.

'It's a bit complicated, but to keep it short, my husband Alan and I came to Durham to visit an old friend, David Tregarth, a retired policeman like Alan. We became involved in helping Mr Tregarth look into a murder at the nursing home where David's great-aunt lives. It's creating a great deal of trouble for the old people living there, and it needs to be resolved quickly. The administration of the home wish as little police involvement as possible, which is why they called on David and he on us.'

'I think that's foolish,' said Sarah firmly. 'Crimes are the business of the police.'

'I quite agree with you, but for the sake of David and his aunt we've agreed to help. I should add that I have a bit of experience in criminal investigation, and of course Alan and David are trained in it, which means we're not totally useless. However, the matter has become crucial. After another incident at the home, the administrators have decided that Great-aunt Amanda may be the culprit, and have said she must leave. Sarah, she's over ninety, and has severe dementia. She can't defend herself, and she's happy and settled there. It might, quite honestly, kill her to have to leave.'

Sarah frowned. 'I still don't see—'

'You will. The man who was killed, Blake Armstrong, was nearby when Nathan Elliot drowned. We think he might have seen something, or heard something, that led to his death. I have been speculating that perhaps Nathan's death wasn't an accident, that someone pushed him into the river. And quite frankly, the only way I can think to learn more about the matter is to find out more about Nathan. Since he was a student of St Jude's, we came to you.'

She thought about that. 'Eileen, how did you get into this?'

'I was the one who saw Dr Armstrong walking away from the scene. He didn't even try to help. I did, but I was too late.'

'So you also saw whatever what's-his-name saw?'

'No. The angle was wrong. I don't know for certain that he saw anything, but he certainly heard the splash, because I saw him turn around, and then rush away.'

Sarah sat silent for a moment, then looked at us very directly. 'I don't know that I can help very much. I didn't know Nathan well. He didn't live here, you know.' She raised an eyebrow, and Eileen nodded. 'I'll tell you what I know of him. It isn't much, and I'll start by saying I can't give an unbiased opinion. I didn't like Nathan Elliot, and to tell the truth I know of very few people who did. He was . . . how shall I put it?'

She hesitated, and I interrupted. 'I hope you'll forget about not speaking ill of the dead. It can't hurt him now, and I don't know about you, but I believe that the truth never hurts, anyway.'

Sarah smiled, the first smile I'd seen since we started talking about the trouble. 'I like the way you think. Very well. Nathan was a snoop and a prig. Holier than thou. I don't know what he was studying; never cared to find out. I hope it wasn't theology!'

'Me, too.' I nodded emphatically. 'That particular attitude seems to me to be absolutely anti-Christian. The antithesis of almost any religion I can think of, actually. But go on. You said no one liked him much. Did he have any actual friends? Or particular enemies?'

She shrugged. 'Enemies would be very much to the point, wouldn't they? But no, I don't know of any. Friends? Again, not that I know of. Most people just ignored him. You can find out a lot more next week when term begins.'

'Sarah, we can't wait until then!' I leaned forward in an attitude of desperation. 'David has been told he must find a new place for his great-aunt in a week. That was yesterday. We have five days after today to work this out!'

'But that's . . . I don't . . . oh, wait. He had some drinking buddies. Not close friends, you understand, but they went out together on occasion. He wasn't much of a drinker, but now and then he'd condescend to lift a glass with the others, and then sometimes got even more objectionable than usual. Sorry to sound catty, but he really was . . . oh, well, the poor sod's dead.'

I opened my mouth, but she held up a hand. 'Wait. I'm trying to think. Two or three of them are first year students, living here. One, I think, stayed here for the vac. I don't know if he's in, of course, but I can find out. Wait here.'

'Dorothy, are you okay?' murmured Eileen when Sarah had left the room.

I discovered that I was twisting my hands together in that motion known as 'wringing'. I stopped. 'It's just that I'm terribly worried about poor Aunt Amanda. She really is the sweetest person, Eileen.'

'I know. I asked to see her when I went to the home. She's a love. Completely gaga, of course, but darling. She thought I was her daughter. I don't want her hurt, either.'

I smiled a little. 'Wishful thinking. She never married or had children. You probably look like her dream daughter. Many of us unlucky enough to have no children have created them in our minds. I imagine that when my mind goes, I'll start seeing my children in every attractive young man and woman.'

'I don't think your mind will – oh.'

Sarah had returned with a young man in tow. He was dressed very casually indeed, and had the look of someone who had just left his bed: tousled hair, a distinct grey shadow on his chin, and eyes that seemed unfocussed.

'This is Charles. I woke him up. I'm going to go get some coffee for him. Anyone else want some?'

Charles slumped down in a chair and yawned widely. My own jaw quivered in sympathy. 'Yes, thank you, I'd love some coffee.'

Charles yawned again and mumbled an apology.

'I'm the one who should apologize, disturbing your Sunday afternoon. If the truth were told, I'd love a nap right now, myself, but that doesn't matter. Did Sarah tell you why I wanted to talk to you?'

He shook his head, and then made an effort to pull himself together. 'Only that it was important.' He yawned again with force that might have cracked his jaw. 'I really am sorry. I didn't get much sleep last night. But I'll try to help with whatever it is you want to know.'

I introduced myself, and by that time our coffee arrived. It probably wasn't the worst I'd ever tasted, and it did have the magical ingredient. I explained my mission, briefly, and was pleased to see Charles's sleepy visage change to a frown. He looked at Sarah.

'You told her I was a friend of Nate's?'

'No. I told her you sometimes went drinking with him.'

'Twice. Exactly twice. And that was once too many.' He drained his coffee mug and set it down with a bang. 'I went the first time because I felt sorry for the bas— for the chap. He didn't seem to know anybody. He didn't live here in college, and he hadn't made friends in his lectures. From what I gathered, he was barely keeping his head above water, academically. Didn't seem to care, and that didn't go down well. Jude's students are rather serious about our work, for the most part. Nathan was serious only about Nathan.'

Charles smothered another yawn. 'Well, he turned up here one evening, and we went to the pub. That time wasn't too bad. He didn't say much, and he bought a round or two. The next time . . .' Charles whistled. 'He started out by giving us a lecture on how wonderful he was, how hard he'd worked to save money and invest it soundly, so he had plenty now and didn't have to take out loans for university – the full Gospel according to Nathan. Oh, and he threw in that sort of thing, too, how he lived according to the word of God and worried about the rest of us poor sinners and where we might spend eternity. All of this while he was drinking our beer!'

'I can see why he was unpopular,' I said mildly.

'Unpopular! He was easily the most hated student in this college. It's no wonder we weren't exactly weeping buckets when he died. Oh, okay, I know I shouldn't say that. But it's absolutely true that he isn't missed.'

'Charles, I have to ask. There's a small possibility that his death wasn't accidental. Did anyone hate him enough to – to push him in the river?'

'To . . . Are you saying he was *murdered*?'

'It's a possibility. Only that, thus far.'

'But – but you don't kill someone just because you can't stand him. There has to be a *reason*. A big reason, like – like – I don't even know what. Like he's sleeping with your wife, or something. But nobody who lives here has a wife.'

'I agree, there has to be a reason, a motive. But my husband, the retired chief constable, will tell you that sometimes the motive is pathetically thin. Shopkeepers have been killed for the few pounds in the till.'

Eileen spoke up. 'Sex, money, power. Aren't those the classic motives?'

'A few of them. Then there's revenge, fear of discovery, fear of almost anything. My favourite soap-box lecture is that fear is at the bottom of almost every crime, but there's no time to go into that. We have to act fast! Charles, think! Go through that list of motives in your mind. Do you know anyone who associated with Nathan Elliot who might have cherished one of those corrosive hatreds in his bosom?'

I could see Charles turning over ideas in his head, thinking of various people, rejecting them. Finally he looked up and said, 'This is beginning to sound like Jacobean tragedy. Revenge, murder. We are living in the twenty-first century, right? I admit it's sometimes easy to forget that in this town, but aren't we getting a bit melodramatic?'

I struggled for a calm, reasoned response, when what I wanted to do was pound this young man's head against the wall. After taking a deep breath, I said, 'Charles. Two people have died. It seems highly possible that their deaths may be related. We are at a dead end in the direct investigation of Dr Armstrong's death. I believe that a searching investigation into Nathan's death is warranted. You can help with that, if you will. If you will not, we will have to turn to someone else, and lose time, and meanwhile a very loveable old woman may be evicted from her home. I have no authority to coerce your cooperation. I rely on your sense of decency.'

He gave me a long look. 'You're retired, right?'

'Yes.' And what does that have to do with anything, I wanted to add.

'Were you a priest or something?'

'Or something. I taught school for many years, children of various ages.'

'That explains it – your air of authority. If I give you a name, will you swear you won't do something drastic?'

'I won't go charging in with bullets flying, if that's what you mean. I won't, for the moment, give the name to the official police. I will pass it, along with any other information you can give me, to my husband and David Tregarth. And we, the three of us, will do our utmost to pursue the question of how Nathan died.'

'Okay. I don't like it. I don't like ratting on friends. On anyone, really. This guy is not a particular friend, but he's a fellow student of this college.' He looked down at his feet, and then up at me. 'His name is Colin Grimsby. He doesn't live in college. I suppose he has rooms somewhere.'

'And why did you think of him, in particular?'

'He's one of the ones who seemed to hate Nathan more than the rest of us. And he's been even more morose than usual after Nathan's death.' He spread his hands. 'I don't really know. It's just a feeling.' He gave me a challenging look.

I nodded. 'Yes. Always trust your instincts.' I stood, with some difficulty, and put out my hand. 'Thank you, Charles. You've been a great help. I promise I won't let anyone know the source of my information.' I looked at the girls. 'I'm sure no one else will, either. And please, Charles, don't say anything at all about this to Colin Grimsby. If he knows something, and passes it along, you could be putting yourself in danger. And don't disparage Jacobean drama! Those plays were popular, and have become popular again, because they speak truth about the wretched human condition – melodrama or not.'

He accepted my handshake, looking embarrassed, and left the room quickly.

'Now what?' Eileen looked at me expectantly.

'Now we have to get Grimsby's address. Can you do that, Sarah, as a fellow St Jude's student?'

'I can. In fact, if you want to come up to my room, I can get it on my laptop.'

More stairs. If I kept this up long enough I'd either be in great shape, or dead.

Armed with a name, address and phone number, I toiled back to the castle. Alan wasn't there. He'd left a note saying he was with David, down at the pub. I called him, saying I was back and too tired to join him. 'This getting old business puts a real damper on my ability to follow up on anything,' I groused. 'But I have some information for you both, if you'd like to come back here. Meanwhile I'm putting my feet up.'

Yes, there was need for haste, but I've learned over the years that neither my brain nor my body works well when I'm tired. Better to snatch a little rest when I could than blunder on doing stupid things that would have to be corrected later. More haste, less speed. Repeating that and other tired adages I lay down and was asleep in seconds.

FOURTEEN

I t seemed only seconds later that the door opened to admit Alan and David, but I looked at the bedside alarm clock and realized I'd slept for about half an hour. Enough to provide a little refreshment and clear my head.

'Awake, love?'

'Almost. No, I don't want any more bad coffee. A little cold water on my face, and I'll be functional again. And then, could we take our discussion down to the courtyard? This room is really too small to hold three comfortably.'

The afternoon was waning, and the sun losing some of its warmth. It was pleasant sitting around a table, with the small sounds of the sparsely populated college around us. 'This must be buzzing in term time,' I commented.

'Indeed. Now, Dorothy, I know you said you had information for us, but I gathered a trifle or two about young Nathan this afternoon, as well. I thought it might be worthwhile to know something about his family, so I checked with the police again. I told you he lived in Birmingham.'

'Yes, but—'

David held up a hand. 'Wait for it. He lived with his mother. An older brother is living on his own. In Bishop Auckland. That's about ten miles from here, as the crow flies, a little longer by road.'

'Oh.' I thought about that for a while. 'Do we know anything about the brother?'

'Only this. When the Birmingham police called on the mother to notify her of her son's death, she said something odd enough that the officers noted it in the record.'

'All right, David, don't make us beg.'

'Apparently she was very controlled. You'll remember, Alan, how much we hated making those visits.'

'The hardest part of the job,' Alan agreed. 'Telling someone a child, or spouse, or sibling is dead . . .' He shuddered. 'It was worst, of course, when it was a death by violence. But an accident could be almost as bad.'

'Yes. Then you'll understand why the officers were surprised at the mother's reaction. She said, and I quote: "It was bound to happen sometime. George can relax now." George being the brother.'

'But that *is* odd. What does it mean, do you think?'

'One thing I'm sure it means,' said Alan, 'is that neither his mother nor his brother was distraught about Nathan's death.'

I shook my head. 'Neither, if what I've learned is true, were his fellow students. He must have been a truly unpleasant person.'

'And I hate to remind you, but his potential as a pushee may have nothing whatever to do with the death we are actually investigating, that of Blake Armstrong.'

'Who also sounds like a pushee, actually. Okay, disclaimer noted and discarded. Now let me tell you what I learned at St Jude's.'

I gave a pretty thorough summary of what Sarah and Charles had told me, and finished with the name and address. 'I must say I hesitated before giving you this. Just because the guy hated Nathan doesn't mean he did anything about it.'

Alan shook his head. 'You can't have it both ways, Dorothy. Either we pursue this investigation or we don't. You've decided there are benefits at the end of the trail. You're caught up in another of the pitfalls of police work: the harassment of possibly innocent people.'

'And remember what's at stake here,' said David, 'the fate of an elderly lady whom I love like a mother.'

I bit my lip. 'You're right, of course. I'm sorry. I won't wimp out. We have two solid leads now, Colin Grimsby and George Elliot. Which shall we tackle first? Or do we split up?'

'Oh, no, we don't!' Alan spoke before David could say a word. 'If you're right, one of these men may be a murderer, and you are *not* going to speak with him alone!'

I rolled my eyes. Alan and I had fought this battle for years. His male protectiveness, enhanced by the English-gentleman code, kicked in every time I wanted to do anything involving the smallest degree of risk. I found his fears both endearing and infuriating. We had worked out an understanding over the years. I would promise to do nothing foolhardy if he would keep his impulses in check, but sometimes he simply couldn't restrain himself.

'I had thought,' I said mildly, 'of going with you to talk to one of the men, and David going to the other. I think I might do best with Grimsby; I do usually get along well with students.'

David had wisely stayed out of the question, but now he nodded. 'That sounds like a reasonable solution. Grimsby's address is nearby, so why don't you phone him, Dorothy? He may well be out of town. And I'll call George Elliot.'

My call went to voicemail. I decided against leaving a message. 'Drat. He isn't there. Maybe away for the break; maybe just down at the pub. I didn't leave a message, since he doesn't know me from Adam and probably doesn't want to. I'll try again later. How'd you do, David?'

'Voicemail. I left a message, a somewhat deceptive one, I fear, just saying I was calling from Durham about the death of his brother. I hope it sounded like a condolence message.'

'Did you keep the policeman out of your voice?'

He smiled. 'I tried.'

'Then we've done all we can for now. Except pray for Amanda, of course. I wonder if the cathedral is still open?'

Alan looked at his watch. 'No, it's well after six. But we can pray anywhere. For now, unless you want a good-sized man fainting at your feet, let's find a meal.'

Since it was Sunday, when the congestion fee didn't apply, David had driven and, wonder of wonders, found a parking place not far from the castle. He drove us to a lovely Indian restaurant quite a way out of town, and just as our food (smelling absolutely wonderful) was served, his phone warbled. He looked at the display and answered immediately.

The end of the conversation we could hear was not illuminating. David clicked off, put his phone away, put a credit card on the table, and stood up. 'George Elliot says he can see me briefly in about half an hour, and is then leaving town. Could you have them box up my dinner? I'll be in touch.'

And he was out the door.

Alan and I ate quickly, not saying much. We were left with

nothing to do until I could reach Colin Grimsby. I tried twice;
still no answer. Alan pocketed David's credit card to give back
to him when we next saw him and paid with his own, getting
a box for David's untouched meal. Then it occurred to us: we
were a few miles from our lodging in the castle, and night
had fallen. How on earth were we to get back?

At home it would have been no problem. Someone we knew
would have given us a ride. Here, we knew no one.

Alan went to the desk and inquired about a taxi. After a
spirited conference among all the restaurant staff, it was agreed
that taxis didn't often come out this far, that they had no phone
number to call a service, and that in any case it was a Sunday.
This seemed to be an unarguable final answer. One of the
waiters, however, said he lived near the castle and would be
happy to take us there when his shift was over. And when
might that be? Around eleven.

It wasn't quite eight o'clock by Alan's watch.

'We could . . . um . . . walk out to the highway and thumb
a ride.' My heart wasn't in the suggestion, and Alan rightly
ignored it. 'It seems we're going to be here for a while,' he
told the man at the till. 'Is there a small table you won't
be likely to need tonight where we can sit and wait?'

'But yes, of course, please! The large tables will be in use,
but there is a table for two – not the best table for dining, you
understand, it is near the kitchen, with much traffic, but for
sitting, with perhaps a bottle of wine?'

We ordered the wine, for lack of anything better to do, and
I dug my notebook out of my purse. 'Is there anything to write
down?' I asked dismally. 'I can't think of a thing to do, or
lists to make, or in fact anything useful. I'm stuck.'

'Take a look at the list you made before. Is there anything
that needs following up?'

I turned back a page to where I'd transcribed the notes I'd
made on the napkin. 'I don't think we ever found out exactly
what time of day it was – the drowning. I don't know that it
matters, actually, and with our police contact out on what is
probably a wild goose chase, we can't check it now, anyway.'

'Excuse me.' I didn't recognize the woman standing by our
table. 'You probably don't remember me, but I work at the

Milton Home, in the kitchen. You came to talk to us a few days ago. Mrs . . . Marlowe, is it?'

'Martin. And yes, I do remember you, but I'm terrible about names.'

'I don't think I ever told you my name. It's Kathleen, Kathleen Anderson. And I was really rude to you. I'm sorry. I didn't quite understand . . . anyway, I overheard you say you're stranded here. If your battery died or something, my husband can help, perhaps. He's very good with cars.'

'Oh, goodness, how kind of you, but it isn't car trouble. Mr Tregarth brought us here and then had to rush off, which means we don't have a way to get back to the castle until he returns, and that may not be for some time.'

'Then we'd be happy to give you a lift. Please! I'd like to make it up to you.'

'There's no need! But we'd be most grateful for the lift. Thank you.'

Alan tried to call David to tell him our plans, but the call went to voicemail. 'He's probably driving back here right now. I left a message.'

We had scarcely settled ourselves in the car before Kathleen turned around. 'I've been wanting to talk to you ever since that day. You were trying to find out about Mr Armstrong, and I was afraid to tell you anything. I need that job. We're trying to save money because . . . well, we're expecting a baby, and I won't be able to work for a while.'

'Congratulations! Your first?'

Her face might have lighted our way down the road. 'I'm really excited. And a little bit scared. Were you scared with your first?'

'Alas, I was never able to have children. But my sisters told me they could never remember afterwards whether they had been afraid. Once that baby was safely in their arms, they forgot the rest.'

'That's what my friends say, too. So anyway. Some of the others at the home said I didn't need to worry about talking to you, that Mr Williams would never sack me for doing the right thing. But I didn't know how to reach you without asking him, and . . .'

'And you still weren't sure it would work out all right. I understand. Well, here I am. What did you want to tell me?'

'Two things. First, I started to tell you that I didn't like Mr Armstrong. None of us did. He was smarmy, and he told lies.'

'About what?' I was suddenly alert. This could be important.

'About everything. He lied about being ill, for a start. He was as healthy as I was. I thought – we all thought – he was hiding out from something. He was a doctor, and we thought maybe he was dodging a malpractice suit. Something like that. He'd moan and groan and carry on when anyone was in his room, any of the staff, I mean, and then be up and out to the garden room first thing. He hid his pills, too, and then said they hadn't given them to him, and raised a great fuss.'

'I thought he wasn't on a nursing regime.'

'He wasn't, but he had a few prescriptions, just like any old person, and the staff were supposed to make sure he took them.'

'Why would he hide them?'

'Just to make trouble, we all thought. But the other thing is really important. Or may be, anyway. I know the talk is that it must have been someone in the home who killed him, because it's very hard to get in. And they're maybe going to make that sweet Miss Amanda leave, and there's no way she could have done it. That's just a crime! So I had to tell you, anybody can get into that place really easily. They'd just have to come in through the kitchen.'

'David didn't mention that there was an outside door in the kitchen.'

'He probably didn't know. No one ever uses it except kitchen staff and delivery men. We don't worry about it, because the residents can't get into the kitchen and then out that way. And it's kept unlocked during the day, because there's always someone in the kitchen.'

'But could a stranger get in without being noticed?'

'Oh, yes, if he was clever about choosing his time. Everyone's madly busy just before mealtimes – any meal, but especially lunch and dinner. And of course we've quite a turnover among the casual staff, just like any commercial kitchen. So even if we did notice a stranger, we'd just think he was a new hire.'

'I see.' I wasn't sure about the implications of all this, except that almost anyone in the universe could have killed Blake Armstrong.

Alan had sat silent, taking all this in. 'Miss Anderson, have you mentioned the kitchen door to anyone else?'

'No. Of course everyone at the home knows about it.'

'Yes. I think it would be as well if you didn't talk about it.'

She wasn't stupid. 'Because anyone out there could be a murderer.'

'Exactly. Will you promise me?'

'She promises.' That was her husband. 'She has two people to look after now.'

'I do promise. And it's three, counting you.' She turned back to the front and grinned at her husband, who reached over and patted her hand.

FIFTEEN

'This changes everything,' I said when we were back in our cosy little castle. 'Now we have to look at anybody who had it in for Blake Armstrong. Unfortunately that includes Tim Hayes. And we can't even eliminate very many of them on the basis of an alibi, since we don't know exactly when he died.'

'Perhaps we'll discover that every medical man in the city was away at a convention in Paris for the whole day.'

'And one of their spouses did the deed.'

We both sighed. 'I wish we'd hear from David. Should we try calling him again?'

Alan glanced at his watch. 'It's a bit late, but perhaps.' He pushed the proper buttons. 'Voicemail,' he said after a moment.

We looked at each other. 'Are we going to start worrying about him?' I asked. 'How long would it take to get to that small town, whatever it's called, have a brief talk, and get back?'

'An hour there and back would be more than ample, I'd think, even if the road is truly terrible. He left us less than two hours ago. So no, we don't start worrying yet. I'm not sure why we'd worry at all, really. David Tregarth is a trained policeman. He knows how to meet most sorts of trouble.'

Alan spoke in the over-confident tone of one who is trying to convince himself. Both of us carefully avoided mentioning the words 'possible murderer'.

Neither did we try to talk about our confusing, unhappy problem. We were tired, we were frustrated with our lack of progress, and no matter what we said, we were worried about David.

Neither of us is a big television fan. I used to watch it years ago in America, when there were some variety shows and sitcoms my first husband and I both enjoyed. Now, I'm told, there's almost nothing back in the States except the 'reality' shows that are anything but. Occasionally, here in England, there's something worth watching. We turned on the small TV in the room and channel-surfed aimlessly, trying to find something to occupy our minds.

I honestly can't remember what we ended up watching. It might have been something about antiques, or perhaps a cooking competition. I couldn't concentrate. I picked up a newspaper, but couldn't remember five minutes later what I'd read.

Where was David? What had he found out about George Elliot? Did Nathan's death have anything to do with Armstrong's, or was I all wrong about that? Where was David? Why didn't he call? What was happening? Where *was* he?

The squirrel went round and round on its wheel, banging against my brain until I developed a nasty headache. I got up to find some Ibuprofen, and Alan's phone rang.

I looked at the alarm clock by the bed. Twelve-fifteen. Very little good news can be expected when the phone rings at that hour.

'Yes, David. Ah.' Alan put it on speaker.

David sounded exhausted, worn to the last shred of endurance. 'Sorry I couldn't call earlier. It's been the hell of a night. I'd like to see you, unless you've already gone to bed.'

'No,' said Alan briefly. 'Come ahead. I'll go down to let you in.'

He went down to wait, and I got out the fresh bottle of Glenfiddich Alan had picked up. I had a strong feeling we might have need of it.

David arrived faster than I'd thought possible. 'I parked on the Palace Green. Strictly illegal.'

I wondered if his car would be there when he went back to it, but sufficient unto the day. 'Always easier to apologize than ask permission,' I propounded. It was one of my favourite adages. He collapsed into a chair and took the glass I offered. He looked even worse than he had sounded.

Alan poured himself a small libation and offered me an even smaller one. I took it, for medicinal purposes, and we waited until David was ready to talk.

'Do you want the saga, or the condensed version?' he finally asked.

'Whatever you want to tell us,' I said, and Alan nodded.

'In short, then, the evening was a disaster start to finish.'

'What's-his-name, George, was combative?'

'Worse. He wasn't there.' David took a pull at his glass. 'I had no trouble finding his house. Posh house, good neighbourhood. I went to ring the bell, but the front door was ajar. Of course that set alarm bells ringing.'

Alan nodded. 'Never a good sign. One might find almost anything inside.'

'What I found was a shambles. Books pulled from shelves and torn apart. Furniture scattered and slashed. Broken glass and china everywhere. One look and I reached for my phone. No way was I going in there to look for the body I expected to find.'

'So you called the police.'

'No. I had my phone out when half a dozen uniforms burst into the room, brandishing guns and shouting. They had me in a hammerlock before I could so much as utter a sound.'

'David! This sounds like a bad movie! The *English* police acting that way?'

Alan heaved a long sigh. 'Dorothy, Agatha Christie died a long time ago, along with the rest of her crowd. There was a time when the police here were gentlemen, courteous to a fault. Some still are, but times have changed. Crime has grown more violent and more prevalent. You have to banish your image of the bobby bicycling round to escort the village sot safely home. Cops have guns now, and tear gas, and the rest of the box of horrors. They meet perceived danger with force.'

'That's all true, Alan, and more's the pity, but wait for it.' David rubbed his eyes and slumped down a little farther in his chair.

'But what *happened*?' I demanded.

'I was manhandled and questioned, rapid-fire questions that gave me no chance to reply. It was a nightmare. Meanwhile the boys in blue roared through the house, both storeys, doubtless destroying evidence left and right. They seemed to be looking for a body in order to arrest me on suspicion of murder. They didn't find one.'

'They finally let you go?' I looked at my empty glass. Alan poured me a minimal refill.

David waved a weary hand. 'It isn't quite that simple. After what seemed like hours, but was probably only a few minutes, someone came on the scene who seemed to know what he was doing, a DI, I think. You should have heard him! Or perhaps not; some of his language . . . anyway, he sent the others away with very sharp words and let me tell my story. When I produced identification, he called the Durham police to check my story.' David managed to produce a tiny smile. 'I gather they were not amused. The DI had a very red face when he ended the call. At that point I showed him the call from Elliot on my phone, with the time. It was too late to call the restaurant to verify the time I'd left, but he was beginning to understand that there'd been a terrible mistake, and that he'd best take seriously the question of Elliot's whereabouts. He called in a forensic team then, but so much damage had been done by the first crowd that they were virtually helpless.'

'So you – they – have no idea where Elliot is now. Or in what condition.' Alan sounded stern.

'No. They're conducting a search, of course.' He finished his drink and waved away Alan's offer of a second. 'I've got to drive home, and at this point I'm not sure I can do that safely.'

'You're not driving home,' I said firmly. 'Alan will drive you to Hotel Indigo.'

'My car—'

'We'll worry about that in the morning. Which is not far away. But before Alan whisks you off, I have one question. Are you absolutely sure that the first gang, the ones who treated you badly and compromised the scene hopelessly, were policemen? Because while we were waiting for you this evening and fretting, I looked at a newspaper. I couldn't give it much attention, but I remember now seeing an ad for a local theatre company, the Auckland Players. They're doing a production of *The Pirates of Penzance*. As I recall, that show involves a chorus of policemen. In uniform.'

'You've caught on. Of course they weren't policemen. I

knew that the moment they started going wild, but there was
nothing I could do. I don't know the whole story. Maybe they
were the Penzance chorus. I'm not sure I care. By the time
the real police finished with me, I was ready to crawl into a
hole.'

'And you thought about us, and knew we'd be frantic, and
used up a little more energy to reassure us. Sort of.'

He laughed a little at that. 'Sort of, yes.'

He was drooping with weariness. Alan supported him, tact-
fully, and they were off, down all those stairs, then the long
walk to the reserved parking area in front of the cathedral. I
hoped his car hadn't been towed away.

I wished we had some snacks in the room, but there was
nothing. I got into my nightgown and fell into bed. The whisky,
on top of a long and stressful day, had made me very sleepy,
but I wanted to stay awake till Alan got back. What a mess!
David manhandled by a group of thugs masquerading as
policemen! I hoped they'd get the book thrown at them.
Probably they would. Assaulting a retired chief constable,
trashing a crime scene . . . or did they perhaps cause the
destruction in the first place? And where was George Elliot?
One suspect lost, maybe dead . . . or maybe he wasn't a suspect
at all. He didn't know Armstrong, after all. Or wait . . . was
that the crime we were investigating? Wasn't it . . .?

I never heard Alan return.

SIXTEEN

Monday has a bad reputation. For those with full-time jobs, it's the day to re-apply one's nose to the grindstone, with the weekend but a distant memory. My first husband and I both enjoyed our teaching jobs, he in a university, I in a public school, but Mondays always found us a little grouchy.

One might think retirement would give Mondays a different complexion, bright, sunny, full of opportunity for adventure.

One might be wrong.

This particular Monday was certainly bright and sunny, at least outside. My inner climate was dark, with thunder imminent.

'Mmph.' My first pronouncement let Alan know that he'd best speak softly and carry no stick at all. He waited until my eyes were open and then approached with a cup of coffee. I don't think I took it graciously, but at least I sat up and drank it. It tasted a lot better than I expected. I must have looked surprised, because he said, 'I went out for some of the good stuff.'

My eyes focussed; I took in the Starbucks logo on the cup. 'How come you're all bright-eyed and bushy-tailed? You got to bed even later than I did.'

'Not much later. I'm fine. Are you ready for some breakfast, or just another coffee?'

I thought about that. 'Breakfast, I guess. What time is it?'

'After ten, I'm afraid, and the breakfast room has closed. But I picked up some pastries, if you'd like those.'

That man, with only a few hours of sleep, had already been out in the town foraging. I would have resented his superior stamina if the coffee hadn't been wonderful. And I love Starbucks pastries. I grimaced and gave up my snit. Alan sat down and ate with me, and poured more coffee out of the thermos he'd found somewhere. I do believe my husband would find a way to provide the basics if we were stranded on a desert island.

It was very late morning indeed by the time I'd showered and dressed. 'Feeling better?' Alan asked, with the smile that told me he knew the answer.

'Much, thanks to you. I'm sorry I was grouchy earlier.'

'Sleep deprivation.'

'And what about you?'

'My dear, I spent many years as a policeman. I learned to snatch rest when I could, and function capably no matter how tired I was. The lessons stuck. Now, are you ready to face the day?'

'Depends on what I have to face. I'm afraid I'm not up for another one like yesterday.'

'Like the curate's egg, surely parts of it were excellent, my dear. We're meeting David downstairs at one o'clock, and we can decide then on an agenda.'

'Do you suppose he's learned any more about – about anything? Oh, and what happened about his car?'

'I left it at the hotel.'

'You didn't walk back! At that hour . . .'

'I could easily have done. Durham is a remarkably safe city. But as it happened, one of the employees was coming off duty and kindly gave me a ride.'

'A female employee, I'll bet.'

'Well . . .'

'I knew it. You're too good-looking by half, you know. All right, it's very nearly noon. A shameful hour for a respectable lady to be starting her day. You can take me down to the market and I'll see if I can find something wildly extravagant to buy as a souvenir of our happy days in Durham.'

'Sarcasm, my dear . . .'

'Right. Lead on, MacDuff.'

A sugar high brings out my silly side.

I did not, in fact, find anything wildly extravagant, but I bought a pretty straw hat to fend off the unexpected sun, and picked up all sorts of tourist brochures from the friendly 'We Can Help' people. Alan called David to tell him we'd meet him at the end of the congestion zone, so he didn't have to park and walk, and by the time we got in his car, I was feeling nearly as sunny as the day.

David took us to lunch at the Court Inn, Tim's pub. Tim wasn't there; this wasn't a day for castle tours. I hoped he was studying, rather than working yet another job. I wasn't really hungry after all the sweet stuff I'd had not long before, but I did full justice to an excellent goat cheese salad while the men had more substantial fare. Alan and I asked David no questions. He was still looking weary and discouraged, and we knew he'd talk when he was ready.

My sunny mood was buried in dense clouds as soon as David began to bring us up to date.

'They haven't found George,' he said heavily. 'His car is there at the house. He didn't show up for work this morning, nor is he with any of his friends – any that they've been able to identify – nor at his mother's in Birmingham. No one of his description has been seen at the railway station here. It's a small station; they'd know.'

'Where does he work?' asked Alan.

'He's an accountant for a manufacturing firm: washing machines, dehumidifiers, that sort of thing.'

'Big outfit?'

'Middling. Perhaps four hundred employees, but mostly in the actual factory. Not many work in the offices, so yes, he'd be missed. Has been missed, in fact.'

I took a deep breath. 'And I don't suppose they've figured out who trashed the house.'

'The invasion of the fake coppers assured that very little useful evidence is left. They're still going through it as best they can, and they're trying to trace how that invasion came about, but the men who did it are extremely reluctant to talk about it.'

'Understandably. They thought they were just pulling a prank, and now they've found out they have committed a crime,' Alan contributed.

'Vandalizing a house is a crime?'

'On that scale, definitely, Dorothy.'

'So . . .' I hesitated. 'So they're not yet assuming that George Elliot is – is dead?'

'Not yet.'

We were silent amid the small noises of the restaurant. Happy, relaxed people having a pleasant luncheon out. And somewhere out there a man was hiding in fear of his life. Or else he was no longer afraid of anything.

'Nothing makes any kind of sense,' I said when Alan and I were back in our room. It was very warm. We had opened the windows to their fullest extent. I felt muzzy, as if the languid air had invaded my brain. 'I can't make things connect. Why did someone attack George?'

'Let's take things in order,' said Alan, tenting his fingers in his lecturing mode. I sometimes resent his orderly, logical policeman's mind. This time I was glad of it. My own mind seemed to have turned to cream cheese.

'David called George and left a voicemail. He told George that he was calling about the death of his brother Nathan. George returned the call, inviting David to come and talk to him. What does that tell us?'

'Search me. I suppose that he wanted to see David.'

'Why would he want to see him? Why not just brush him off with a brief phone call?'

I thought about that. 'You know, Alan, that *is* odd. People in mourning usually want to talk about their loss, about the person they'll miss so dearly. But from what his mother said, if our third-hand report is accurate, it sounded as if George wasn't exactly devastated by his brother's death.'

'We've speculated that perhaps he caused it. Brothers have been known to kill brothers.'

'From time immemorial,' I agreed. 'But it's usually for jealousy. Cain killed Abel because God apparently liked him better. In this case, though, George is the one doing well, holding down a responsible job, living independently. Nathan sounds like a dilettante, going to university but not studying much. He claimed to have a lot of money, but I'll bet he was lying. Do we know anything about his lifestyle?'

'I don't, at any rate. Make a note, darling.'

I pulled out my trusty notebook. *Nathan – rich?* I scribbled.

'I think even his mother was fed up with him. Anyway, it sounded that way. Why would George want to kill him?'

'There are other motives besides jealousy, Dorothy. Forget Cain and Abel.'

'It takes a lot for brother to kill brother,' I said stubbornly. 'That's a close tie. I've forgotten which one was older.'

'George. I don't know by how much.'

I made another note. 'There might well have been some hero worship on the part of the kid brother.'

'Or, as you posited earlier, jealousy. George who got on well in life. George who won the approval of his parents. George who was everything Nathan wanted to be.'

'Aha! You're doing what you always accuse me of doing – inventing fairy tales. We don't know a thing about the brotherly attitudes towards each other. And anyway, what you've just dreamed up would be a motive for Nathan hating George, not the other way round.'

Alan shook his head. 'We're talking in circles. We've lost our focus – why did George want to talk to David? And before we go off on another tangent, I can think of only one reason: he knew something about Nathan's death, or at any rate had a theory about it, and he wanted to try it out on someone only semi-official before he went to the police.'

I thought about that. 'And maybe someone didn't want him to have that talk. Someone like Nathan's murderer.'

'If in fact Nathan was murdered. And how would that person have known George's intentions?'

'Oh, dear! Alan, we're getting nowhere! All we have is speculation. We don't even know, not positively *know*, that Nathan's death and Armstrong's have anything to do with each other. We need some solid facts, some evidence, a little straw for our bricks. Just a little! And while we're trying to find it, Great-aunt Amanda is one day closer to eviction.'

Alan sighed. 'Perhaps, after all, the police will find something useful in George's house. It will take some time, though, and as you point out, time is running out. It seems we're just going to have to carry on speculating.'

I groaned and picked up my notebook. 'Okay. We were

beginning to organize a chronology of last night. I didn't write all that down, but we'd only got as far as George returning David's call and asking him to come over.'

'And David went, incidentally leaving us in the lurch. Which reminds me; I didn't return his credit card, and we never gave him the dinner he left behind.'

'Which hasn't been refrigerated for hours. It'll have to be thrown out. What a pity. All right. David went to – wait a minute, I'll get it – to Bishop Auckland. Very odd name, but then England specializes in peculiar place names.'

'Says a woman who lived near Stoney Lonesome and Gnaw Bone, Indiana.'

'All right, all right! David arrives at George's house. I suppose George gave him directions?'

'Probably. Or satnav. At any rate, he got there, and discovered chaos.'

'And no George. Before he'd even set foot in the house, he was attacked by a gang of hooligans dressed as policemen. Why, Alan? Why would anyone do such an idiotic thing?'

'If we knew that, my dear, we might hold the key to the whole incident. Clearly someone put them up to it. And we can guess the motivation from the result. Evidence was destroyed, perhaps by accident, perhaps not. The invaders made it much more difficult for the police to identify the person – or persons – who caused the damage.'

'Was David a target of the invasion?'

'Make a note of that question, love. It's one for David to answer; he would know if it felt personal. Myself, I'd say not. This little timetable exercise has started some wheels turning, and I'm beginning to get the notion that David's visit had nothing to do with the destruction.'

He settled back, hands tented and touching his mouth. If Rodin had seen him, *The Thinker* would have adopted a similar posture. Then his hands returned to the desk. 'Consider this scenario. George calls, invites David to meet with him. He ends the call; the doorbell rings. He's taken aback; David could not possibly have got there that fast.'

'Does George know where David is coming from?'

'I don't know, and we'll want to ask, but he certainly knows he isn't just around the corner. All right, the bell rings. I'm not going to speculate about who's at the door, except that George isn't worried about letting him in. That means he knows the person, or at least he/she doesn't have a threatening appearance. The person comes in. Now I confess I'm reaching a bit here, but I think they talk for a bit, and the conversation escalates into a quarrel, then a fight. Visitor loses his temper entirely and starts throwing things.'

'Is George injured in all this? Injured, or—'

'I don't know. I can't even guess. David made no mention of blood, but anything is possible. Perhaps he just gets out, gets away from this maniac who's destroying his house.'

'But not in his car.'

'As you say. We don't know why. He leaves, either of his own volition, or . . . not. The maniac also leaves, having expended his fury. Being once more in something resembling a right mind, the person sees costumed actors leaving the pub on their way back to rehearsal, and has the bright idea of creating a diversion. He offers to pay them for entering the house and making the mess even worse. They're a bit tipsy, and it sounds like fun.'

'And just as they're heading over there, David arrives. Alan, that would mean he just missed catching the guy! He must have been getting out of there just as David was going in.'

'By a few minutes, yes. If David has worked that out, he must be feeling a bit frustrated just now. If I'm right about this, of course. It's all spun out of air.'

'Not quite. Somebody did trash the house; somebody did get the bobby chorus to invade. It's a wonder they didn't break into song while they were at it. I can just hear them bellowing "With catlike tread upon our prey we steal" while tromping through the house.'

'That's the chorus of pirates, dear, not the coppers, but they might have done. Perhaps they did. Though I imagine David would have mentioned it. We're sliding into silliness, my dear.'

'We are. I don't know about you, but I badly need a nap. Let's resume this not-very-fruitful exercise a bit later.'

SEVENTEEN

When my phone rang and woke me from a nap, I expected some new tale of calamity from David. Instead it was Eileen who greeted me.

'You sound a bit foggy. Did I wake you?'

I sighed. 'I admit it. The past few days have been . . . sort of trying. But it wasn't a restful nap, so I'm just as glad you called. What's up?'

'Nothing good, I'm afraid. I shouldn't bother you with this, but I thought . . . well, you've been kind to Tim, and—'

'Is something wrong with Tim? He's not hurt!' My voice was sharp. On the other side of the bed, Alan sat up, his brow furrowed.

'No, nothing like that. It's just that . . . oh, it's dreadfully unfair!'

'Tell me.' I turned on the speaker to let Alan hear.

'Tim's flatmates have moved out. No warning, they just said they wanted a better place. Maybe they can afford it. Tim can't. And the rent is due, and the landlord won't give Tim time to find new flatmates. He's going to be out on the street!' She was fighting back tears, not very successfully.

'All right, dear, calm down. I think we may be able to help.' Alan had picked up his phone and moved to the bathroom. I shut off the speaker, just to make sure Eileen wouldn't hear; I had a good idea what Alan was doing. 'Why don't the two of you come over for tea? I know you should both be studying, but I wouldn't imagine your concentration is at its best just now.'

Eileen drew in a long, shuddering breath, the remnant of a sob. 'I'll go and persuade him. He's not with me now; I didn't want him to hear this call. I'll tell him – oh, dear, what shall I tell him?'

'Tell him I called you and invited you both to tea. It's only a half-lie, and we can tell the whole truth if necessary. Come as soon as you can; I'll send Alan out for some goodies.'

I clicked off before she could object and waited for Alan to end his call.

'You called David?'

'Yes. He's on his way. With tea cakes. I think it may work out, Dorothy.'

'Can we lend Tim some money, meanwhile? I doubt he'd accept an outright gift, but it's going to take David a while to find a new place. That's if he agrees. What did you tell him?'

'Only that our friend had a dire housing problem, and we thought his needs and David's might mesh. He jumped on it. He hasn't said much about his living situation. He's loyal to his family. But we've both felt his unrest.'

'I hope he gets here first, to let us lay a little groundwork.'

But as it worked out, Tim and Eileen were the first to knock on our door. I explained that we were going to have another guest, who was bringing the tea cakes, and Alan went to filch another couple of chairs from somewhere. A party of five was going to stretch the capacity of our room to the limit.

David arrived. Everyone was introduced. I made tea; David, bless his heart, had brought a larger pot and a few teabags. 'I knew B&B facilities weren't going to be adequate for a tea party,' he said with a grin. Bless the man! He was beset by worries, and was still thoughtful and able to smile.

He passed around the large box of food. He had brought not only scones and fruit tarts and luscious-looking cakes, but tea sandwiches in great variety – and some paper plates to put them on. 'David, this is a feast!' I exclaimed. 'I won't need to eat for a week.'

'You told me students would be here. Students are perpetually hungry. Do help yourselves, everyone.'

When we all had full plates (all except David, who had taken one modest sandwich), David began the conversation. I held my breath. Was he going to spill the beans?

'I'm glad you're here, you two,' he addressed Eileen and Tim. 'I have a problem you may be able to help me solve. Don't be offended, Alan and Dorothy, but you don't know Durham well.'

'Not at all,' I put in.

'Precisely. And I don't know it well, either; I've lived here only a few months. I've been living with a granddaughter, and while she is all that is kind, I know that she longs for a little privacy, as well as more room. She and her husband have two young children, and we're a bit squashed. As I've hinted to Dorothy and Alan, I've been hoping to move, and have found a pleasant house not far from here, with a bit of garden. It's too big just for me, though. I'd like to find someone, preferably a student, who would share with me. The cost would be nominal; I'm wanting company and some help about the house more than help with the rent. Do you, either of you, know a student who isn't afraid of a bit of work and wouldn't mind sharing with an old duffer like me?'

Tim put down the strawberry tart he was about to devour. 'Sir, did someone put you up to this?'

David smiled. 'In a sense. Alan did mention that he knew someone who might be looking for housing. But I found this house some days ago and signed a lease. I'm looking to move in any day now. Are you telling me you're interested?'

'Interested! Sir, you are the direct answer to prayer! I've always believed the Lord protected his lambs; now I know for certain. This morning my flatmates moved out, leaving me with full responsibility for the rent, which is due tomorrow. I can help you with moving, if you're seriously wanting me to share? You don't know a thing about me. I can get references, but it will take a little time, and—'

'I know you're a friend of my great friends. That's enough reference for me.' He looked at his watch. 'It's a bit late in the day to begin a relocation, but if you'll come with me – after you've finished your tea – I'll have another key made and show you the house, and you can bring your things any time you want. Then we'll set a time tomorrow to begin my move. I imagine it will be more troublesome than yours. I've had a good many more years to collect barnacles.'

'I'll bet you've been careful about scraping them off, though. I'm guessing you're a practical sort of chap, more attached to people than things.'

'You'll have to watch your step, David, with this lad in your house,' said Alan. 'He can see further through a brick wall than most people. I've told him he'd make a splendid policeman if he ever decided to give up his theological ambitions.'

'Not a chance of that, I'd say.' David looked Tim over with an amiable eye, while Eileen gave Alan and me a look of such gratitude I was hard put not to cry.

We settled down to our tea. We all, especially the kids, did full justice to the bounteous spread, but they ate fast, plainly eager to be on their way. David pushed his plate aside first. 'Right. You two, come with me to my car. We have a lot to do! Alan, Dorothy, I'll ring later.' I put the few leftovers in a box and handed it to Eileen, who gave me a hug on her way out. At that I did shed a tear or two.

When they had left Alan and I did what we could to tidy up the mess. The wastebasket in the room was entirely inadequate to deal with crumby, jammy paper plates and napkins and bits of tarts and sandwiches and scones. Alan crammed it all into a Tesco bag I'd been saving and put it outside the door to carry down to the breakfast room in the morning, and we relaxed.

'That's one mission accomplished, anyway,' I said smugly. 'Tim's found a safe home, cheap and secure.'

'And David's his own man again. He and Tim will be good for each other, I think. I always thought it a pity David and Gwen never had children. Now David has a son.'

'Not quite yet – but they're headed that way, I agree. But he also has a real great-aunt in deep trouble. We're one day closer to the deadline, and no closer to exonerating that poor old dear.'

'No. I meant to ask David if he'd found another place for Amanda to stay, but there was no chance.'

'Maybe when he calls later. But Alan, nobody wants that for her! We want her to stay where she is, where she's safe and contented and loved. We need to stop wasting time and solve the . . . er . . . the confounded problem!' The cathedral bell, chiming out the near approach of evensong, took the stronger adjective from my lips.

'Ah – a reminder. Let's go seek some help and consolation, and then tackle the problem afresh.'

There is something about evensong. The prayers and the

readings are all designed to envelop one in a sense of security, all anxiety banished, all fears swept away. And when the service is sung by a superb choir, those of us who love music are left feeling that heaven is not very far away at all.

We came out into a perfectly lovely evening, pink and gold and green, and soft, fragrant with the scent of just-opened lilacs and new-mown grass. I took a deep breath. 'Alan, I don't want to go back up to the room. I'm getting cabin fever in that place. We need to find a quiet, friendly place where we can sit and think about our problem. Is the little library open in the evening, do you think?'

A student who was hurrying by heard us and stopped. 'I'm afraid the Palace Green library closes at five. Are you staying in the castle?'

We smiled back. 'Yes, in the building – I don't know the name of it – the one where the Great Hall is.'

'Ah, then come with me. It's not far.' He kindly slowed to our more elderly pace and led us down toward the market square to a pleasant place called The Shakespeare.

'A pub?' I said dubiously. 'We were looking for a quiet place to sit and talk and think.'

The young man grinned. 'In term time it's mobbed. Everybody's favourite place just before exams! But just now it'll be as quiet as you like. And the beer is good! Enjoy the peace while you can.' He waved and hurried away before we could even ask his name.

Once we got inside, I was delighted. The upstairs room was spacious, comfortable, well-lit, and deserted. It was the ideal space for studying, or for mulling over a knotty problem, and no one seemed to care that we didn't want to order food or drink.

'Right,' said Alan briskly. 'To work. Shall we resume our timeline for last night, or take a new tack?'

'New. We were going around in circles. I'd like to note down questions we need answered, and then work out how to answer them.'

'That last is easier said than done, love.'

'Yes, but the questions come first. We'll find the answers. We always do!' I was buoyed up by evensong, optimistic and cheerful. I got out my notebook. 'I propose we concentrate for now on what happened last night, because it's the most recent event.'

'We don't know that it has any bearing on who killed Blake Armstrong.'

'We don't know anything,' I retorted, 'but we never will unless we start asking the right questions. And the first question I want answered is where is George Elliot?'

'The police will be working on that, Dorothy. And they have the resources.'

'Yes, but you're forever saying they don't have enough resources, enough manpower, enough anything. It can't hurt for us to ask around. Second question: why didn't he take his car to wherever he went?'

Alan thought about that and listed several possibilities, ticking them off on his fingers. 'He was thinking only about escaping the madman who was tearing up his house. His car wasn't running properly, or it was out of petrol. He was dead.'

'There's another one, and I just thought of it. Alan, where do you keep your car keys?'

'In my pocket.'

'Not when you're at home, you don't. When you get ready for bed you put them in that wooden tray on the dresser, along with everything else from your pockets. And half the time in the morning you forget to put everything back *in* your pockets until you're ready to leave the house, and then you have to go back upstairs to get it all. Suppose George didn't have his car keys handy? He sure wouldn't have taken time to go get them, not if he was running in fear of his life.'

Alan slapped the table. 'Full marks for that one, Dorothy! We can't know if that's what happened, but it's a *very* intelligent suggestion.'

'And if the team searching George's house finds his keys—'

'In some spot far from the door—'

'Then we still won't know for sure, but the odds go up considerably.'

We exchanged smug looks. and I made a note: *query car keys*. 'Now, next question. How can we find and talk to the men in the *Pirates* chorus?'

'That's another item the police are chasing down.'

'Ah, but I propose to go about it in a different way. First, I'd bet money that most of them are students. That means we talk to Eileen and Tim. If they know any of the choristers, we can get an introduction, and they'll talk to us, or at least to me, more readily than to the police.' Alan grinned. 'Well, you're the one who always says people find it easy to talk to me!'

'And it's true, my love. We do need the kids' help. Which reminds me: we have to get Tim and David's new address. He forgot to give it to us.'

'Right. We'll have to do that when we see him this evening. But first I'm going to get us two tickets to the *Pirates* performance.'

'Dorothy, we don't even know when it's on. We may be back home by then.'

'Don't be silly. The dress rehearsal was last night; we know that because the chorus was in costume. We're probably missing the first performance right now, but there's bound to be at least one more. We've always enjoyed G&S, and this way, even if our two students don't happen to know anyone in the cast, we have the best possible reason to go to the theatre and talk to them afterward. And you see, if we can find the ringleader of that exceedingly stupid prank, we'll know who put them up to it. Ta-da!'

'That's if the pseudo-bobbies know the chap. That's anything but given.'

'Oh.' I hadn't thought of that. 'But would they – the singers, I mean – would they have invaded someone's house on the suggestion of a stranger?'

'If our speculation is right, they were all reeling a bit, and were offered a bribe. Under those circumstances, yes, I think they'd have agreed eagerly.'

'Oh,' I said again. 'Well, we can but try. If we don't learn anything, we've lost nothing but a few pounds for the tickets.'

'And an evening.' Alan soberly reminded me that time was short.

Wordlessly we struggled out of our too-comfortable chairs and went back to the castle.

EIGHTEEN

David called me just as we arrived, panting a bit, at our lofty room. He inquired about dinner.

'I'm still full of that marvellous tea. I can't even think of food. How did it go with Tim?'

'That lad has certainly gathered very little moss thus far on his journey through life. His belongings fit easily into one suitcase and three boxes, two of which held books.'

'Well, of course. You remember Erasmus' famous saying: "When I get a little money, I buy books. If any is left, I buy food and clothes." Tim has the same priorities. And I have to say I agree with him, within reason.'

Alan looked over at me, grinned, and shook his head. I ignored him. 'He's settled in, then?'

'As if he's lived there all his life. When I left him to start packing up my own things, he was busy scrubbing the kitchen floor and arranging the cupboards to suit him. We agreed he's to be cook and gardener and I'll manage the finances and light housecleaning. I think it's going to work out splendidly.'

'And then he'll graduate, and marry Eileen, and you'll be alone again.'

'Bridges to cross, Dorothy. If you're not hungry, would you enjoy a pint at our favourite pub?'

'Sounds good to me. Fifteen minutes or so?'

We ambled down. With the students still on break, the place, like The Shakespeare, was nice and quiet. 'Next week we won't be able to hear ourselves think in here,' I commented as we found a table and waited for David.

'Next week I devoutly hope we'll have dealt with all the problems and be back home.'

'Amen. Ah, here he is.'

'The usual?' he called from the door, and came to the table expertly carrying three foaming glasses on a not-quite-big-enough tray. 'It was easier back in the days of the mugs. I could carry three in each hand then.'

'And they were pretty, too, that heavy, dimpled glass. Ah, well.' I lifted my brimming glass. 'Confusion to our enemies!'

'At least as much as they've given to all of us,' said David ruefully. 'I wish I had any good news to give you, but there are no new developments. And I won't be able to pursue it at all tomorrow; I've got to spend the day finding a place for poor Amanda to live.'

'We all hope it won't come to that,' said Alan, sounding (I was sure) more confident than he felt. 'Dorothy came up with a couple of ideas today that might help.' He gestured at me with his glass.

'Well, one idea won't help all that much.' I explained about the car keys. 'Of course, they may not find them. But I think they will, and that would fill in quite a few gaps in our understanding of what happened last night.'

'Indeed. Good thinking. I'll pass it along. It won't help find Elliot, though – alive or dead.'

'No. But my other idea might help find his attacker. We're going to go to a performance of *Pirates of Penzance* to meet and talk with the chorus, to see if they can't identify the person who sicced them on you!'

'The police—' David began.

'The police are official, and therefore threatening. I'm not. I'm just a dotty, little, old American lady – I can strengthen the accent when I need to – who heard about their high jinks and thinks it's funny. I'll wear a hat and look as frumpy as I can. I'm pretty sure I can get them to talk.'

David laughed. 'You might, at that. So you're harking back to Nathan's death, still thinking it was murder, still thinking it has to do with Armstrong's death.'

'I am. I know you're not at all certain, but you haven't lived your life by Goldstein's Theorem of Interconnected Monkey Business.'

Alan chuckled; David looked confused.

'I'll explain. It goes back to some wonderful mystery novels by Aaron Elkins. He created a character, in every sense of the word, named Abe Goldstein, who claims that when several strange things happen in close proximity of time and space, there's virtually bound to be some connection between them, even though it may not be obvious. Interconnected Monkey Business. I have nearly always found that to be true. And since we have in this case no other notions to chase, why not follow this one? Can't hurt.'

I was to remember that remark.

We ended up having a couple of Scotch eggs, my favourite pub snack, and then David brought his car round and took us to his new home. It was near enough to the castle that Tim could bike there easily, though I thought of all the steep hills and was very glad it was him and not me.

Tim was home. Eileen was with him; big surprise! We stopped in for just a minute to let him show off his new pad, after which he carried in the first load of David's stuff, firmly refusing any help from anyone, even Eileen, who was certainly young and strong enough to carry heavy loads. She and I exchanged looks that clearly said, 'Men!'

David was ready to call it a day, take us home and get to bed himself, but before we left I asked Tim and Eileen about the *Pirates* cast. No luck. Not students, so far as they knew. We were just going to have to see the show. What a sacrifice!

Dropped off at the corner of Dun Cow Lane, we toiled up the hill and across the Palace Green and collapsed gratefully into our bed.

I didn't sleep well, though, and woke long before I wanted to on Tuesday morning. After I made the necessary trip to the bathroom (fuming about the more annoying aspects of ageing) I found I couldn't get back to sleep. The weather had changed in the night. Clouds hung low in the sky and the air was heavy and damp. The sheets were damp, too; I couldn't get comfortable. Alan slept soundly, which irritated me. I wanted somebody to talk to. And I was hungry, and the dining room wouldn't open for hours.

I reminded myself that I wasn't a helpless Victorian sort of woman. I was perfectly capable of finding coffee and pastries. I knew there was a Starbucks nearby, but wasn't sure exactly where, so I pulled out my phone to check. Sure enough, it wasn't far away, but it wasn't open yet. I showered and dressed, hoping I was making enough noise to wake the slumbering love of my life, but no. Sighing, I grabbed my purse and my cane, and the umbrella just in case, and went down the stairs and out into the world.

It wasn't exactly hot outside, but there was barely a breath of air stirring, and the clouds looked heavier every moment. I hurried as much as I safely could on the treacherous cobblestones and reached the coffee shop just as it opened, and the storm began.

It was a doozey. Reminded me of the storms that used to scare me half to death when I was a little girl in Indiana. Lightning, thunder loud enough to make me nervous, sure something nearby had been struck, rain that made Niagara look like an also-ran. The lights flickered once or twice, but mercifully didn't go out. Starbucks without electricity to make coffee was not a pretty thought.

That kind of intense storm seldom lasts long. When the thunder had rumbled away and the rain diminished to a drizzle, I chose some pastries, packed everything up in the handy cardboard carrier, and had started out the door when the boy at the counter called me back. 'Madam, is your name Dorothy Martin?' He held out a telephone.

What on earth? I took the phone.

'Ah, Dorothy, there you are. I thought I might catch you.'

'Alan? Why are you calling me here? I'm just about to head back with breakfast.'

'Yes, love, but you see you left your phone in the bathroom, and as the storm was bad, I wanted to be sure you weren't in some sort of trouble. Don't let the coffee get cold.' And he clicked off.

Oh, dear. My protective English husband, trying to pretend he hadn't been worried sick about me, off in a serious storm, and without a phone, with a murderer running loose somewhere. And I'd been cross because he'd been able to sleep when I couldn't.

There was no doubt about it: I didn't deserve this man. I hurried back up the hill with coffee and goodies; he met me halfway.

'Alan, I'm sorry! I should have left a note. But you were sound asleep, and I was sure I'd get back before you woke.'

'The thunder woke me. It didn't take me long to work out where you must have gone. But next time you disappear into the blue, love, do take your phone.'

And that was all. No ranting, no recrimination. How did I ever get so lucky?

We ate our very unhealthy but very satisfying breakfast in amity, speaking only in trivialities. When I'd downed the last crumb of a cheese Danish and the last sip of coffee, I sighed with satisfaction. 'It does feel good to break the rules occasionally.'

My model husband didn't remind me of how often I break the rules. He dusted off his fingers and said, 'Right, chief. What's on the agenda for today?'

'I was thinking about that most of the night. Bearing in mind Poirot's maxim that it's always best to know as much as possible about a victim, I thought we might go and visit Nathan's mother.'

Alan looked dubious. 'I'm not sure that's doable, love. Birmingham is a good long way from here, and I'm not sure what the rail connections might be. And we're due in Bishop Auckland at eight, don't forget. With a car we might manage it, but I fear not otherwise. You might phone his mother.'

I shook my head. 'No. That wouldn't work at all. Would you talk on the phone about one of your children with a woman you didn't know from Adam? Well, Eve, I suppose. No, it has to be in person. If not today, then what about tomorrow?'

'Hmm. It might work, if there's an early-morning train headed that direction. It's possible we might have to spend the night.'

'That would take it to Thursday. We've got to move faster than that.'

'Yes. Amanda's deadline.'

We sat in a depressed silence. Not only had the sugar high worn off, it seemed less and less likely that we would be able to help solve Armstrong's murder in time to help Amanda.

The cathedral bells began to ring, and I stood up. 'We're going to morning prayer. Can't hurt. Might help.'

There was no music at this simple service, only the old familiar prayers. Somehow, in a place that had heard those prayers for centuries, they seemed a part of the fabric. If the presider had lost his voice, one felt that the very stones would carry on. For at least four hundred years monks had chanted them in this very choir, had sat in these very stalls. In the nave, the people had brought their fears and woes to God, their joy and worship, their thanksgivings, and had gone away knowing that their prayers had been heard, and secure in that knowledge.

Nowadays there were no monks, and the congregations, except on Sundays, fit in the choir, with room to spare. The Age of Faith is long gone. But Alan and I carried some of that ancient peace away with us when the service was over. He turned and smiled at me. 'I don't know about you, but that very early breakfast has vanished as though it had never been. I'd like some real food!'

'You are a snare and a delusion. I'll never get thin this way. Lead on!'

We were just in time for breakfast, and over the sausages I made a decision. 'Alan, I've got to call her – Nathan's mother. She may not want to talk to me at all, but I have to make the attempt. We can't waste a day. Can you get her number from the police, do you think?'

He considered. 'If not the number, perhaps her full name. Or I could find that in an obituary, if we knew the date of his death.'

My twentieth-century mind immediately sprang to thoughts of the public library and old newspaper files – and then I remembered my phone and the Internet. I wasn't very good yet at searching on my phone – I still thought of the device as a way to call people – but I'm learning. 'OK, I'll look it up. Or no! Better idea. I'll call Eileen. She was there! She'll remember.'

She even, having read Nathan's obituary, remembered the name of his parents. 'I never look at obituaries, but I was interested in this one, for obvious reasons. His father's name is Thomas Elliot. His mother's name wasn't given, of course.' I heard the annoyance in her voice. Women so often didn't count, even in this somewhat progressive age.

'Mrs Thomas Elliot. All right, that's useful. Are you still helping with the move?'

'Nearly done!' She sounded smug. 'David is gone for the day, searching for a home for poor dear Aunt Amanda, but his granddaughter has been good about letting us come and go as we liked.'

'She's probably glad to be rid of him!'

Eileen laughed. 'She tries not to show it. They truly do love each other, but three generations in one house is a bit much, especially when the youngest of them is very young indeed. About two, I'd say, and in perpetual motion. I do bless you for working out this new arrangement. Much better for all concerned!'

'I'm glad it's working out. I must go. Carry on!'

It was Alan, much more adept than I with the mysteries of cyberspace, who eventually found a phone number for one Thomas Elliot of Birmingham. Praying that it was the right one, I made the call.

A woman answered. She sounded about the right age to be the mother of a college student. She also sounded wary, as one does when answering a call from an unfamiliar number.

'Mrs Elliot, you don't know me, but I'm not a telemarketer or anything like that, so please don't hang up. My name is Dorothy Martin and I'm trying to get some answers about your son Nathan's death. You'll think this is ridiculous, but I believe he was murdered.'

There was a long silence. Finally: 'Who are you and why is my son's death any business of yours? You're not with the police, or you would have said. I suppose you're one of those tabloid reporters!'

'No, I'm not, but a friend here in Durham is a retired policeman, as is my husband. We heard of Nathan's death through a related matter, too long to go into. My husband and our friend are not enthusiastic about my . . . call it instinct about Nathan's death, and the police here in Durham aren't interested, but I'm quite sure in my own mind, and I want to see his killer found. I'm also very worried about his brother George.' I took a deep breath. 'Would you have time to talk with me a little about your sons?'

Again the long pause. 'You're American, aren't you?'

I raised my eyes heavenward, a foolish gesture since she couldn't see me. 'I was born there. I've lived in England for some time, and am now a British subject.'

'You live in Durham?'

'No, in Sherebury. My husband and I are visiting here.'

'I see. Mrs Martin, there's no sensible reason why I should trust you, but somehow I'm inclined to do so. As it happens, I'm in Bishop Auckland at the moment, hoping to find some trace of George.'

'Oh, so this is your mobile number.'

'Yes, of course. The landline forwards to this number.' She sounded impatient. 'There's a reasonably pleasant café near his house. If you would care to join me for lunch, perhaps we could talk.'

'That's very good of you. Where and when?'

NINETEEN

After we'd settled on a time and place, I ended the call and sat down to work out logistics with my ever-resourceful husband. A quick Internet search told him there was a train that would set me down in Bishop Auckland in time to meet Mrs Elliot, and then I might as well stay there cooling my heels until time for the opera at eight.

'We're lucky, you know. The trains don't run that often anymore. The rail service in this country . . .' And he went off into the familiar English rant about the terrible state of the railways. Coming from a country where train travel is nearly non-existent, I wasn't inclined to be terribly sympathetic.

'The real question is how we're to get home after *Pirates*. That is, I suppose you'll come with me? Though you could come later. I can't see Mrs Elliot as posing a mortal threat, and I'm sure she won't want you to sit in on lunch.'

He made a face. 'No. I can see that's to be ladies only. But I'll have to come with you, as the only other train will be too late for the opera. And there doesn't seem to be one coming back afterward till tomorrow morning. It's a wonder they've kept that station open at all!'

'Yes, dear.' And I turned my mind to the tricky question of wardrobe – something nice enough to wear to the performance but not too dressy for lunch at a 'reasonably pleasant café' with a woman whose social and financial status were completely unknown. These things seem to matter a lot more in England than they used to at home.

As usual, I compromised on a pair of black pants and an inconspicuous top, with a colourful scarf I could put on, or not, depending. Along with shoes that didn't look quite as comfortable as they actually were, I was set.

The train was late. Alan groused some more, but we made it in time, if only just. We had planned to explore the town a bit, but instead I had to hail a taxi to the café. Arriving just as a smartly dressed woman entered, I decided she was Mrs Elliot, and added the scarf to my ensemble.

Smartly-Dressed was standing near the doorway. She looked up as I entered, and I took a chance. 'Mrs Elliot?'

'Mrs Martin.' Her tone was neutral. If not exactly welcoming, it wasn't hostile, either. 'There's a corner booth that will suit us nicely, I think.'

I meekly followed. If she wanted to call the shots, I would go along. Up to a point.

'I looked you up,' she said, holding up her phone. 'You are not unknown,' she added, almost accusingly.

The only way to play this was straight. This woman was not to be won over by charm. 'No,' I replied.

'Is it accurate, what the newspapers say?'

'Not entirely. Newspaper accounts seldom are, don't you find? But if you've read that I've been involved in untangling a fair number of problems, mostly in and around Sherebury, it's perfectly true.'

'Why? Why have you meddled in that sort of thing?'

I bristled a little at her tone, but I tried not to let it show. 'Usually because someone was in trouble and I wanted to try to help them out of it. After a while I found out I was good at asking questions, and people often seemed willing to talk to me.'

'Why?' she asked again.

I shrugged. 'I don't know. Maybe they think I'm harmless.' I gave her my most disarming smile.

She did not smile in return. 'I don't think you're harmless. Quite the contrary. But I said I'd decided to trust you. Oh, yes' – to the waitress who had appeared – 'I'll have the chicken salad and tea.' She raised her eyebrows at me and I nodded agreement. After two breakfasts I wasn't actually hungry, but I could pick at my salad as long as I needed to finish our talk. If she decided to talk.

The waitress dismissed, Mrs Elliot pushed her shoulders back. She didn't have a lorgnette, but the effect was exactly as if she was staring at me through one. I met her gaze. 'Very well. What do you want to know?'

'Anything you can tell me about your sons. I want to know what they're like. Were like. Sorry, I can't get the tenses right.'

She dismissed that. 'I may shock you. My feelings are not what you may think of as maternal, or appropriate.'

'I doubt that, Mrs Elliot. I have no children of my own, but I was a teacher for most of my life and have known many hundreds of children. I am aware that they come in plenty of varieties, some more easily acceptable than others.'

Her laugh held no humour. 'Yes, you might put it that way. I did not like my younger son, Mrs Martin, and the older one is not a great deal more satisfactory. When I talked to the police about Nathan, I think they found my attitude peculiar.'

'I was told what you said to them. To me it sounded as though you weren't entirely surprised by Nathan's death. Now I must ask you if you are surprised that I believe it was murder.' I had lowered my voice, though the noise level in the busy little café easily covered our conversation.

This remarkable woman pursed her lips. 'No,' she said at last, 'not astonished, at least. He was a most infuriating person. He was always right, you see, and never shy about letting you know. Saint Nathan.'

The Gospel according to Nathan, the boy at St Jude's had said.

'And underneath it all,' his mother went on, 'he was a nasty, sneaking person. Even as a child he would spy on his school-mates and then threaten to tell the teacher or their parents unless they gave him something he wanted.'

'Juvenile blackmail.'

'Exactly. He made quite a nice little thing out of it, actually. It progressed rapidly from toys and trinkets to cash, larger amounts as he grew older. He never squandered it on sweets and ices, as another child might have done. No, he hoarded it and gloated over it.'

'I see. A miser as well as a blackmailer. I agree he doesn't sound like an attractive child. But how did you find out about his activities?'

'It was his father, actually. I am a fairly recent widow, Mrs Martin, and not entirely devastated by the fact. My husband was in many ways very like his sons – or they like him, I suppose. Nathan was quite sure that his father would approve of his cleverness when he told him some of what he was doing.

Tom looked into it, verified that Nathan was telling the truth, caned him severely, and then took the money.'

'To give back to the victims?'

'Surely you jest. Tom said it was part of the punishment. It went into his own pocket, of course, and thence to his wine merchant.'

Our food arrived. I had lost whatever appetite I'd had, but I drank the tea thirstily. 'And was the punishment effective?' I asked when I had finished my cup of tea and poured another.

'In a way. Nathan never told his father anything important ever again. He had never trusted me, so communication foundered in our household. I believe he used to talk to his brother now and then.'

'And he continued his unsavoury enterprise?'

'I think he did. He used to brag about how much money he had, how he'd never had to take out student loans even though we'd never given him a penny (this with mournful violins playing softly in the background). But he would never tell us what sort of job, or jobs, he had. "This and that," he'd say. "I work very hard."'

'What was he studying?'

'I don't know that, either. We quarrelled about it. He said quite frankly that since I wasn't paying for it, it was his business.'

'Was he succeeding academically?'

She shrugged. I thought I knew the answer. The student at St Jude's had said Nathan was sloughing off his work. But it was interesting that his mother either didn't know that or didn't care. I took a bite of my salad and tried to decide where to take this.

Mrs Elliot made the decision for me. 'You said you wanted to know about both my sons.'

'Yes, because I'm quite worried about George. Do you have any idea where he might have gone?'

She shook her head impatiently. 'The police already asked me that. If I'd had an idea I would have told them, wouldn't I? He's a grown man, a successful businessman. Almost as close-mouthed and difficult as Nathan, but at least he's made something of himself. Why are you worried about him? He'll fall on his feet; he always does.'

I was becoming more and more annoyed with this woman's cavalier attitude toward her sons. Maybe they weren't the nicest people in the world, but they were her *children*, for Pete's sake! And she'd never see one of them again in this world. Perhaps not in the next, either. 'I am worried about him, Mrs Elliot, because someone killed Nathan. I am more than ever sure of that, now that you've told me about his illegal activities.' She glared at me. 'Blackmail is a crime, you know, and a very dangerous one. I think he went a bit too far with one of his victims, who put an end to the extortion in a very effective way. And if George, who you say was sometimes in his brother's confidence, if George knows something about Nathan's death, he could be in very great danger. He left home in a great hurry, and from all appearances in the middle of a violent confrontation. Yes, I'm worried about him!'

'And you think I should be, too.'

'I do. The fact that you are not leads me to believe you do know something about his whereabouts, though you deny it. I have just one more question for you, a quick one. Have you any idea who might have hated and/or feared Nathan enough to kill him?'

She looked me straight in the eye. 'I do not. If I did, I would tell the police. I may not have loved my son, madam, but I am not such an unnatural mother as to condone his murder.' She stood and tossed some money on the table. 'Enjoy the rest of your meal.'

Whew! I began to wonder if Nathan had perhaps committed suicide. With a mother like that . . .

As difficult a woman as she was, though, she'd given me one useful piece of information: Nathan was a blackmailer. I shook my head in exasperation. Of all forms of crime, that's one of the stupidest. Making enemies left and right for the sake of a little money. Okay, maybe a lot of money, but at what a cost! A cornered rat will bite. A blackmailer may think himself safe, but in fact he's terribly vulnerable. Nathan had paid for his extortion with his life.

But at whose hands? I was no closer to knowing that, or to

finding George. I wished I'd had the ability to follow Mrs Elliot. I was certain she knew where her remaining son was hiding out. I also wished I'd learned more about George, whom his mother didn't like, either. She approved of his success in life, however. And she'd come a considerable distance to 'find some trace of George', she said. Now what did that mean?

I discovered that my teapot was empty and hailed the waitress to ask for more. 'You didn't care for the salad, madam?' she asked, sounding as if she cared.

'It's very good. What I actually didn't care for was my companion.'

The waitress, who was quite young, nodded sympathetically. 'A rather . . . um . . . cold lady. To tell you the truth, I always hope she won't come to this table, but she nearly always does.'

'It's quite private. She comes in here often, then?'

'Not to say often. A few times, with a younger man. Her son, I think. I'll be right back with your tea.'

Drat. I wanted to talk about the son. The café was nearly empty, and I wasn't due to meet Alan for another half hour.

She did come back quickly, and I was able, without much difficulty, to persuade her to sit down for a moment. 'I expect your feet hurt. Mine always did, decades ago when I did a little waitressing.'

'You were a waitress?' She could hardly have sounded more astonished if I'd told her I'd ridden in a Wild West show.

'Not really. I mean, I just had a part-time job when I was in college . . . university. I wasn't very good at it. What I mostly remember is the sore feet!'

The girl stretched hers out, after giving a quick glance around. 'I'm closing today, so I can relax for a minute.'

'Good. I wanted to ask you about Mrs Elliot – the woman I was with. I've never met her before, and I wondered if I'd done something to offend her.'

'Oh, she's always like that. Cold, like I said. And her son – if that's who he was – not much better. Stingy, too.'

I reminded myself to add a bit to the money Mrs Elliot had left. 'Did you know he'd gone missing?'

'Oh, is he the one! Well, who'd have thought! He seemed

like a respectable sort. The kind that make a parade of being respectable, you know?'

'Uriah Heep,' I suggested, but that brought only a puzzled expression. 'I mean, yes, I know the type. They always look like they've smelled something unpleasant.'

She giggled. 'Exactly like that! I'd never have thought he'd be one to do a runner.'

That was a new idea. 'You think that's what he's done? Run away from something, maybe debts?'

She nodded sagely. 'Now I think about it, it is high mucky-mucks, sometimes, who come a cropper. Good at putting on a front, you know. I heard his house was in a frightful state. Maybe a bill-collector trying to find some money?'

That seemed pretty far-fetched to me, but I nodded thoughtfully. At least the bill-collector idea was an interesting one. There are all kinds of bills.

I looked at the name badge pinned to her uniform pocket. 'I'm a stranger to these parts, Melanie.'

She nodded. 'American. Or maybe Canadian?'

'More or less. Anyway, if you wanted to get lost quickly, where would you go?'

She wrinkled a cute, turned-up nose. 'Never thought about it. There are some places up in the hills, caves and that. It wouldn't be very comfortable, though, and you'd have to know the area. I don't think this man lives here, does he?'

'He does now, but he's from Birmingham originally.' Oops.

Her face changed. 'You know more about him than you pretended! What are you after?'

'I'm trying to find him, Melanie. I'm not sure he went away of his own free will, and I'm worried about him. I'm sorry if I led you to believe otherwise. I really am on the side of the angels.'

'Yes, well . . . I have to go.'

She picked up the cash from the table and disappeared into the kitchen. I drank a little of my now lukewarm and unwanted tea, put down a handsome tip, and went to find Alan at the imposing town hall.

'Nice lunch?' he asked innocently.

'Bits of a salad, dressed with vitriol.' I looked around to make sure Mrs Elliot wasn't lurking somewhere. 'Given a choice between lunching with her and with a tarantula, I'd choose the latter. And you know how much I love spiders.'

'That bad, eh? Was it worth it?'

I made the rocking 'maybe' gesture with my hand. 'I got a few things. Did you eat at all?'

'Found a good pub and had an excellent ploughman's. Shall we go and find you some proper sustenance, and you can tell me all about it?'

TWENTY

I opted for a lovely beef sandwich on a crusty roll, with lots of horseradish. While I devoured it, with eyes streaming, I told Alan about the blackmail. 'Remember I told you he bragged about having plenty of money? Now we know where he got it. How often in your career did you have a case involving a blackmailer who got himself dead?' I gulped some of my pint to counteract the horseradish.

'Not quite as often as in the fiction you dearly love, but often enough. Blackmail as a profession is fraught with occupational hazard.'

'Indeed. And since the law is often helpless in such cases, because the victim is afraid to tell the police about it, perhaps – but no, I won't say the punishment is merited. Nothing justifies murder. However, are you now ready to accept my certainty that Nathan was deliberately pushed into the river?'

'Yes. We have nothing that could make a case, though. It's all supposition and theory, and while I do now find it convincing, there's nothing to get hold of.'

'I know. And time is running out for Amanda. Have you heard from David at all?'

'No.'

We finished our beer in dispirited silence.

As we got up, Alan looked at his watch. 'Still hours before the opera. What would you like to do?'

'Well. This isn't a market day, so there's not a lot of interesting shopping to be done, and anyway shopping bores you to tears. I wonder where George's house is.'

'I knew you'd ask that,' said Alan smugly. 'I checked with David before we left Durham. It's a bit far to walk, and I'm sure it's sealed off as a crime scene, but we can take a taxi if you like.'

'I like. I know it's silly. The police will have seen anything there is to see, but I'd feel like a shirker if I didn't at least look.'

It was indeed sealed off, as we discovered when the cab dropped us off, with strict instructions to be back in half an hour. The cabby darted a significant glance at a nearby pub, grinned, and took off.

'Is that *the* pub? The one the pseudo policemen came out of?'

'Grammar, darling!'

'I'm with Winston Churchill on that one. "A silly rule, up with which I will not put."'

'Right. As to the pub being *the* pub, I don't know, but I assume it is. It's the only one nearby.'

'Okay, then, I don't understand. The show tonight is in the theatre at the town hall. What was part of the cast doing here?'

'Don't know that, either. We'll have to ask when we see them tonight. Meanwhile, the garden isn't sealed off, only the house. Do you want to walk round and peer in the windows?'

'The neighbours will probably call the police. Of course I want to, but let me take this scarf off. I don't want to snag the silk, and those roses look pretty fierce.'

The house was in good repair, the roof sound, the trim recently painted, but George had neglected the garden. There was a scrap of grass on either side of the front walk, and it was neatly mowed, but the only flowers to be seen at either front or back of the house were rambler roses which had lived up to their name. The one over the front door had covered the small porch-like enclosure on both sides and the roof, and hung down to assault the unwary with needle-like thorns.

Alan and I skirted the thorns carefully to peer through the window in the door. Or we tried to peer. The window was covered with a curtain, and although it hung askew, we could see almost nothing in the dark interior.

We circled the house. More roses, more curtains. A few of the roses bore half-open blooms in a rich yellow; the effect would have been beautiful if the plants had been pruned and properly trellised. As it was, I was reminded of the Secret Garden: wild, unchecked growth, almost savage in its intensity. 'Nature red in tooth and claw,' Alan commented as a thorn caught the back of his hand and made a small gash.

'Ouch!' was my elegant reply. It had got me on the arm.

And the exercise was futile. We could see almost nothing of the inside of the house. I glimpsed clutter here and there, but the curtains had shut out light as well as prying eyes, and nowhere were we able to see enough of any room to help us at all.

'Well.' We gave up before our cab was due to return. 'That was a sheer waste of time.'

'But it might not have been,' Alan comforted. 'One never knows.'

'My father used to say, "One never knows, does one, and even then one can't be sure." I realize now he was being funny, but at the time I didn't get it at all.' I pulled out my phone and glanced at the time. 'Still five minutes, if he's back on time. I'm going to take another look in that window on the front door. I thought I maybe saw a handkerchief on the floor. That could be a source of information – DNA and all that.'

Alan just smiled.

The sun had shifted slightly, enough to show through the small opening in the curtain that what I had seen was a piece of paper. I backed away from the door and stopped, my hair caught in the welter of roses. I couldn't get myself loose. 'Alan, help!' I called. 'The monster's got me!'

He came and carefully untangled my hair, collecting a few more scratches in the process. 'We deserve hazardous duty pay,' he growled. 'Hello, what's this?' He stopped tugging at my hair; I couldn't turn around to see what had attracted his attention.

'Alan, I'm still stuck!'

'Sorry, love. One second. Do you still carry that Swiss Army knife around with you?'

'Of course. It's in my purse.' Which was dangling from my arm. He reached inside, fumbled around, and apparently found the knife and its tiny pair of scissors. I heard a couple of snips, and then one more, and my head was free.

'I had to cut only one small lock; I don't think I've ruined your hair.'

I dismissed that; my hair at its best looks extremely casual. 'What's that you've got?'

'A button.' He held it out on the palm of his hand. It was still attached to a bit of rose cane and could, at first glance, be mistaken for a rosebud. I reached out to touch it; Alan pulled his hand back. 'I don't travel with evidence bags these days. Would you perhaps have an envelope or something similar in that capacious purse of yours?'

Oh. Evidence. Yes, of course. I mentally smote myself on the forehead and rummaged in my purse, pulling out the aged Tesco bag I always carry with me. 'Will this do?'

'Nicely, thank you. Not chemically clean, of course, and far too big, but it serves the purpose.'

He let me take one more look before he consigned the button to the bag. It was small, about a half-inch in diameter, made of a yellowish plastic, with four holes, the sort of button one might find on the cuff of a man's jacket. A few scraps of tan thread still clung to it. 'A clue!' I exclaimed in awe. 'A real clue!'

'Was you wantin' to go someplace, mate?' The cabby had arrived without our noticing, and was growing impatient.

'Yes, sorry.' We clambered into the cab. Alan said, 'The police station, please, and wait for us. We won't be long.'

'All the same to me, mate.' He gestured toward the meter, which was running up an appalling total. I hoped he accepted credit cards; we never carry much cash and hadn't anticipated spending a fortune on transportation in a town even smaller than Sherebury.

'I suppose we do have to take it to the police,' I said wistfully.

Alan just looked at me.

'I mean – yes, of course we do. It's just that it's *our* discovery, and – oh, okay, forget it. But can I take a picture first?'

He carefully opened the bag and exposed the unexceptional button to the light. I took a couple of pictures. He put the button back.

'I suppose you'll get scolded for removing it,' I said.

'Almost certainly. But I did cut away part of the rose, and can show them where it was. And you saw me remove it.' He looked at me over the top of his glasses and I nodded agreement to the fib. I *heard* him remove it, at least. I smiled to myself at the thought of my utterly truthful, law-abiding husband stretching a point. I was teaching him bad habits.

The Bishop Auckland police were frigidly polite. *Yes, sir. I see, sir. And you removed it because? Ah, tangled in your wife's hair. I see.*

I winced a little at that one, but made no comment. The conversation went on. *And you were searching the property for what reason, sir?*

All their questions were directed at Alan, of course. Women are necessary, but are not important. Still, in the twenty-first century . . . Ah, well.

Alan refrained from pulling rank on them for as long as he could stand it, but was finally obliged to let them know that he was a retired chief constable, that he was still a sworn police officer, that he was aware of the rules about evidence collection, that he was happy to have been of service, good afternoon.

It was doubtless a good thing that we couldn't hear their comments after we left.

'Ungrateful bunch, aren't they?'

Alan slammed the door of the taxi with unnecessary vigour. 'We found something their people missed. Of course they're not happy about that, and I'm sure someone will get a wigging. But they could have been more respectful, I agree.'

'They didn't know who you were until the end,' I pointed out.

'That shouldn't matter. Any member of the public . . . oh, very well.' He relaxed and grinned. 'I would almost certainly have done the same with an interfering busybody who turned up with a bit of rubbish my officers should have found. They were insufferable toward you, however. I would not have taken that attitude.'

'No. You are always courteous to women. Overprotective at times, but never rude.'

'Where next, mate?' He had driven away from the police station, which was on a one-way street, but had now reached a corner where a decision had to be made.

Alan looked at me.

'I don't know any more than you do about the town, dear.

Is there,' I asked the cabby, 'some place we as tourists shouldn't miss?'

'There's Bishop's Castle. Being restored, but worth a visit. The bishops of Durham lived there back in the old days.'

'Um . . . I thought they lived in the castle at Durham.'

'Both, but they liked this one better. Lived there until a few years ago. You want to see it?'

'Certainly,' said Alan. 'We can lay claim to two bishops' residences during our visit. We're staying in Durham Castle at present.'

'Oh, yes? Wouldn't be my choice. Cold, damp places, castles.'

'This one is actually very nice,' I put in. 'Of course it's been remodelled a bit.'

And we talked about castles for the rest of the brief ride. I don't use taxis much, and I'd forgotten the delights of cabby conversation. Even here, far to the north of London, the drivers are a breed of their own, independent and fascinating.

The castle was very nice. Though the restoration was not yet complete, one could get a good idea of how lovely the place would soon be. More of a palace than a castle, actually, it had little of the fortified feeling of Durham Castle. I could easily see it as the palatial home of the prince-bishops of past centuries. The deer park was lovely and the art gallery stuffed with remarkable paintings, and I was more than ready for a substantial tea after we'd walked for what seemed like miles and seen all there was to see.

'I wish,' I said after I'd downed about a month's worth of carbohydrates, 'that we could take a nap. I'm tired, and my feet hurt.'

'Have another cup of tea. Or order some coffee. That should keep you awake.'

'Yes, because I'll be looking for the loo every half hour!'

But I ordered the coffee anyway, and waiting for it and drinking it helped to pass the time until we needed to head for the theatre.

In my years of teaching, I'd assisted at enough amateur dramatic presentations to know that there was no point in trying to talk to the cast beforehand. Even though these were adults and not excited children, and even though this was the second night of the run, everyone would be nervous, anxious about forgetting cues, or lines, about watching the baton without being obvious about it, about that tricky lighting cue in the second act, about all the thousand things that can go wrong in a complex production. They would have no attention to spare for a nosy outsider. Alan and I meekly paid an extra pound for a programme, found our seats, and settled down hoping that all would go reasonably well.

As it worked out, we enjoyed ourselves. *The Pirates of Penzance* has always been one of my favourites of the G&S canon, and this production was well done. True, the stage was a bit small for the large cast, and some of the choreography had to be ingeniously devised to fit in the confines, but the acting and singing were good, and the small orchestra played their hearts out. Most of Gilbert's plots are pretty silly, and *Pirates* is one of the silliest yet, but it's all great fun. Alan and I were delighted that the audience were invited to join in the well-known chorus that 'A policeman's lot is not a happy one', a sentiment that Alan could echo with considerable feeling.

We did not stay for the several curtain calls but rose as soon as the applause began (to the irritation of those seated between us and the aisle) and headed for the stage door. I would have been shy about asking to go backstage, but Alan's training as a policeman had given him a commanding manner when necessary, and he was not above flashing his old warrant card in a pinch. This time his strongly voiced request did the trick, and as soon as the cast left the stage for the last time, we found ourselves surrounded by noise, movement, and the mingled smells of greasepaint and warm bodies.

It was all a bit overwhelming, but again Alan's experience with crowd control worked a small miracle. Without appearing to push, without discourtesy, he managed to cut off one of the singers dressed as a policeman and draw him into a relatively quiet spot behind one of the scenery flats. He shook hands with the man and turned on his charm. 'Well done, sir! Before I retired I was a real policeman, and I must congratulate you and your colleagues on your portrayals!'

The man looked embarrassed. 'We had to play them as bumbling idiots, as per the script. No insult intended, of course . . .'

'Certainly not, and none taken. This is my wife, by the way, an American who knows quite a lot about idiotic police.'

I accepted the slur on my native country and picked up my cue. 'Yes, I've known a few American constables who weren't maybe the brightest bulbs in the chandelier. Your interpretation of the type was terrific.'

'In fact,' Alan went on genially, 'we were hoping to treat you and your colleagues to a congratulatory pint when you've freed yourselves from your costumes and makeup and all.'

'Oh, please do!' I chimed in when I saw the hesitation on his face. 'You must be hot and dry after all that work, and we'd love to talk with you!'

'Well . . . it's very kind of you. I'll ask the others, shall I?'

Alan didn't leave it to chance, but accompanied the man to the men's chorus dressing room while I tried to look inconspicuous among the jostling crowd backstage, cast members as well as stage hands trying to strike the set without trampling on each other or dropping a sandbag on anyone's head. I enjoyed it. Our school productions were never anything like as professional as this one, nor had our theatre been nearly as well equipped, but the atmosphere was identical, and to me intoxicating.

Evidently Alan managed to persuade the bobby chorus that the other sort of intoxication sounded like a good idea, for in remarkably little time we were joined by seven somewhat dishevelled and malodorous men, all expressing thanks.

'Right,' said Alan when we had picked our way to the outside door and stood enjoying the fresh air. 'I don't know Auckland at all. Where's the best pub near here? We're staying in Durham and came here by train, so I don't have a car at hand.'

'The Mitre has the best beer,' volunteered one of the group. 'Not as fancy for the lady, though.'

I expressed my preference for good beer over pretty surroundings, and we headed down the street to an establishment whose décor could best be described as basic. It had a bar, a dartboard, tables, chairs that looked ancient and teetery, and one or two lamps waging a losing battle against the stygian gloom.

Our new friend had been quite right. Not at all my kind of place. The beer would have to be very good indeed to make up. However, this gathering was not intended for my entertainment, but for investigation. Onward, Dorothy!

Alan guided me through the dimness to the largest table they had, and pulled over another, and he and two of the other men went to the bar to fetch our drinks.

TWENTY-ONE

When we had settled in our chairs, one of the men raised his head and sniffed ostentatiously. 'Bit of a pong, isn't there? Sorry about that. It was warm under those lights, and our costumes were wool.'

'Can't be helped. At least it's draughty in here.'

I hadn't intended a pun, but the men took it as such and laughed, and I felt that friendly relations had been established. Our pints arrived, Alan made a toast, and we drank and chatted about nothing for an amiable interval.

I was sure Alan would have worked out a subtle way to approach the subject of the 'prank' a few nights before, and I was right. We were on our third round (Alan and I still working on our first) when he said, 'I read in the programme a listing of events at the hall. Busy place. I wonder that you were able to work out rehearsal times.'

'Oh, we don't rehearse there,' said the baritone who'd led the chorus and sung the solo bits. 'Too expensive, for one. The Players operates on a shoestring. And you're right, they couldn't have fit us in anyway. No, we rehearse in an old church hall. The church moved out years ago, but the building is still sound, if a bit dingy. Much cheaper than a real performance space.'

'But not really equipped for opera,' said the bass. 'It's fine for drama, with a small cast. But bobbies, pirates, and daughters popping up everywhere—'

'Not to mention a portly major general—' interjected a tenor, to laughter.

'It was all a bit crowded,' concluded the bass. 'And hot!'

'Ah,' said Alan sympathetically. 'I hope you've a good pub near there, as well.'

The laughter and chattering died. The leader cleared his throat. 'Yes, but we . . . um—'

'We may not be welcome back there,' said a small man who

had not yet contributed any comments, a tenor, by the sound
of his speaking voice. 'We . . . there was a bit of a fuss.'

I shook my head, smiling. 'Had a few drops too many, did
you?'

'Not really. We only—'

'It wasn't our fault,' said the other tenor hotly, the one who
had joked about the major general.

I made a disbelieving face. 'Of course not,' I said, laughing.
'It never is!' I held my breath. Were we going to get it?

'You may laugh, but this time we weren't to blame.' The
tenor was getting a bit belligerent; he'd finished his second
pint and was well into his third, and as small as he was, it
probably took less beer to get him well lubricated.

'Back off, Reilly,' said the bass. 'No rudeness to a lady.
And it's not quite true. We could have said no to the chap.'

'But what *happened*?' I put as much puzzlement as I could
dredge up into my voice and face. 'A bar fight?'

'No. Not as bad as that. Or maybe worse; I don't know.' A
chorus arose, taking sides one way or the other. 'Shut it!' the
bass roared. 'I'm trying to explain to the lady. We were taking
a break during rehearsal,' he said when the babble subsided a
bit. 'It was dress rehearsal, and they'd run into a spot of trouble
with one of the pirates' choruses. We were all hot and thirsty,
so we popped across the road, still in our costumes, of course,
and had a couple of quick ones. We were just heading back
when a chap came along with a bright idea. He wanted to play
a trick on one of his friends, he said. We were dressed like
policemen. He'd give us twenty pounds each if we'd pretend
to stage a raid on a house just over the road. We were all a bit
tipsy, and it sounded like easy money, so naturally we agreed.
He handed Reilly a wad of notes and we charged ahead.'

He finished his pint in one massive gulp. 'But it didn't work
out quite as well as we'd hoped. The chap who answered the
door wasn't the one who lived there. That one was gone, no
one seemed to know where. And the one we talked to was a
retired copper.' He paused and looked at Alan, and I could
see wheels turning. He wasn't exactly drunk, but his mental
processes were a bit fuddled. 'Didn't you say you were once
a copper, too?'

'I did, and I was, a good many years ago now. But I can't help being curious about this chap who got you and your mates into trouble. Did any of you know him?'

No response except for headshakes.

I sighed, but silently. We'd lost their confidence with the revelation of Alan's past profession. Now they wouldn't tell us a thing.

'Pity,' said Alan. 'He did you a bad turn and deserves to be disciplined. Ah, well. Who's for another?'

But no one seemed thirsty anymore. Almost as one man they stood and mumbled excuses and melted away.

Alan stood, too. 'All for naught,' he said. 'Shall we?'

I'd been sitting for too long in that wretchedly uncomfortable chair. He had to help me to my feet. 'It really was good beer, though.'

'A trifle costly,' he said, putting away his now distressingly slim wallet.

Night had fallen, making the interior even darker than before. We stumbled out and stopped, wondering what to do next. We hadn't booked a room anywhere, and it seemed much too late to try to find a car to hire.

'Excuse me.' We turned. It was the bass. 'I'm sorry I blew the gaffe. You're serious about this, aren't you?'

He had sobered, quickly. I nodded. 'Don't worry, though. Will your friends hold it against you that you led them into the situation?'

'No. They're good chaps, and honest, but not over-fond of the police after what happened that night. They tore us off a strip, more than we deserved, we thought, though we were daft to take on that prank. But you're looking for the tyke who put us up to it?'

'Yes,' said Alan. Just that. No explanation.

'We weren't lying when we said we didn't know him. Never set eyes on him before. But he was young, and I'd lay odds he was a student from Durham.'

'What makes you say that?'

'There's a look. I can't describe it. Scruffy but snobby. And he was flash with the cash. Not a working lout, for sure.'

'Can you describe him at all?'

'Nothing to stand out. It was all too quick. Caught us, threw his money about, vanished.'

'Anything? Tall, short, thin, fat?'

The bass shook his head. 'Ordinary. Wearing jeans and a tee, like everyone else.'

'Accent?' I put that one in.

'Not from here. Southern. But I can't say more than that.'

Alan shook his hand. 'Even that much is a help. Thank you.'

The man sketched a salute and walked quickly away, and Alan's phone rang.

The conversation was brief and when he ended the call he was smiling. 'David, wondering where we were, and when I told him, he said he'd come pick us up.'

I sighed with relief. 'And so the old woman got home that night.'

We tried to talk over what we'd learned on the way home, hoping David would have some suggestions, but he was in a defeatist mood and didn't want to talk about it. I gathered he'd had no luck finding a suitable home for Amanda and was growing desperate, but he didn't want to talk about that, either. He dropped us off at the top of Owengate and we made our way up the hill and across the cobbles and up the many stairs to our room in glum silence.

'A better day tomorrow, love.' Alan fell into bed without even brushing his teeth.

'I sure hope so. I thought we'd make some real progress today, but we're nowhere. And poor Amanda!'

Alan's reply was drowned in a yawn.

Wednesday morning I woke early, far earlier than I intended. The cool evening had prompted us to open our windows wide, and the birds were joyously greeting a lovely dawn. Their racket was enough to wake the dead in the nearby churchyard.

I was considerably less joyous about the whole thing. I got up to go to the bathroom, firmly intending to go back to sleep. But Alan was awake, too, and ready to start the day. After one look at my face he wisely said nothing, but simply made coffee and presented it to me with a kiss. I growled something, but the stuff smelled good, so I sat up and drank some, and then some more, and sleep gradually receded.

'Oh, well, I suppose . . .' I got up and showered, grumbling all the while. Alan slipped out to find a newspaper and came back with better coffee and some pastries, as it was too early for breakfast in our splendid hall.

'We've got to stop eating like this,' I snarled, trying to button my pants. 'I'm getting *terribly* fat.'

'Perhaps we need to take more exercise.' He was still a little short of breath from the stairs, which made me laugh – as he had intended.

'I remember,' I said, 'when I was a little girl, I was mad about something and was sulking, and my sisters decided to make me laugh, to shake me out of it. They succeeded, and that made me madder than ever. I *wanted* to be in a snit.'

'Oh, dear, I'd best be careful, then. Almond croissant?'

My very favourite pastry. I bit into the flaky sweetness, gave up my snit, and smiled. 'I can't imagine why you put up with me.'

'You have a few redeeming qualities. Curiosity and persistence, among them.'

I shook my head. 'I'm about to give up on this one. We're getting nowhere.'

'I don't agree. We know a good deal more about Nathan Elliot, and what we know makes it extremely likely that he was murdered.'

I brightened a little. 'Which also makes it much more likely that Armstrong was murdered for what he saw that day.'

Alan grinned. 'And since you've been convinced of both those scenarios from the first, isn't it nice that you've been confirmed? Almost.' He dodged the pillow I brandished. 'And we have one solid piece of evidence.'

'The button. I'd forgotten the button. The police didn't think much of it, though.'

'The gentlemen at the station house were extremely annoyed that they hadn't found it. They were obliged to disparage our discovery in order to save their honour. I'll wager anything

you like that they are at this moment exploring every possible
way to identify that button. Laundries, dry-cleaning establish-
ments, shops – anything they can think of.'

'Ooh, wouldn't it be fun if we figured it out first!'

'Which we have very little chance of doing, love. We are
limited in our power to go about asking questions.'

'True. Or at least of getting people to answer them. Witness
Mrs Elliot. I'll swear she knows where George is, or at any
rate where he's likely to be, but she's refused to tell me or
the police, and I wonder why.'

'Oh, that's an easy one. She isn't worried about him
because she knows he's not in danger, and she doesn't want
him mixed up with the police because she knows, or suspects,
that some of his activities wouldn't bear close scrutiny. Don't
forget she said he's a lot like his brother.'

'Ah. His brother the blackmailer. What do you suppose
George has been up to?'

'He's an accountant, didn't you say?'

'Oh, my, yes. A profession that offers countless
opportunities—'

Alan's groan interrupted me, and I heard what I'd said.

'Drat it, I never mean these things! That's just the way my
mind works. Anyway, opportunities for anyone who's smart
and not overly concerned about legality and ethics.'

'And that, since we're now back in the realm of unsupported
speculation, makes me wonder what sort of hold he had on
the man who tossed his house.'

I finished my coffee along with another pastry, knowing I'd
be sorry later, and dusted off my hands. 'And until we find
George and/or his intruder, we're stuck.'

'So, to that end, I think we should invite Tim and Eileen
to lunch. They're our link to the student world.'

'You think our informant – darn it, we forgot to ask his
name – you think he was right about the instigator being a
student?'

'I think he's a keen observer, at any rate. And what other
lead do we have?'

The breakfast room downstairs was now open, but as we
were both stuffed with carbs, we went for a walk until we could

decently call Tim or Eileen. Seven thirty of a lovely summery morning was far too early to disturb anyone, even someone as mature and responsible as both these kids.

We walked, of course, down to the river. This time I was paying close attention to the bushes near the path.

'Looking for another button?' asked Alan.

'Yes, I am, and don't laugh. Or if not a button, something – anything – that might give us a lead.'

But there was nothing. Not so much as a beer can or a cigarette butt. Evidently the maintenance crew had taken advantage of the students' absence to do a thorough clean-up. 'It looks like they ran a vacuum cleaner along the path,' I said in disgust. 'Even Sherlock Holmes couldn't find anything here.'

'We can't get lucky every time, you know. Real villains aren't as eager as the fictional sort to strew their belongings about.'

When we came near to the place where Nathan went into the river I stopped, looking at the river and its bank as if they could tell me something.

'Meditating?'

'Not exactly, just . . . oh, it's silly. I thought I might pick up some vibes or something.'

'I'm not laughing, love. You do have a keen sense of atmosphere.'

'In old churches, anyway. But not here. I'm feeling nothing except impatience.'

Alan looked at his watch. 'Let's walk on toward the bridge and go up that way, and then we'll phone the kids.'

As we neared the bridge we saw a little knot of people standing on the riverbank looking down. 'Oh, Alan, no! Don't tell me someone else has drowned!'

My agitated voice carried, and one of the bystanders turned to me. 'Don't worry, ma'am. It's nothing like that. A chap's doing a bit of diving.'

'But . . . are there interesting creatures down there or something?'

My informant laughed. 'No, the fellow's an archaeologist, and he's found all sorts in the river. Old coins and that. Telling us a lot about what life was like hereabouts hundreds of years ago.'

'Oh, yes,' said Alan. 'I was reading something about it in the newspaper this morning. It said there used to be shops on one of the bridges, and one poor shopkeeper lost everything when his shop collapsed into the river.'

'S'right. Some of it don't look like much when he brings it out, but clean it up and it's amazing.'

'Goodness. Like a dig, but he's digging in water, so to speak.'

'S'right.' The man beamed at us and went back to his observation.

I couldn't see that there was anything much to observe, as all the activity was under the surface, but to each his own. We moved on. 'Alan, could we call now, do you think?'

He pulled out his phone. Yes, Tim was home. Eileen had just got there; they were helping David get organized in his new digs. Yes, they'd love to have lunch, thank you. No, David wouldn't be able to join us – still searching for a home for Amanda. The Italian place? Super.

TWENTY-TWO

I killed part of the morning reading the newspaper account of the diving archaeologist, and the rest shopping for gifts. We would be going home soon, whether the problems were solved or not. The summer university term began on Monday, so students would be moving back into their rooms on Sunday, and we would be evicted. David had offered to put us up in a hotel, but a retired policeman isn't made of money. We declined with thanks, and I started thinking about what Jane, our neighbour and pet-sitter, would love.

Durham's Market Square is small but crammed with shops. I usually enjoy shopping, but I had a hard time keeping my mind on what I was doing. I wandered into the indoor market and went from stall to stall in a fog. I'd pick up a pair of gardening gloves I thought Jane would like, and stand staring at them, wondering how David was doing in his frantic search. I found a wooden train I was sure she'd love to give to her great-grandson and wondered if the police had checked with the railways for signs of George.

I pulled myself together in time to buy the gloves and the train and a marked-down spring jacket that looked just right for Jane (and big enough), and trundled heavily laden to the Italian restaurant to meet Alan and the kids. Tim and Alan helped me stow my parcels and sat down. I was a little late; they had already ordered a huge plate of antipasto which arrived the moment I sat down.

The waiter also brought us a large bottle of white wine. I looked at Alan, eyebrows raised. We had planned to have a discussion over our meal, and lots of wine doesn't usually aid serious thinking.

Eileen caught the look and chuckled. 'We know, Dorothy, but we insisted on treating everyone to a nice wine. We're celebrating!'

I glanced at her left hand, but it wasn't that. This time Tim joined in the laughter. 'Not yet, Dorothy. But soon! Right now, the good news is that I'm a wealthy man! Or nearly.'

'Your aunt's will has been reversed?'

'Not yet, though my lawyer is hopeful. No, I told you about my sister, who's comfortably fixed. She's a dear, and we've always been close. Well – wait for it – she just won the lottery!'

'Tim! Not one of those multi-million ones!'

'No, but a very nice sum indeed. And she's going halves with me! What with that and my grand, new, rent-free rooms, I can give up my night job. I'll still do the tours of the castle, but that's usually only once or twice a week. I'm a free man!'

'What wonderful luck!' I enthused.

'Or pure grace. So here's to a brighter future.' We raised our glasses. 'It's a pity David can't be here to celebrate with us,' said Eileen. 'Tim would still have to work the other job if not for his generosity.'

'He's a good man, David,' said Alan, 'but you know you're doing him a favour, too. He needed to get away from his family, dearly as he loves them, and he wouldn't be able to maintain that house without help.'

'Yes, well.' Tim shrugged that off, the typical English reaction to anything resembling praise. 'I'm sure you didn't invite us to lunch for us to crow. Are we making any progress?'

'Some,' said Alan, and after the waiter took our orders Alan related what we'd learned over the past few hours. 'What with the revelations of Nathan's not very savoury character, and a few more details about the prank at George's house, I've come round to Dorothy's point of view. I think it's almost certain that Nathan was pushed into the river and that Dr Armstrong was a witness to at least some part of the event.'

'And that he was killed because of that,' I finished.

'I'm not ready to go quite that far, not yet,' said Alan, 'but it's certainly within the realm of possibility.'

'That means all we have to do,' said Eileen, swallowing a black olive, 'is prove all that, and find the murderer, and Amanda is home free.'

'Yes,' said Tim gently, 'that's all.'

I didn't want to dwell on the enormity of the task still in front of us. 'We did find one tangible clue,' I said, 'or at least a possible one. There was a button caught in a man-eating rose by George's front door. My theory is that the villain lost it when he fled from the house, but of course it could have been George's.'

'Ooh! Do you have it with you?'

Alan smiled at Eileen. 'We left it with the police, of course, but Dorothy took a picture.'

I pulled my phone out of my pocket, but the picture wasn't very good. 'I'm afraid it just looks like a button, any old button.'

Tim and Eileen studied it closely but could make nothing of it. 'If we had the actual button, we could show it around, but this . . . I'm sorry, Dorothy, I don't mean to insult your picture—'

'I'm a terrible photographer, and a phone isn't a wonderful camera. I wish we had the real thing, too, but Alan is a policeman first and last.' I smiled at him to take away the sting.

Our food arrived then, smelling as marvellous as Italian food always does, and for a few minutes we concentrated on the joy of gluttony. I stopped before I had to undo the button on my jeans, but it was a near thing.

Tim pushed his plate away. 'I won't need to eat for several days,' he said. 'Thank you, Dorothy and Alan. Now, what can we do to help with the investigation?'

Alan slipped into his lecturing mode. 'We have only the slightest description of the man who caused the brouhaha at George's house, the one who incited the chorus men to wreak their destruction, but our informant was certain he was a student, of average height and build, and not from these parts. A southern accent, he said.'

Tim whistled silently. 'Not a great deal of help, is it? Amongst thousands of students . . .'

'We can narrow it down a bit,' I said. 'The man we're looking for is presumably one of Nathan's blackmail victims, therefore someone he knew. Wouldn't that make it more likely to be a student from his own college, St Jude's?'

'Somewhat more likely, I agree.' Tim was very thoughtful. 'But you know we take classes and attend lectures with men and women from all the colleges. What would help a great deal is knowing what he's studying.'

I sighed. 'I suppose we'll have to find out somehow. More delay.'

We declined dessert and polished off the wine, but our celebratory mood had dimmed. Two more days, plus one afternoon, to free Amanda from suspicion and allow her to keep her home.

Standing up gets to be more and more of a problem the older I get, especially from a comfortable seat. I struggled out of the booth, dropping one of my parcels in the process. The jacket I'd bought for Jane slithered out onto the floor. Alan picked it up, shook it out, and raised his eyebrows. 'Have you a secret admirer, dear heart?'

'Don't be silly. It's for Jane.'

'It's intended for a man. Look at the way it's cut. Look at the way it buttons. Left over right.'

'Oh. I didn't notice. It was on sale and it looked sturdy, and big enough for Jane, and anyway she goes in for masculine styles . . .' I stopped, looking more closely at the buttons. 'Alan!'

'Let's get it out into the light.' Our companions followed us eagerly.

'Yes, I think you're right,' Alan said when he had taken a good look.

'And see,' I added, 'the sleeve buttons aren't sewn on very tightly. One could easily be wrenched off.'

'So you think it was a jacket like this one?' asked Eileen.

'Or one with the same buttons. There must be thousands of them out there.' My initial excitement was rapidly subsiding.

'Never mind, love.' Alan patted my shoulder. 'It's a tiny step, but in the right direction.'

'And we'll keep a close watch for a jacket like this,' said Tim, 'or buttons like these. It will all come right in the end. Try not to worry too much.'

'Easy for him to say,' I grumbled as we walked back to the castle. I was beginning to get used to hills; my legs weren't aching much anymore. 'He's young. Nothing seems as urgent when your whole life is in front of you.'

'I think you've forgotten how desperately large small matters could loom when you were that age,' said Alan, taking my arm as we hit a steep bit. 'The next examination was a life-or-death ordeal. A problem with one's love life could be shattering. No, I think the reason Tim is hopeful lies not in his youth, but in his faith. Don't forget he's planning to enter the priesthood.'

The cathedral bells rang out just then, as if in agreement.

'Oh, dear. And Hope is a virtue. That's one in the eye for me, isn't it? Very well. I'll try to be more hopeful. But even if God sees to the design, we're the ones who have to work it out, and I have no idea what to do next!'

'That is the problem,' Alan admitted. 'Let's have some coffee and make a plan.'

We'd gone over and over the same ground so often that we had the steps memorized. 'Let's go back to the beginning,' Alan suggested. 'Or the point at which we entered the scene. Armstrong's death. Is there some path we've neglected to follow?'

'Not that I can think of. We, or the police, have questioned everybody at the Milton Home. All we've learned is that someone could have come in the back way, through the kitchen, but that doesn't tell us much. Oh, but wait!' If we'd been in a comic strip, a light bulb would have appeared over my head. 'We have something to show them now. We could ask if anyone's seen a man wearing this jacket! Only . . .' I sighed. 'With David running around all day with the car, we don't have a way to get out there.' I hadn't fully appreciated the convenience of a car until we were without one. Going anywhere was much more complicated and time-consuming, and in cases like this, impossible.

Alan stood, pulled out his phone and began poking at it. 'It's time we hired a car.' One more poke and he was talking to someone. 'Yes. Good. As soon as possible, please. We're in the castle. Yes. Yes. Right.'

He put the phone back in his pocket. 'Enterprise. They deliver, and are allowed to come to the Palace Green to pick us up. Get your skates on, woman!'

It was lovely to be in a car again, with Alan at the wheel. True, it was smaller than ours, and not quite as comfortable, but it didn't matter. We were independent again! With satnav on my phone, we got to the home without a hitch. Alan having called to say we were coming, the woman at the front desk greeted us with a smile and phoned Mr Williams to say we were there.

When he came down to meet us, it was obvious he wasn't best pleased. Though courteous, he was less than cordial. 'I hope you haven't come to discuss Miss Bowen's situation. We of course regret the necessity, but I assure you we have no alternative but to ask her to find another home.'

I caught up. 'Oh. Great-aunt Amanda, you mean. I didn't know her surname. No, we don't intend to argue with you, though *I* assure *you* that you've made the wrong decision.'

Alan gave me a warning look and took over the conversation. 'We know that you are as unhappy as we are about the circumstances of Dr Armstrong's death, and we've found a new piece of evidence that may help to uncover the truth of the matter. We hoped you might allow us to ask your staff a few more questions. I believe this is the time of day when most of them have a brief respite from their duties?'

'Mr Nesbitt, we *have* uncovered the truth of the matter, as you put it. Unhappily, there is no doubt that Miss Bowen is to blame. It isn't her fault, of course, and she could never stand trial, poor dear, but you must see that we can't continue to put the lives of our other residents at risk.'

Alan pulled out his phone. 'In that case, sir, I have no recourse but to call my solicitor. I have discussed the matter with him, and he agrees that you may be acting in an unreasonably obstructive manner.'

Gosh. Even I fell back. Alan in full chief-constable mode can be extremely intimidating. The director's face changed. He held out a hand. 'I do not agree with you, Mr Nesbitt, but if you wish to waste your time in this fashion, you are free to do so. I ask only that you not waste the time of my staff. They work very hard and are entitled to their rest at this time of day. Good afternoon.'

He strode off. The receptionist let out her breath in a gust. 'He doesn't mean to be rude, you know. This whole thing has upset him enormously. This place is his pride and joy, and he hates the thought of its reputation being damaged. And the worse of it is' – she looked around and lowered her voice, though there was no one in sight – 'the worst of it is he doesn't really believe himself that poor Amanda had anything to do with all this, but he has to do something, and he doesn't see anything else to do.'

Alan was still not quite ready to unbend. 'Perhaps. Now, before we go elsewhere, we should ask you if you recognize this.'

I pulled the jacket out of my carrier bag. 'Not this particular one – it's new – but have you seen anyone wearing a jacket like this recently?'

She looked it over carefully. 'Hmm. Wool?'

'Acrylic, I think. It was on sale, but even at sale prices, wool would be more expensive.'

'Yes, I see. Meant for warmish weather, then. For spring, probably. Smart, but not too expensive. No, I can't say I remember seeing it before.'

'Don't worry,' I said. 'There are lots of other people to ask. Are you on duty every day, by the way?'

'No, I'm off on weekends.'

'We'll need to talk to your replacement, then, but that can wait a bit. For now, can you give us the key codes for the kitchen and the elev— the lift?'

She chuckled. 'I do speak some American, you know. Here are the codes, and good luck to you!'

TWENTY-THREE

The kitchen door was very near the elevator. We flipped a mental coin and chose to go upstairs first.

The staff room was crowded when we knocked on the door and looked in. Some of the people didn't look familiar. Either they hadn't been there when I visited before, or I simply didn't remember them. (A growing possibility these days.) But several remembered me.

'Mrs Martin!' The attractive woman who'd been so pleasant before jumped up with a huge smile on her face. 'We were just talking about you. Well, talking about Amanda, and hoping you'd been able to clear her name. We can't bear the thought of her leaving. I know we're not supposed to have favourites, but . . .'

There was a subdued buzz of agreement.

'Thank you – oh, I've forgotten your name.'

'Dharani.'

'Lovely name. I should have remembered. I'm sorry to tell you we haven't yet found out who really did kill Dr Armstrong. This is my husband, incidentally – Alan Nesbitt.'

Everyone murmured something polite. The men stood to shake his hand. Even after living in England for years, I still haven't quite got used to that little courtesy. My native countrymen have a few things to learn.

Miss Manners having been satisfied, Alan and I took the seats we were offered and turned down the cups of tea. Velma (I remembered *her*, for sure) said in her usual irascible way, 'If you haven't come to give us good news, why have you come? I'll bet it isn't for the pleasure of our company.'

'Not entirely,' I said, sweetly as you please, 'though I did enjoy meeting you all. No, I have something to show you.' I pulled out the jacket and held it up. 'Does anyone recognize this?'

Velma, of course, spotted the tags immediately and pounced. 'How could we? It's straight from the shop.'

'This one is, you're quite right. But we have reason to believe that someone wearing one like this is . . . well, at least, not an entirely pleasant character.'

'You mean he killed Armstrong.'

'That's an inference we're not quite yet ready to make, although you could well be right,' said Alan smoothly. I watched with interest. If he could charm Velma out of her gleeful malice, he deserved the Nobel Peace Prize. 'You seem to be an observant woman. Take a good look.'

He handed her the coat. She inspected every seam, every pocket, every button, and finally rendered her verdict. 'Showy but cheap. Not a jacket for a *gentleman*. I'm quite sure I've never seen one like it before.' She handed it back to Alan and said no more, but I thought perhaps her movements showed a grudging respect.

Of course after Velma's pronouncement no one else would have dared admitting to recognizing the jacket, so we took our leave, with thanks, and went to the elevator, where I trimmed the tags off the jacket before we returned to the main floor and the kitchen.

Tea was being prepared we saw when we let ourselves in. Cakes had been set out on attractive plates. Bread was being sliced thin and assembled into sandwiches: cucumber, tomato, egg and cress. A large fruitcake had been cut into generous wedges which were also being placed on plates. Trays stood ready with sugar, milk, and thin slices of lemon, along with cups and spoons and fat-bellied china teapots. This time of day might be restful for the caregivers, but not for the caterers. I had no doubt that for many of the elderly residents, tea was the most important and most enjoyable meal of the day. They could doubtless remember the teas of their youth, when it was an important social ritual for people of their class. I had to admit that the sight of all those delightful treats made my insides rumble, despite the huge lunch I'd just finished.

The woman who had rescued us from the Indian restaurant when David vanished – Kathleen, that was her name – was making dainty tomato sandwiches and carefully trimming off the crusts. She looked up, covered a plateful with a damp tea towel, and came over to us with a smile. 'Did your friend ever turn up? Mr Tregarth?'

'He did. Quite late, and with an extraordinary tale to tell. Do you have a minute?'

'I've nearly finished with these, and then I can sit down with my own cuppa.' She gestured toward a table in a corner. 'If you'd like to wait for me?'

She joined us in only a few minutes, bearing a tray with cups, teapot, and a plate of fruitcake. 'The cook always makes extra,' she explained, 'as it just gets better as it ages.'

I am immune to fruitcake, a fact my English friends find incomprehensible, so I refused it with thanks, blaming lunch. I was glad of the tea, though.

'Now. You've questions for me, I don't doubt.'

'Only one, actually, but let Alan tell you the story of that night first.'

He finished by relating our inspection of the outside of George Elliot's house and the discovery of the button. 'And then,' I picked up the story, 'I came across this jacket on a sale rack in the market, and bought it for a friend of mine, and believe it or not, it has buttons that look identical to the one we found. That makes us think that the man who arranged that dreadful raid on the house might have been wearing a jacket like this. And we think, or anyway I think, that he's very probably the man who killed Dr Armstrong. It's a long and complicated chain of reasoning, and I have to admit that Alan doesn't entirely buy it, but the point is we need to know if someone wearing a jacket like this has visited the Milton Home recently.'

Her face fell. 'Oh, dear. I don't think so. I'd remember. It's quite a nice one, isn't it? Good colour, well cut. Many of the men who work or visit here are dressed really casually, so it's unusual to see someone in an attractive sport coat. Oh, I'm really sorry, but I don't think I can help you.'

She was near tears. I hastened to reassure her. 'Oh, don't worry, dear. There are lots of other people to talk to. If he was here, wearing this, we'll find someone who saw him. Ask around, will you? Wait, I just got an idea.'

I gave Alan the jacket and told him to put it on, then took

a picture. 'Give me your phone number.' She recited it to me; I sent her the picture and waited to make sure she had it. 'There. Now you can show the others. And it looks like the pace is picking up a bit in here, so I expect you have to get back to work. Hang in there, dear!'

I have never believed in coincidence. Things happen for a reason. Thus I refuse to call it coincidence that one of the aides, a young, dark-skinned man I'd noticed before, was stepping from the elevator just as we left the kitchen. He looked around quickly and came over to us.

'I didn't like to say anything before,' he said quietly. 'Velma can be . . . well, you have seen what she's like.'

'Skin you alive if she's annoyed, right?'

He grinned. 'Something like that. But I had to tell you. I have seen a man wearing that jacket, or I mean one just like it, right here.'

I gasped. 'Here? Here in the home?'

'Exactly here.' He pointed to the floor. 'He was standing by the kitchen door. This is not a part of the building where visitors come, so I was a bit sharp when I asked if I could help. I thought he had no business here. He was very apologetic, said he was looking for – a room number, I forget what – and he had got lost and thought he needed to go through the door. The kitchen door. I lied and said I was not sure where to find the room he wanted and told him to go back to the reception desk, where they could help him.'

'But that's exciting!' I began, but he held up a hand.

'That is not all, Mrs Martin. He pretended he was trying to go into the kitchen, but I am sure he had just come *out* of the kitchen. The door was just closing behind him.'

I was ready to jump up and down with glee, but Alan retained his composure. 'Can you give us a description of this man?'

Here he hesitated. 'Young, white. Well-dressed.' He spread his hands. 'He looked like anyone.'

I would have pursued it, but Alan shushed me. 'Can you tell me when this happened? Day and time, if you remember.'

Now he was on steady ground again. 'Yes! I remember very clearly, because of what happened later. It was in the morning, late morning, of the day Mrs Carly was attacked.'

Alan held out a hand. 'We thank you very much . . .'

He let the sentence trail off, and the man responded with a brilliant smile. 'My name is Jabulani, but please call me Jabu.'

'*Thank* you, Jabu!' I wanted to say much more, but Alan led me away. He managed to restrain my enthusiasm while we asked everyone we came across, but no one we talked to had seen the jacket being worn. That dampened my spirits a little, but only a little. I let loose when we got back to the car. 'But Alan, this is huge! We have to tell the director!'

'Dorothy, love, calm down. What do we have? One man saw someone wearing a jacket like this. No one else did. We have no proof that there is any connection whatever to any of the other parts of this tangle. And we have no identification of the person.'

'I wanted to press Jabu about that, but you stopped me.'

'Think, love. He is from Africa. He hasn't been in this country very long, I think. He still speaks the clipped, precise African English. He is surrounded by unfamiliar faces, and he's had no training in identifying people, as I have, for example. It's asking a lot to expect him to come up with a clear description of someone he saw for a minute or two, at most.'

'Oh.' I thought about that. 'But all the same, we need to tell Williams.'

Alan started the car. 'Not yet. Not until we have some proof. We need a strong case to set before him, and as yet we have no case at all.'

I fumed all the way back to the city. The fact that Alan was right, and I knew it, didn't help at all. I wanted action!

We decided to stop at David's before going to a car park near the castle. Alan had me call to get the address and find out if anyone was home. Tim was; David was not. Satnav got us there easily, though finding a place to park was another question. Alan finally dropped me at the door and went a little farther afield. I was beginning to see another reason why walking was very popular in this city.

Tim was still riding his riches-induced high. He offered me a choice of coffee, tea, or a nice glass of wine. I was about to decline with thanks, when I saw how pleased he was to be able to play host, and accepted coffee that I didn't want. 'Only, where's the loo? I had a lot of tea just now.'

'I just called Eileen,' Tim said when I came back to the front room. 'She wants to hear the latest; she's coming over straightaway.'

'I'll wait to tell you anything, then. Anyway, Alan will probably be a while. The parking situation in this town is incredible!'

Tim grinned. 'Oh, but you should see it in term time! Just one more reason to ride a bike. Poverty has its points, you know.' He poured my coffee and offered milk and sugar.

'You're a fraud, Timothy Hayes! Now you have this great gift from your sister, you're not poor anymore. Just hard up. There's a difference. And any man who makes coffee this wonderful can get a job as barista any time.'

'Which would be lovely, except I want a job as a priest.' He raised his coffee cup in a salute.

'Doesn't pay as well.'

'Oh, stipends are not bad nowadays. And oh, the perks! Free bread and wine, free housing . . .'

'In a draughty old vicarage with seventeen rooms and a leaky roof, all to be maintained on a salary that wouldn't keep the vicarage cat alive, if it weren't for the bounty of the church mice. Oh, yes, a cushy job indeed! Have you given any thought to where you might like to . . . er, is "practice" the word?'

'That's for doctors. Priests serve. At least, I hope to.' He was serious now. 'Your ideas about parsons' living conditions are a bit out of date, you know. There are a lot of perfectly decent livings available. The thing is, though – well, I don't know if I'll be of any use to anybody, but I'd like to work in a poor parish somewhere, a place where I might really be able to help.'

'And what does Eileen think about that? Is she willing to scrimp and starve in a good cause?'

'She would be,' said the lady in question, who had just walked in the door, 'except I'll probably be earning enough to keep us in modest comfort, if not luxury. Tim, I haven't had a chance to tell you. The Hayes-Walsh star is definitely in the ascendant. I got that internship at Kew!'

'Oh, how lovely for you!' I cheered. 'Kew is one of my

favourite places.' The Royal Botanic Gardens, just a few miles from central London, are glorious, even though badly damaged by a terrible storm some years ago. Rare two-hundred-year-old trees were uprooted, among other disasters, but the English, who think in centuries rather than years or decades, calmly replanted them, reasoning that in another two hundred years they'd be as good as before. 'When do you start, Eileen? What will you be doing? All the details, please!'

We were still hearing all about it when Alan came in, rather hot and tired. 'Oh, you poor dear. Did you have to park miles away?'

'Bottom of a hill. A *long* hill.' He dropped into an armchair.

'Ah, then I expect you'd rather have a beer,' said Tim. 'There's a nice lager just waiting for you.'

Lager is the only beer that is routinely served chilled in England, and I find it far more refreshing than ale on a hot day. Tim saw the look on my face, winked, and silently traded my coffee cup for a lovely cold glass.

'All right now,' said Tim when he had met everyone's needs. 'Eileen and I are dying by inches. Tell us the news.'

I opened my mouth, but Alan forestalled me. 'Let me give them the basics first, love. Then you can embroider.'

'Ha!' I devoted myself to my beer.

'We've learned that a man wearing a jacket like this one was seen at the Milton Home very close to the time that the woman was attacked.'

'Wait,' said Eileen. 'This is the woman who wasn't badly hurt? But the management blamed her attack on poor Amanda?'

'Yes.' He waited, but she gestured for him to go on. 'Further, it appears probable that he entered the building through the kitchen, which would suggest that he didn't want to pass the receptionist and sign in. He was seen next to the kitchen door.'

'And where else? Near the woman's room?'

'Nowhere else. That in turn might suggest that he took great care not to be seen.'

'No one else in the kitchen saw him?'

'Not that we know of. It was shortly before lunchtime, when the staff would have been very busy. It's quite possible that someone could enter then, pretending to be making a delivery, and could pass unnoticed through the busy workspace.'

'In a sport jacket?' Tim sounded sceptical.

Alan shrugged. 'I don't know what their suppliers usually wear.'

I'd had enough. 'All right, I've let you have the cautious policeman's version. He won't let me tell that director the story, because he says there's no proof of anything. I admit he's right, technically, but putting together all the bits and pieces, I think we have plenty to create a reasonable doubt about Amanda's involvement, and I think we ought to tell him the whole thing.'

'What whole thing? What have I missed?' David walked in looking exhausted, and certainly not ready to find a party going on in his house.

'Oh, David, I'm sorry. I've not even started supper. I wasn't expecting you until a bit later.'

'I gave up.' He plopped down in the chair Alan relinquished. 'There is simply no facility within a reasonable radius where they would give Amanda the loving care she deserves. I'm going to have to move her to one of the horrid places to live out her last years in squalor.' He was near tears. Tim put a glass in his hand. It had something amber in it. David downed it in one gulp.

Alan was silent, but his body language was eloquent. He took several deep breaths, looked at the floor, the ceiling, his clasped hands. He pursed his lips, took one more deep breath, and spoke. His voice was quiet, but authoritative. 'I've made a decision which may surprise you all. David, I'm going to tell you a story, a scenario. As a policeman, I recognize, as you will, that the story is thin. But between the two of us, we ought to be able to present it to Mr Williams in a convincing manner. At the very least, I think we can buy Amanda a bit of time.' He explained in careful detail, from the very beginning as we saw it, Nathan's death.

'It's certainly complex,' he finished, 'but I have come to believe that it hangs together. I propose to go with you to set the case before Mr Williams and ask him to give your great-aunt a stay of execution while the police continue to trace the man who ruined George Elliot's house and who, we believe, was responsible for all the other crimes in the web.'

'And to help in that trace,' I said to Tim and Eileen, having recovered from my astonishment, 'I'm sending both of you the picture of the jacket. The more people we have looking for the man who wore its duplicate, the better chance we have of finding him.'

'Send it to us as well, love, and we can pass it along to Mr Williams. The kitchen staff already have it, but as Dorothy says, the more the better.' Alan stood. 'Now. I hired a car today, but yours may be nearer. Shall we?'

TWENTY-FOUR

I kissed Alan as he left. I didn't say a word, but he understood.

'Well, that was an about-face!' said Eileen. 'I wonder why he changed his mind so suddenly.'

'Amanda's plight,' I answered. 'Alan tries hard to conceal it, but underneath that austere policeman's façade is a heart of marshmallow. He couldn't bear the thought of that sweet old lady losing her home. As long as he thought David might find another good place for her, he was sticking to his professional caution. Now that hope for that is gone, he had to act.'

'Well, here's to Alan!' Tim raised his empty glass, and then offered us refills.

'Now then,' he asked when we refused anything more to drink, 'what did this chap look like? The one who wore the jacket clone?'

'We don't know. That's the worst part. The man in the chorus – we never did get his name – couldn't say any more than that he was young and had what he described as a southern accent. And that he was a student. Our informant was certain of that, though his reasons were vague.'

'A student.' Eileen sighed. 'That narrows it down to perhaps 18,000 people.'

'Less,' said Tim. 'A lot of the students are women.'

That struck us as funny, for some reason. We were getting punchy, I thought.

'All right, a male student who lives somewhere south of, say, York. What did the man at the home say?'

'Unfortunately he couldn't tell us much, either. He was sure about the details of exactly when and where he saw the man, but he couldn't describe him. Alan thinks it's because he's new to this country and surrounded by unfamiliar faces.'

Eileen nodded. 'That makes sense. I'm not good at describing people I don't know well. All we have is the student category, then. If the chap was right.'

'But there's the almost certain fact that he is someone whom Nathan was blackmailing. Does that cut it down at all?'

'No idea,' they replied in chorus. 'We didn't know him, remember,' said Eileen. 'I'll get busy asking my friend at Jude's. Someone will know something. It will be easier when everyone comes back on Sunday. And now that we have more time—'

'We hope!'

'Yes, but I'm sure David and Alan will prevail. There's not all that hurry now.'

'No.' But I said it sadly. Yes, unless something went badly wrong, Amanda was safe for a bit longer, maybe forever if Mr Williams could be made to see reason. But Alan and I didn't have extra time. We were going to have to leave by Sunday, when our room in the castle would revert back to its rightful occupant. It was foolish of me, but I wanted to see this through.

Ego, Dorothy! I scolded myself. It doesn't matter who catches the murderer, only that he be caught.

Tim, as Alan had noted, was very observant. 'You want to do something more, don't you?'

'I do. But I can't think what. It's all in the hands of the police now, or will be as soon as David presents them with the new evidence. Scanty as it is.'

'What about Nathan's brother?' asked Eileen. 'You think his mother knows where he is.'

'I'd bet on it. But she's a difficult woman. I don't think I can get her to tell me anything more.'

'Hmm.' Tim's face fell into an expression so like Alan's when he's thinking hard, that I almost laughed. 'People seem to like to talk to me. I wonder if she's still in Auckland, or has she gone back home?'

'I've no idea. I have her phone number. You might try her, though I don't know whether she'll answer. I'm sure she won't if I try. She has my number and she doesn't like me.' I pulled up the number on my phone and read it to Tim.

Once the phone on the other end was ringing, Tim put his phone on speaker, gesturing us to silence.

'Yes?' That same wary tone.

'Mrs Elliot, you don't know me, but my name's Timothy Hayes, I'm a student at Durham, and I knew your son Nathan.'

'Yes?' Slightly warmer.

'We weren't in the same college, but we met now and then, and the fact is – this is embarrassing – I borrowed some money from him.'

Eileen and I looked at him in astonishment. He shook his head at us and continued.

'And I never had a chance to repay him before he had that dreadful accident. So I was wondering. I just now came into a little money. That means I can pay back the loan, and I wondered if I should give it to you or his brother. He mentioned his brother to me, and I thought perhaps . . .?'

He artistically left it hanging.

'Hmph. Honest young man, aren't you?'

'Well, you see, I'm a theology student, and . . .'

Again, he let the sentence taper off.

'I see. What did you say your name is?'

He repeated it.

'I never heard Nathan mention you. But then, he talked to me very little. Yes, he has a brother. He lives in Bishop Auckland, but he's not there now. He's taking a little break at the seaside. I can give you his address, if you'd like to send him a cheque. I'm sure he'd be delighted to have the money.'

Eileen and I raised our fists in a silent cheer.

She gave him the name of a hotel in Hartlepool and hung up.

'Wow! You *are* a persuasive person! But what a lot of shocking lies!' I shook my head in pretended dismay.

'We're told to be wise as serpents,' he said with a grin. 'And some of it was true. Of course I never met Nathan, let alone borrowed money from him, but that's minor. The important thing is that we know where George is.'

'If his mother is telling the truth,' said Eileen. 'I must say Hartlepool isn't my idea of a seaside resort.'

'But that's an excellent reason for him to choose to go there,' I pointed out. 'It isn't at all likely. Where is it, by the way?'

'Not far from here at all. About – what would you say, Eileen? Twenty miles?'

'About that. And nothing in particular to do when you get there.'

'All right. Tim, I think you'd better call David right away and have him call the police. They can follow up, and once they talk to George, we'll know a lot more.'

Of course, it wasn't that easy. When David and Alan returned (with Indian takeaway), they caught us up to date, between bites.

'Good news/bad news,' Alan summed up. 'We did manage to persuade Williams to put off any action with Amanda.'

'Does she know that?' I asked with a frown.

'There's no need to tell her,' said David. 'No one told her that she was going to be moved, so now there's no point in telling her that she *won't* be moved. It would only upset her, and she wouldn't remember anyway. The staff will be told, and I know they'll be happy about it.'

'Okay, that's the good news. Are we strong enough to hear the bad news?' I tore off a piece of garlic naan and ate it.

'The bad news is only provisionally bad.' My husband paused for a mouthful of curried lamb. 'The Durham police are not optimistic about finding George Elliot. It seemed the Hartlepool force is even more understaffed than most. The city has suffered severe budget cuts in recent years because of loss of major industries. It's beginning to come back, but at present the police can deal only with critical matters. Finding a man who is charged with nothing, just to oblige another authority, is not a high priority. That's not to say they won't try, but they can only do so much. It may sit on a back burner for a few days.'

'Oh, but if they don't act right now, he might move on, and then it's all to do over again!' I put down my plate of chicken tikka masala, not hungry anymore. 'It's really frustrating!'

David and Alan looked at each other, sighed, and stood up. 'Ought we to call first?' asked David.

'I think not. We don't want to scare him off. Either he'll be there, or he won't, and it's not far away. Are you coming, light of my life?'

'Try and stop me.' I turned to Tim and Eileen. 'Kids, I think you'd better not come this time. We don't want to descend on George with a delegation. He's in hiding, or so it seems, and until we know more about the situation we need to walk on eggs. We'll keep you informed!'

'And meanwhile,' said Eileen, 'I'm going to call Sarah, at Jude's, and see what she can find out. Good luck!'

'Do we have a plan of action?' I asked when Alan had negotiated Durham dinnertime traffic and made it to the A181 heading southeast. 'He went into hiding for a reason.'

'Yes, and though we're not sure of the reason, we can assume he was fleeing whoever came to his house that night. Ergo, that man posed a threat of some kind.'

'We've assumed that the caller had something to do with Nathan's death.'

Alan sighed. 'And it's an almost totally unjustified assumption. Even if he did, how would George have known that? Or are you assuming that the chap knocked on his door and said, "Hello, I killed your brother"?'

Of course, I ignored that. 'So George is afraid of someone. A male. Does that mean that he's less likely to run away if I go knocking at his door, rather than one of you? I don't really look very threatening.'

'That, my dear, is why I asked you to come along.'

'That, and you knew I'd come anyway.'

David snickered in the back seat.

The day was waning when we came into Hartlepool. Even in northern latitudes, a May evening ends eventually. In the dusk I had to admit that the city wasn't terribly attractive. Gigantic cranes silhouetted against the deep purple sky at the waterfront looked ominous, like monsters ready to devour all in their path. 'Godzilla,' I said, and pointed. I wasn't feeling welcome in this place.

Neither man laughed. They seemed intimidated, too.

We found the hotel easily enough, a Victorian pile in the centre of town. Parking wasn't difficult. Alan pulled into a space, shut off the engine, engaged the brake, and looked at us. At me.

I sighed. 'Right. My turn, is it? Anybody have an idea what I should say? If he's here, that is.'

'You might,' said Alan mildly, 'try the truth.'

'Which is?'

'You know about his brother's death, you believe Nathan to have been pushed into the river, you heard that he had disappeared, and you were worried about him.'

'And when he wants to know how I found him?'

'I'm sure you can improvise something. But the truth there might not hurt either. His mother gave the information to a friend of yours.'

'And then play it by ear. Very well. Are you coming in, or are you going to lurk out here?'

'We'll lurk in the lobby, or the bar, whichever seems less conspicuous. I don't like the idea of you being in there entirely unaccompanied.'

I took a deep breath. 'Very well. Nothing ventured, nothing gained. Pray for me.'

I went in alone, David and Alan following after an interval, trying to pretend they weren't with me. I went to the front desk. Mr Elliot? Yes, madam, he was still registered. Room 324. Certainly, madam. The lifts are just there.

In an American hotel, I thought, or even in London, they wouldn't have given me the room number. Perhaps they were less security-minded here, or else I simply looked too old and dotty to pose a threat. At any rate, they paid no attention when I turned in the direction of the elevators. I looked over at the men and finger-signed three-two-four. Alan nodded.

I knocked at the door, half-hoping he wouldn't be in. There was no answer for a moment, and my hopes went up, but then a man's voice growled, 'Yes? What is it?'

'Mr Elliot, my name is Dorothy Martin. May I come in?'

Silence. Maybe I should have lied and said I was the maid. But then he would have expected me to open the door with my own key. I waited.

Eventually heavy steps sounded and the door opened a crack. 'What is it? I'm busy.'

'I can see that you are.' I looked beyond him to the rumpled bed, the can of beer, the bag of crisps, the game show on the television screen. 'I won't be a moment. May I come in?'

'I was getting ready to go out to dinner.'

Really, the man should polish up his lies. Unless he didn't care whether I believed him or not. 'I won't detain you. I want to say, first of all, that I'm very happy to find you in good health. A number of people have been very worried about you since your disappearance, you know.'

I had raised my voice a trifle, and he pulled me hurriedly inside. 'Here! You needn't tell the world! Who are you, and what do you want?'

Reasonable questions, actually, but they could have been phrased more courteously. However . . . 'As I said, my name is Dorothy Martin. I live in Sherebury, in Belleshire. My husband and I came to Durham to visit with an old friend, Mr David Tregarth.'

Recognition dawned. 'The copper.'

'Retired policeman, yes. He came to your house on Sunday evening, at your invitation, only to find you gone and your house in a shambles. Then he was set upon by a gang of rowdy men dressed as policemen, who did further damage to your house. When the real police arrived on the scene, can you wonder that they, and we, became very interested in your whereabouts? We weren't at all sure you were still among the living! Why did you tell no one where you had gone?'

'But you found out. How did you manage that? And why do you care? What possible business is it of yours?'

This man was his mother's son, all right. Ignoring his first question, I held onto my temper, and sat down, uninvited. 'It is my concern because of your brother's death. We believe he was killed, and that his murderer has also killed one other person, a defenceless old man.' That was stretching a point, but never mind. 'We further believe that the killer was the man who called on you on Sunday night and did such damage to your home.'

'"We." Who is "we"? Are you connected with the police?'

'Unofficially, yes. And we, the police and several others, have been unable to find anyone who can identify the killer. You saw him and talked with him. Who is he?'

TWENTY-FIVE

Geroge dropped onto the bed smack on the bag of
crisps, crushing them to bits. I swallowed a laugh.

'I – I don't know his name. He was a student, a
friend of Nathan's. I'd never met him before.'

I'd had enough. 'Mr Elliot, I taught school for many years
in America. I've had a great deal of experience separating
truth from lies. It is vital that we find this man, before he
decides that someone else is inconvenient to him. His name,
please.'

'Why should I tell you? The man is dangerous. If he knows
I told you, he might—'

'He might, indeed. Which is why he needs to be appre-
hended. His name, Mr Elliot.'

'You have no right!'

'That, at least, is a true statement. You may certainly refuse
to tell me. In that case I will remain here, further delaying
your dinner, while Mr Tregarth and my husband, who are
waiting downstairs, summon the police to come and talk to
you. And they, sir, do have the right to ask you questions and
require answers. They also have the duty to protect you once
you've said your piece. It's your choice. Tell me, or tell them.'

Either my school-teacher persona intimidated him enough
to overcome his cowardice, or he was too hungry to wait
further for his meal. 'Bloody hell! His name is Colin something. I don't remember his surname. He's a thoroughly nasty
little toe rag, and I wish you joy of him. Now, get out!'

I got. With alacrity.

'I wish,' I said with feeling, 'that we could charge George
with something! Talk about nasty!'

'But you got a name out of him. Here's to you, Dorothy!'

He raised his glass. We were sitting in the lounge of the
hotel, having (from a nice dark corner) watched George stomp

out. David had a stiff Scotch; I was enjoying some excellent bourbon. Alan, who was driving, was sticking to soda.

'A name,' David repeated. 'Only a Christian name, but it's a start.'

'It's more than that,' I said, purring.

Alan looked at me suspiciously. 'You're concealing something, woman!'

'No, just gloating. For once I've remembered something you forgot. We had two leads to follow up a little while back. George Elliot and . . .' I paused invitingly.

Alan smacked the table. 'And Colin Grimsby. And you tried to phone him Sunday night and got no answer. Do you think he was on his way to George's house?'

'I think,' interposed David, 'that the police need to know about this immediately. George could disappear again, and we badly need his testimony. There are too many questions. Why did Nathan turn up at his door? Did George ask him there? If so, why? And what exactly happened?'

I sighed. 'I wanted to ask all those questions, but George threw me out. Almost literally.' Alan scowled. 'No, my dear, he never laid a hand on me, but he was working up a temper. When he roared at me to get out, I stood not upon the order of my going.'

'Someone should teach him manners,' muttered Alan.

'I can't imagine who might do that. His mother would certainly not be qualified.'

David, meanwhile, had taken out his phone and retired to a quiet corner. We heard murmurs, but could distinguish no words. When he came back to us, though, his expression was not joyful.

'The bureaucracy strikes again,' he moaned, sitting down heavily. 'Durham can't act in Hartlepool without permission from the local authority. Which, as I said before—'

'Is too busy and understaffed to pay much attention,' Alan finished.

Silence. 'Are the Durham people going to look for Colin Grimsby, anyway?' I asked, finally.

'They are. But without George Elliot's evidence they can't charge him with anything. He can simply deny it all.'

'And my statement is worth nothing,' I said bitterly. 'Hearsay,' I added before they could get the word out. 'There are times when I long for the good old days of frontier justice.'

'You wouldn't like it really, you know,' said Alan. 'And even in your country, those days are long gone. The Wild West is paved over with freeways and parking lots, and the OK Corral is a Disneyfied tourist trap.'

'All right. I take your point. And in fact I'm not in favour of settling matters with a gun. But it would be nice if the lawfully appointed police could deal with malefactors without such a lot of pettifogging rules!'

'But we can't,' said David. 'Even before I retired, I longed sometimes to bend the rules.'

'Yes.' Alan nodded. 'One did yearn to expedite matters. I never did, but the temptation was often strong. The worst times were when I and my whole force knew quite well who the guilty party was, and could do nothing about it because we hadn't a case strong enough to stand up in court.'

We looked at each other and stood in unison. 'David,' said Alan, 'perhaps you'd be willing to wait here, in case the chap returns, while Dorothy and I sweep the town.'

If you want a thing done right, do it yourself. I didn't say it aloud. I didn't have to. We were all of one mind.

It was quite dark by now, and I realized I was hungry. That interrupted meal of takeout we'd had back in Durham seemed a very long time ago. Adrenaline had kept me going until now, but searching a dark and pretty well deserted city at night provides limited excitement. Alan seemed of the same mind. 'The man *said* he was going out for a meal. Shall we take him at his word and explore some restaurants?'

'Given his tastes, I'd think pubs would be more likely.'

'You're probably right. Let's pop into the first one we find, the first respectable one, that is, and see if we can get some grub.'

'Thus killing two birds with one stone.'

'Or at least,' said Alan with a grin, 'doing a bit of hunting. In the American sense.'

'And hoping it's not for wild geese.'

'Enough, woman. Let's find that pub.'

That part wasn't hard. We didn't even have to get the car; the pub was a few steps from the hotel. It was clean and attractive, and had only a few customers. Plainly this part of town went home as soon as office hours were over. We chatted a bit with the barmaid, bought two ham rolls, and sipped a little of the half-pints we felt obliged to order. We didn't linger. George wasn't there, and apparently hadn't been there.

'You know,' I commented as we went to the car, looking over a pub or two on the way, 'if we have to drink something everywhere we go, we're both going to be in trouble. You won't be safe to drive, and I won't dare get ten feet away from the loo.'

'Cheer up. Maybe we'll find him in the next one.'

But we didn't. Skipping a few unsavoury dives, there weren't all that many pubs near the hotel. The two cafés we saw were closed. Daytime only spots, evidently.

Then there were the actual restaurants. Only two of those were open, except for the takeaway places. If George had opted for Thai, Indian, Chinese, or pizza, we were out of luck. It had been, by that time, over an hour since George left the hotel. He'd have had plenty of time to buy a meal, take it somewhere, eat, and vanish again. And neither the Italian nor the French restaurant had seen anyone who matched our careful description.

'One last possibility,' said Alan, weary and still hungry, despite the ham roll. 'There's bound to be food of one sort or another at the railway station.'

'Do you know where it is?'

'That question, my dear, has become in this day and age more or less irrelevant.' He held up his phone, gave it a command, and started following its directions.

The last train of the evening had just left the station, and the small refreshment bar was closing. One look at the offerings told us it wasn't George's sort of place.

We were heading back to the car when Alan's phone rang. It was David; Alan turned on the speaker.

'You haven't found him?'

'No. I would have called you. He hasn't come back?'

'That's why I called. He isn't coming back. He called to

check out a few minutes ago. When a maid came up to clean the room, I left the alcove where I was lurking. I told her I needed to talk to him and asked her when she expected him back, and she told me.'

I stifled the exclamation that came to mind. 'Then your vigil, and our search – all a waste of time.'

'We'll be there in five minutes to pick you up,' said Alan, and hung up.

I made an exasperated noise. 'Of all the . . . is that man so stupid that he can't see his only safety lies in telling the police everything?'

'That's possible.' We got in the car. Alan turned it toward the hotel. 'You might be surprised how many people are exactly that stupid. The other possibility is that he has his own reasons not to go to the police.'

'You mean he's a villain, too? How could that fit into the pattern?'

'I have no idea. I merely mention it as a possibility. His efforts to vanish seem a bit extreme for the excuses he's given.'

I thought about that. 'Actually,' I said slowly, 'he's said very little by way of excuse, except to say that he thought the man was dangerous and might retaliate in some unspecified way if he, George, talked to the police.'

'Hmm. Not "He said he would kill me" or anything of that sort?'

'No. In fact, I believe I was the one who mentioned that his vandal might be his brother's murderer. I suppose I shouldn't have said that, but it seemed at the time to be the only way to pry out a name.'

'It might have been better not to say that, but you did what you thought you had to do. There's never any point to second-guessing, love. Ah, there's David, waiting for us.'

He was not happy. 'Fool that I am, I should have told them at the registration desk to delay him if he tried to leave.'

'But you haven't the authority to do that anymore,' Alan reminded him. 'The first matter of importance is: have you had anything to eat?'

He held up a package that had contained a thin cheese-and-chutney sandwich. Half of it was left. 'If you don't mind?'

'Finish it. I wish we could all go somewhere for a proper meal, but everything seems to be closed.'

'Never mind. My house is not much more than a half-hour away, and I've plenty of food there. Alan, what's the plan now?'

'First, we strongly suggest to Durham that they put out an all-points call for George Elliot. They won't be stepping on Hartlepool toes now that the chap has done us a favour by leaving there.'

'Do we know that?' I interrupted.

'It's a safe assumption, and for the purposes of the argument we'll state it as fact. David, if you'll make that call, you might also check on any progress they've made in finding the unpleasant Mr Grimsby.'

The highway traffic was light and moving smoothly, so we were nearly halfway home when David ended his call. 'They're on the lookout for George. He drives a white Tesla, by the way.'

Alan whistled. 'Not a poor man, then.'

'No.'

'But he left that behind in Bishop Auckland.'

'He doubled back and got it, apparently. Or sent someone for it.'

'His mother, maybe.'

'Perhaps. One can see why he'd be reluctant to leave it behind. As you say, Alan, it's an expensive vehicle. And it's only a few months old. Dorothy, I'll read you the registration number if you want to write it down. I doubt we'll see it, but one never knows.'

'If I were George, Durham would be the last place I'd want to go. Or no, the second-to-last. Home is certainly the first place he'll want to avoid.' I wrote down the number he read off.

'And Mummy's house in Birmingham, of course. That leaves a good bit of territory where he *can* hide out.'

'But how far can he go in an electric car?' I asked. 'Don't they need recharging every couple of hours?'

'Not as often as you'd think, not the new ones,' replied David. 'Turn right at this next intersection, Alan. It'll avoid traffic and get us there sooner. I've been reading up on this new Tesla, Dorothy. On a full charge it has a range of over three hundred miles.'

'Oh, that's not very far.'

Alan laughed. 'Every now and then you forget you're not in America with its vast distances, my love. The United Kingdom stretches only a little over six hundred miles, as the crow flies, from Land's End to John O'Groats. Farther over the roads, of course. We're a bit north and east of the middle of the country here, so his possibilities are almost endless. He probably couldn't get quite to Penzance, but three hundred miles would take him to Scotland, to Wales, to London, to most port cities, to any airport.'

'Oh.' I sat back, deflated. 'Well, maybe the Tesla doesn't have a full charge. Maybe it'll run out of juice and he'll have to sit someplace waiting for the AA. A delightful thought!'

We sped on through the night, looking closely at every car we saw, but none was a white Tesla.

TWENTY-SIX

E ileen had gone home by the time we got back to David's house, but Tim had waited up for us. 'I'll heat the curries and all if you want, or make you an omelette, or whatever you like.'

'Tim, if I weren't already married, I'd try to wrest you away from Eileen. I don't know about the others, but an omelette sounds perfect for me.'

David fetched a bottle of a nice white wine from the fridge, and we sat enjoying our late supper in a weary haze. When Tim had offered ice cream, and we had refused, he sat down with us. 'I don't want to keep you. You all look tired and I'm sure you're longing for your beds. But was the trip worth the effort?'

We told him all we'd learned. 'So we're still searching, but at least now we know who we're searching for.' I shot a glance at Alan, but he forbore, this time, to criticize my grammar. 'We're still not quite sure why George Elliot is behaving so strangely. Alan thinks maybe it's more than just fear of Colin, that maybe he, George, has something he doesn't want the police to know about. And Colin – well, we can't prove Colin is a murderer. Yet.'

'At least Amanda is safe. That's the main thing.' Alan yawned hugely, and apologized.

'Go home,' said David. 'Shall I drive you, so you won't have to worry about finding a spot to park?'

'Do you reckon your car will be available tomorrow?'

'It's at your disposal, now I'm not chasing wild geese, or wild caregivers.'

'Then, yes, we'll take you up on the offer.' Alan yawned again. 'Sorry. And tomorrow I'll call Enterprise and turn the thing in.'

We said goodnight to Tim. David brought his car around and we were asleep almost before we reached our room in the castle.

* * *

Find George. Talk to Colin. Those were the two thoughts that popped into my head the moment I woke on Thursday morning.

I was, for once, wide awake, even though the day was not the sort that prompts one to spring out of bed carolling happily. The sky was heavily overcast, and it was cold enough in our room that the central heating had kicked in.

'I used to think Indiana had widely variable weather,' I remarked to Alan when I got out of the shower.

'"If you don't like the weather, wait a minute",' Alan quoted. 'Wasn't it an American who said that?'

'Sounds like Mark Twain. But it could certainly have been an Englishman. Anyway, I'm grateful this morning for the central heating, though it's all wrong in a twelfth-century castle.'

At breakfast in the Great Hall (where they'd turned on the chandeliers against the lowering darkness), we made plans.

'I'm going to walk over to St Jude's,' I said, 'and see what I can find out about Colin Grimsby.'

'They won't tell you much,' said Alan, finishing a bite of sausage. 'Privacy rules, you know.'

'I wasn't planning to talk to anyone official. I'll bet the students will tell me plenty. I'll have to call Eileen first, to get the names of the students I talked to before. I only remember their first names. Meanwhile, what are you going to do?'

'As soon as David and I fetch my car and I've returned it, he and I will plot out our next step. There's not a lot we can do, actually. Drat it! It's frustrating to have no official status!'

'Yes, dear. I know.'

He grinned. 'You do, don't you? But you have that disarming air of innocence in your favour. I can never hope to look anything but official.'

'That "air" didn't disarm Mrs Elliot, or not for long. It didn't work for George at all; I had to pull out the dragon-schoolteacher to get anywhere with him.'

Alan finished his coffee. 'Let's hope one persona or the other works its magic on the students at St Jude's. Don't go too early, dear. Remember they're still on holiday and probably went out partying last night, while they still can.'

David called just then to say he was ready to fetch Alan any time he wanted. He offered to drive me to St Jude's, but I declined. 'It's kind of you, but it's too early for students, and there'd be a bit of a way to walk, anyway. Unless it absolutely starts to pour, I'll be fine.'

I dilly-dallied over a second cup of coffee after Alan had left, wondering how to approach the students at St Jude's – or just 'Jude's', as I'd noticed it was called locally. Seemed a bit disrespectful to me. After all, a saint deserved . . . I pulled myself together and went up to my room to make a list of questions.

Where does Colin live? What is his course of study? Where is he from? Who are his friends?

I didn't plan to pose the questions baldly, but if I could get a student talking, or better yet a group of students, I could surely nudge the conversation in those directions.

At that point in my cogitations Tim called.

'Hi, Dorothy. David tells me you're planning to talk to some of the students at Jude's. If you think I might be useful, I'll come along. I know some of them slightly.'

'And people find it easy to talk to you! That would be an enormous help, Tim. What time, would you say?'

We settled on early afternoon, leaving me with several hours to try to organize our departure on Saturday. It's amazing how much stuff one can accumulate on even a brief holiday. Not that this had exactly been a holiday. Amongst the souvenir leaflets and the knick-knacks picked up for reasons I could no longer remember were schedules of services at the cathedral, phone numbers on bits of paper (with no names attached – a truly stupid habit of mine) and an address in Bishop Auckland that I presumed was George's. Into the bin!

Alan called to say he was off with David to the police station to check on their progress. And, I guessed, prod them fairly stiffly! Would I be all right left to my own devices for a bit? 'Tim and I are going to St Jude's later. Meanwhile, I'm trying to tidy up this place. I'll see you when I see you.'

I hung up wondering what I ever did without a mobile phone and went back to my depressing job.

Alan came back bearing sandwiches but no real news, and

shortly after that I dragged myself off to St Jude's, with little enthusiasm for my chore. I could sympathize more than ever with Alan's biggest frustration in his days as a policeman. We knew, or at least I was sure we knew, who was responsible for all the recent mayhem, but I could see no way to prove it even when we found the guy.

There was an unusual amount of vehicular traffic in Bailey Street, where St Jude's is located, and when I neared the college I saw two police cars standing outside, blue lights flashing. What on earth?

A sturdy uniformed police officer stood at the foot of the steps up to the front door. 'Sorry, ma'am. No one is allowed inside.'

'But – but I'm meeting someone here. What's happened?'

'There's been a spot of trouble. Move along, please.'

My phone rang. Shaken, I moved away from the policeman and answered.

It was Tim. 'Dorothy! Where are you?'

'Just outside St Jude's. There are police all over the place and they won't let me in. Where are *you*?'

'Inside. I couldn't call earlier; it's a huge mess.'

'But what's happened?'

'There's been . . . oh, it's too complicated. I'll try to get them to let you in or let me out, one or the other. Sit tight.'

I put the phone away and confronted the stalwart guard. 'Young man, the person I was to meet is inside those doors. My name is Dorothy Martin, I am the wife of a retired chief constable, and I do know the rules. I don't intend to cause any trouble, but until you let me in or he is allowed out, I'm going to sit right here. I'm an old woman and I'm tired.' I plumped myself down on a step, well to the side, and gazed down the street, trying to look rooted to the spot.

'But ma'am, you can't . . . I'm supposed to . . .'

I took my phone out of my purse. 'Give me the phone number of your superior, please. Or should I simply call 999?'

'No! Don't do that!'

'You seem to think that my presence here constitutes an emergency,' I pointed out.

'No, but—'

The impressive front door opened. A man impressive enough to match the door came out. 'Thank you, Sergeant,' he said to the distressed guard. 'Is this Mrs Martin?'

I stood, not without difficulty. 'It is.'

'Then come with me, please.'

I was escorted inside. I refrained from giving the sergeant a triumphant look, which I hope counts in my favour at the pearly gates.

Inside all was chaos. The reception desk was occupied by a uniformed policeman, a second line of defence, I assumed. More uniforms milled about in the foyer, along with young people I presumed were students.

Tim made his way through the mob. 'Dorothy! I'm sorry I couldn't get to you in time, but they were asking me questions – and then they wouldn't let me leave—'

'Mrs Martin,' said the gentleman who had admitted me, 'perhaps we could find a quieter place to talk.'

'The middle of Piccadilly Circus?' I suggested, and was rewarded with a wintry smile.

He led Tim and me down a hallway into a small room equipped with a table, three straight chairs, and one lamp that had seen better days. He shut the door. 'Not the Ritz, but private, at least. Mrs Martin, my name is Peter Simms. I'm the liaison between university and city authorities here in Durham. I understand your husband is a highly ranked police officer in Belleshire?'

'He was the chief constable there for many years. His name is Alan Nesbitt. He retired some years ago, but he assists in investigations now and again, and right now he's helping his long-time friend David Tregarth with a town-and-gown matter here in Durham.' Plainly flim-flam would not work with this man.

'I see. And you are assisting him in this matter?'

'I do what I can. People sometimes seem to find me easy to talk to.'

'Ah.' He considered that for a moment.

'Mr Simms, plainly something fairly drastic has happened here. Can you tell me what?'

I could feel Tim, sitting beside me, grow tense.

'Yes, you need to know. A student has been viciously attacked.' He ignored my gasp and continued. 'A man whom we presume to be another student assaulted him with a broken beer bottle, inflicting severe cuts to his face and arms. A large vein was severed, and the boy lost a good deal of blood before the chap living in the next room heard the disturbance and came to check. That's when the police were called.'

'And will he be all right?'

'It's touch and go at the moment, I'm told.'

'Did the attacker get away?'

'Unfortunately, yes. But the police have a positive identification, and he is being sought.'

Tim could bear it no longer. 'Dorothy, it was Colin Grimsby! And the student he half-killed is roommate to the one who told you about him, Charles Lambert.'

TWENTY-SEVEN

Of course that meant a long explanation of our suspicions and conclusions about the deaths of Nathan and Dr Armstrong, and how Alan and I became involved, and had sought the help of Tim and other students, and the few bits of actual evidence we had gathered. It all took a while. Mr Simms took careful notes.

'And I take it the police have all this information?' he said when we'd finished.

'Yes. David and Alan spent much of the morning with them. The problem was that, although we had a moral certainty that Colin was the villain of the piece, there was no evidence that would stand up in court. Now that he's attacked this poor boy, everything's different. And he even got the wrong one, if he was after Charles!'

'Yes. Thank you, Mrs Martin, and Mr Hayes. You may both leave now, if you wish. In fact, the traffic prohibitions have probably been lifted while we talked. The boys' room will be sealed off for some time, I imagine, but the rest of college will have to be opened up. Term begins on Monday, as you would know, Mr Hayes, and the returning students must be allowed in their rooms.'

'What is his name, Mr Simms?' asked Tim. 'The victim, I mean.'

'Mark Ziegler. I don't believe he can be visited in hospital, though. Not yet.'

'Probably not. I just want to add him to prayers. At the cathedral,' he explained.

Mr Simms looked slightly taken aback. 'I'm not sure – that is, I think he's Jewish.'

Tim smiled. 'So was Jesus.'

We were very subdued as we left the college. Tim came back to the castle with me, walking his bicycle. It was getting colder by the minute, and windy. I invited Tim up for a cup of tea.

Alan was there. 'I heard,' he said. He handed me a cup of tea as soon as I sat down. 'Laced with a tot of bourbon. I thought you'd want something hot and sustaining. What about you, Tim?'

'Just tea, thanks.'

I kept shaking my head as I thought over the multiple crimes one young man had committed, the lives he had ended, the ones he had disrupted. 'I can't help wondering why,' I said at last.

Both men knew what I meant. 'I didn't have a chance to talk to anyone before all hell broke loose at Jude's,' said Tim, 'but in the midst of all the confusion when the police came, I heard a few students talking about Colin. He wasn't well-liked, and that's unusual at Jude's. They're a small college and a pretty close-knit group. One chap said he'd wondered if the man was quite sane. Well, what he actually said was that he thought he was a bit loopy.'

'More than a bit, I'd say,' said Alan with a sigh. 'His actions have become increasingly violent. I think George Elliot was lucky he wasn't badly hurt. Grimsby seems to have slipped a cog. The police are taking no chances. The bulletin states that he is to be regarded as extremely dangerous and approached with caution.'

I held out my cup; Alan filled it with the mixture as before. 'Do we know anything about his background? Where he's from, anything like that?'

'The police are looking into that, assuming that he might head for home,' said Alan. 'All David and I could glean was that he lives in a village in Sussex, apparently with elderly grandparents, and that the family is not very well off.'

'Oh, dear! They've probably sacrificed a lot to send him to university, and now he's blown it. I do feel sorry for the grandparents.'

The bells sounded from the cathedral next door, calling us to evensong. We didn't even need to consult each other, but stood, put our raincoats on, and headed out. It was beginning to rain, but the distance was short, and we were dressed for it. As we entered the choir, I caught hold of Tim's arm. 'Mark Ziegler,' he said. I do love it when someone understands without a word.

So we prayed for Mark's recovery, and I at least for his miserable, confused attacker, and for the messy, confused world we live in, and heard lovely music, and went out into the cold evening somewhat restored.

The rain had that steady, determined aspect that makes one sure it's going to last all night, unabated. The wind had picked up as well, and no matter what direction I turned it was in my face. 'Oh, dear, Tim, I wish one could get a car up here.' I had to shout over the din of the storm, and I held tight to Alan's arm as I slithered over the wet cobblestones. 'We're going to be drowned rats by the time— What was *that*!'

It sounded like an explosion, loud enough to dominate even the noise of wind and rain. Alan peered into the blinding rain, uttered an expression unsuited to his surroundings, and pulled us both back. 'Inside! Back in the church! NOW!'

The verger was just closing the door. 'Let us in!' Alan demanded in his best policeman voice. 'Keep everyone in the building. Send someone to the other doors, or put a message on the speakers. A dangerous criminal is at large in the car park!'

In the instant before Tim and I rushed inside, the wind shifted for a moment and I saw what he had seen. A car had ploughed into a van and was backing up, apparently ready to have another go.

Alan had shouted to everyone outside in his most stentorian tones, and as they ran to the shelter of the church, he pulled out his phone, punched 999, and began to issue crisp orders.

Tim and I told the verger briefly what was happening, and then we did our best to calm the frightened crowd. It helped when a priest appeared, the one who had officiated at evensong. I didn't know if he was the dean or one of the canons, but his presence was soothing. Someone had explained to him.

'My dear friends,' he said, 'you could be in no safer place, no matter what danger threatens outside. This church has stood for over nine hundred years, and is as much a fortress as the castle next door. Come away from the doors into light and warmth, and I'm sure our excellent police will deal with the situation.'

And faintly, from beyond the solid stone walls and the solid oak doors, we could hear the stentorian sounds of sirens and see, through stained glass, a hint of flashing blue light.

Alan stayed on the phone with the police. Tim and I spoke with the priest, telling all we knew and nothing of what we speculated. He nodded sadly. 'These things are beginning to happen here, though nothing like as frequently as in your country.' I was too upset to correct him about my misleading accent. He disappeared for a few minutes and soon gentle, quiet organ music filled the space. Several clergy joined him. The frightened crowd took seats at the back of the nave, soothed by the music and the unruffled clerics.

If I had to take refuge from a homicidal maniac, I thought a trifle wildly, I couldn't imagine a nicer place to do it. It wasn't too long before the choir drifted in. Shorn of their vestments, the boys looked like the ordinary mischievous urchins that choir boys usually are, but their director rounded them up, along with the men, gave a cue to the organist, and they launched (by memory) into a lovely anthem by Purcell, 'Rejoice in the Lord Alway'. This was an edited version, without the solos, but words and music were both lovely, and we were further comforted.

We were all beginning to get a bit restive when Alan finally put down his phone and went to speak to the officiant. The priest nodded and stood in front of the congregation, motioning for silence and asking us to move closer to him.

'I hope you can hear me. Voices rather echo in here, I'm afraid. I have good news. The danger is past, and you may all go on your way.'

A subdued cheer. One man stood and asked, 'Did they get the scoundrel, then?'

Alan answered, 'Unfortunately, not. He was away before the police arrived. They know who he is, however, and have made sure he has left the area. You need not fear. The police are confident that they will capture him soon.'

The crowd muttered at that, not quite reassured. The priest

took over, dismissing us with a lovely prayer and a beaming smile.

'You and the reverend whoever-he-is make a good tag team,' I said as we made our way out into the now-gentle rain. 'Secular and sacred arms of authority.'

'Do you really think they'll catch up with him?' asked Tim quietly.

'I'm certain they will. Eventually. He's made it easier for them, now that his car is badly damaged.'

'Why did he do such a crazy thing?'

'You said it, my dear. Crazy. My guess is he's gone completely off the rails.'

'He never had too far to go, if what I overheard at Jude's is true,' said Tim. 'But where do you think he is?'

Alan sighed. 'I couldn't say this earlier. The people in the cathedral needed reassurance. Stirring up fear is almost never a good idea. But I think he isn't far away. My guess is that his mad fury is directed toward those he thinks have shopped him, and that would most likely be the students at St Jude's. They're under police surveillance, which should not only keep them safe but make it easier to capture poor Colin.'

In which suppositions my husband was both right and dangerously wrong.

We had reached the car park, and David got out of a car, hailed Tim, and hurried over to us. 'Tim, I drove up to save you a bike ride in the rain, but in view of what's happened, I'd like to give you all a ride to my house. Tim, we can put your bike in the boot – but I don't see it.'

'It's up at the castle. But I can easily ride. It's not far, and the rain's almost stopped.'

'I'd rather you collected it later,' David said firmly. 'Eileen's waiting for us, and I think she's cooking something that shouldn't be kept waiting. Come along.'

Tim shrugged and got into the car with us.

'He isn't worried about a meal, is he?' I whispered to Alan. He shook his head.

Eileen had made a delicious soup, just right for a chilly evening. It would only have improved with standing, a fact nobody mentioned. There was crusty bread and a chunk of wonderful cheese to go with it, and strawberries and cream to follow, and we left the table sated and content. By common consent we had said nothing about the disasters of the day. We were only too happy to set them aside for a little while.

It was still quite early when Alan stood. 'That was a perfect meal, Eileen, and we thank you for your gracious hospitality, David, but I think it's time we made our way back to the castle, if it's convenient for you to give us a ride.'

'Of course. And Eileen, I'd like you to let me take you home as well, after I return. Not a pleasant evening for walking.'

Especially, everyone was careful not to say, with a murderer on the loose.

David drove us to the cathedral car park, as close as he could get to our lodgings. 'Be careful,' he said as we thanked him and got out of the car. He might have been referring to the slippery cobbles.

So dark was the sky that it might have been midnight instead of early evening. We hurried as best we could. The rain had turned into that sort of drizzle that seems simply to hang in the air and penetrate to one's very pores.

The massive gate to the castle forecourt was closed; we had to enter through the small, low door cut into the big one. As we turned toward our staircase I saw Tim's bicycle looking forlorn. It had been propped up against a wall but had fallen into a puddle, probably blown over by the wind. 'Oh, poor thing! All that wet isn't going to do it a bit of good!' I moved toward it to pick it up, and a shadow, detaching itself from behind a buttress, was upon me before I could even scream.

TWENTY-EIGHT

I woke up in a strange bed in a strange room, feeling as though I'd had a ride in a gigantic rock-tumbler. There wasn't an inch of me that didn't hurt. I blinked bleary eyes and tried to focus.

'Ah. You're with us again.' It was Alan's voice, sounding a bit thin, but definitely his voice. 'Have a little lovely chipped ice.'

'Water,' I croaked. My mouth was so dry my tongue stuck to my teeth.

'They won't let you have water quite yet, love, until they're sure you won't choke. Open your mouth.'

He spooned in a piece or two of ice. I crunched them obediently, and they did help. 'Where . . .?' It came out as a cough. I tried again. 'Where am I? And who's "they"?'

'You're in hospital. "They" are the doctors and nurses attending you, and an officious lot they are, I must say.'

I would have pursued that, rather enjoying the idea of my husband being bossed around, but I fell asleep in the middle of a sentence.

The next time I woke my mind was in much better working order, though my body still felt perfectly awful. Alan was still there.

I worked myself up, painfully, into a half-sitting position. Alan helped, finding the button that raised the head of the bed. 'I feel like death warmed over,' I said.

'I'll bet you do,' he said, still in that odd voice. He cleared his throat. 'It's a bit of a miracle that nothing is broken, but you seem to have bruises on your bruises.'

'But what happened? The last thing I remember is walking through that funny little door into the castle courtyard. Did I slip on the cobblestones or something?'

'Or something. You were attacked, my dear, by our old nemesis Colin Grimsby.'

'No! But why would he attack me? Or has he gone right round the bend, attacking anyone in sight?'

'He's not making a great deal of sense at the moment, but—'

I interrupted. 'He's in custody, then?'

'Oh, yes, and booked on a list of charges as long as your arm. As I say, he's rambling, but from what anyone can make out, he finally worked out that it was you pursuing him and causing him all sorts of inconvenience, so he decided to settle you once and for all.' Alan swallowed again. 'He nearly did, you know, darling. It took four of us to pull him away. The porter was in his lodge, heard the mêlée and came to help me, and two brawny students came in just then. If it hadn't been for them . . .' He took a swallow from the glass at my bedside, water this time.

'You poor dear! You must be bruised and battered, too.'

He tossed that aside. 'I only wish there were something to be done about your pain. I had to tell them you couldn't take any of the opiates; they were all ready to give you a hefty jab of morphine.'

I shuddered. 'That would really have done it. If anything could make me feel worse, it would be being desperately sick for hours on end. Thank you for stopping them. I must say, I do sometimes feel sorry for myself, being unable to take any really effective painkillers.'

'At least you'll never become addicted to them; that's one blessing.'

I shifted position in a vain attempt to get comfortable. 'And another one is that Colin hadn't armed himself with a broken bottle this time. Oh! Is that student all right? What was his name?'

'Mark something. Yes, he's still in hospital, but he'll be fine once his blood level is back to normal. The young bounce back very quickly. I'm told he'll need plastic surgery, though, to repair his face. It was very badly cut. As you say, you are fortunate.'

'I suppose. I don't feel very fortunate at the moment, just sore. Oh, well, anyway now we can go home with a clear conscience, as soon as they'll let me go. Problem solved, Amanda in the clear, everybody happy.'

Alan cleared his throat. 'Well . . . I'm afraid not quite. Certainly we've been able to run several crimes to earth and lay them at Colin's door. Good grief, I'm not at my best with metaphors today, am I? What I mean to say is that Colin is definitely to blame for the attack on poor Mark at St Jude's, for the idiotic rampage in the cathedral car park, and for the attack on you. With eyewitnesses in each case, he could do little but admit to those incidents.'

'I suppose some lawyer will file an insanity defence.'

'Probably. The point is that he has stated absolutely that he had nothing to do with Nathan's death, or Dr Armstrong's, or the attack on Mrs Carly at the home.'

'And the destruction at George's house?'

'He won't talk about that.'

I lay back among the pillows with a groan. 'Blast! We're back where we started!'

The nurse came in then and glared at Alan. She'd heard the groan. 'I can't have you upsetting my patient! And it's time for her medicine. Doctor has ordered a proper painkiller.'

'Your patient,' said my husband in his steeliest tones, 'is my wife. We understand one another perfectly. If she wishes me to leave, I will leave. If she wishes me to stay, I will stay. And you will administer no opiate medication to my wife, or I will sue you, the doctor, and this hospital for malpractice!'

Not even an officious nurse can stand up to my husband in that mood. I was spared the medicine that would have made me miserably sick, but I did consent to a sleeping pill. For a few hours I was removed from the vale of pain, and from distress about unsolved crimes.

The next time I surfaced it was morning. Bright sunshine flooded the room. Alan and the nurse arrived at the same time, each regarding the other with suspicion.

'I suppose,' said the nurse haughtily, 'you have no objection to my giving *your wife* her breakfast.'

The level of sarcasm in those two words would have withered a lesser man. Alan simply smiled. 'None at all. As I assume you have no objection to my doing the same.'

He held up a bag with the familiar mermaid logo. The nurse

sniffed, set down a tray with a clatter, and marched out, her face stiff with indignation.

Alan lifted the dish-cover on the tray. Beneath it lurked a plate with some tough-looking scrambled eggs and discouraged toast. Some withered orange sections and a cup of tepid water with a tea bag in it completed my repast.

Alan lifted the tray and deposited it on the floor.

'She'll trip over it when she comes back,' I said.

'Good. Now, do you want this it bed, or would you rather eat in the comfort of your chair?'

'I want to get up. If I can. I'm stiff as old oak.'

'The only cure for that is activity. Take my arm. And I brought your dressing gown.'

'I didn't pack one.'

'I know. It was time you had a new one, anyway.'

He helped me out of bed, ignoring my piteous groans. Before he assisted me to the recliner in the corner, he pulled a handsome brocade bathrobe out of a bag and slipped it over my fetching hospital gown.

'How's that?'

'Positively regal. But I have to sit down before I fall down.'

More groans, but once settled in the chair, I actually did feel a bit better. He pulled the tray table away from the bed and put it in front of me, spread with a veritable feast of pastry, along with coffee that smelled like heaven.

'Starbucks is going to miss you when we go home.'

'Indeed. I've become quite chatty with the baristas. I believe they think, from the quantity of food that I buy, that I have a household full of starving children. Or else nine wives.'

'Mm,' I replied, through a mouthful of croissant.

The doctor came in just as I finished eating. He looked at the remains on the table and chuckled. 'I see our catering doesn't meet with your approval. By the way, you'd best move that tray. Someone will come a cropper.'

I was hard put not to laugh as Alan hastily put it on top of the radiator. I refrained, however. Laughing hurt.

'Have I forgotten something?' the doctor went on. 'I don't recall giving orders that you should be up.'

'You didn't. I just couldn't stay in that bed another minute.

Have you ever tried to get comfortable in a hospital bed? Even without a thousand bruises?'

'I have not. You have a point.' He looked at my chart. 'You've come off amazingly well, you know, considering the violence you suffered. No broken bones, no internal injuries. Bruises heal, you know, though at your age it takes time. You'd do well to consider a good painkiller to help you through.'

'Maybe no one explained to you, doctor. Painkillers make me violently sick. I'm not happy about it, but I'll just have to tough it out with over-the-counter stuff until the pain goes away.'

'Ah.' He made a note on the chart. 'I see. Well, assuming you have a good supply of ibuprofen or whatever you prefer, I see no reason why you shouldn't be discharged.'

Alan spoke up. 'We had planned to leave Durham tomorrow to go home. We're staying at the castle, and the students will be returning and reclaiming their rooms.'

He frowned. 'Where's home? America? I can't possibly allow a transatlantic flight.'

Alan and I sighed together. I suppose my accent and vocabulary had reverted, under stress. 'No, no,' I assured him. 'I'm American originally, but I've lived in Belleshire for many years now. Sherebury. It's about five hours by train.'

Another frown. 'With a change in London. I'm afraid that won't do. You'll need to stay the night in London and go on in the morning, or you'll be in real trouble by journey's end.'

We accepted that after a silent consultation, and Alan went back to the castle to get me some clothes. The ones I had worn were, they told me, fit for nothing but rags after Colin had done his work. 'And that's one more thing to add to his bill,' I thought bitterly. 'He owes me a new set of clothes.'

David was at the wheel when Alan took me downstairs in the wheelchair the hospital insisted on. 'The walking wounded?' David queried.

'More like the wheeled wounded. But I can walk, really. This confounded place wouldn't let me.' To prove it I stood, slowly, tottered to the car on Alan's arm, and collapsed in the front seat.

I still didn't know Durham well enough to wonder where we were going, until David pulled up in front of the Indigo.

'You're not climbing all those stairs at the castle,' said Alan firmly. 'You'll be far more comfortable here.'

I thought about protesting. Alan and I are certainly not among the wealthy of the world, and this hotel positively shouted its luxury status. Then I thought about the stairs to the small room we'd been calling home, and shut up.

Alan had got me a walker, or 'Zimmer frame' as I'd had to learn to call them here. I found I could walk fairly well with it, while deploring how much it made me look like an old lady. I don't mind pulling the 'old' card when I find it useful, but I hate to think it's really true.

The staff fussed over me, making me feel more senile every minute, but I had to admit the room was marvellously comfortable. Alan had managed to pack everything we needed for the night and said he'd go back for the rest tomorrow. Then he ordered a light lunch from room service, an indulgence we seldom allow ourselves, and when we had disposed of that he sat down with a purposeful look on his face.

'I have news,' he said.

To tell the truth, I didn't want news. I wanted a hot shower to help with the aches and pains, and then a nap. A long nap. I suppose my face showed my lack of enthusiasm. Alan always says I should never play poker; my face is too easily read.

'I'll be brief, but I think this will interest you. They've found George.'

For a moment I couldn't remember who George was. 'George? Oh, *George*! Where? How?'

Alan smiled. Well, it was more of a smirk, actually. 'Things worked out well. As you predicted, or at least hoped, his car ran out of . . . I don't suppose one can say petrol, since it doesn't use any. At any rate, it stopped, miles from any charging station. They're fairly thin on the ground, you know.'

Well, no, I didn't, but it didn't matter.

'He had also forgotten to charge his mobile. Understandable, but unfortunate. He's no great walker, our George. He walked for some distance before someone took pity on him and gave him a ride to the nearest garage. They towed his car back in to charge it, but because the police had put out a bulletin, they were called. They arrived just as the Tesla did.'

'When did all this happen? And where?'

'Yesterday evening, a few hours before . . . Well, yesterday. I only just heard about it this morning, being otherwise occupied. As to where, the car gave up a few miles outside Birmingham. He was apparently going home to Mummy.'

'Given her temperament, I wouldn't have thought she'd welcome him with open arms.'

'David tells me she was quite frosty when the police phoned her. Said she wasn't totally surprised that he had proved himself incompetent once again, and hung up.'

'The psychiatrists would love to get their hands on him, I'm sure. Deprived childhood, plenty of money but no love, and see what a mixed-up mess resulted. Actually, I'm not sure they're totally wrong. Neither he nor Nathan turned out very well. But have the police been able to get any kind of sensible story out of him? Why he led them such a chase, for example?'

'I gather he's sticking to his story about being afraid for his life.'

'But if he thought his attacker wanted to silence him for fear he'd tell someone, once he *had* told someone – me – he was safe.'

'Perhaps logic is not his strong point. Or perhaps, as we've surmised, he has some other reason to avoid the authorities. At any rate, if you'll be settled here for a bit, I propose to go back on the trail this afternoon.'

'I'm in the lap of luxury. Go, hound – nose to the ground.'

He'd better not be slow about it, either, I thought drowsily as I went down for my nap. By this time tomorrow we'd be on a train back home. Well, London first. I'd have to call Jane to tell her we were coming. Maybe we'd skip the stopover in London. I was feeling quite a lot better. I shifted position, found a few more sore spots, and changed my mind.

George would tell us it was Colin who ruined his house. And left his button caught in the roses. His jacket. We had to find his jacket, with a missing button. That would clinch that part of it. Button. Button, button, who's got the button . . .

'Nice nap, darling?'

I swam up out of my dream and tried to sit up. 'Ouch.

Lovely dream. Something about . . . no, I don't remember, but it was pleasant. Nothing hurt.'

'Ah, yes, after a certain age that can be the essence of a good dream. No pain. How do you feel now you're awake?'

I took a mental inventory. 'Not awful. Not great. Much better than yesterday. But if I ever get to talk to that young man, I have quite a few things to say to him. What luck with George?'

'I didn't talk to him, as you can imagine. They're being a bit stuffy about non-police getting into the act.'

I snorted. 'Non-police, indeed! You outrank them all!'

'I used to. Not anymore. They did allow David to sit in, however. George has been willing to state, for the record, that it was Colin who did all the damage at his house. Or most of it. The ersatz policemen contributed a bit.'

'But what happened? Why was Colin even there?'

'David says George isn't telling the whole story. The way he tells it, the boy knocked on his door just after George talked to him, David.'

I nodded. 'On the phone, when we were at the restaurant.'

'Right. And he came in, saying he'd been in Nathan's college with him and wanted to express his condolences. They talked for a bit, and then, George says, he was trying to hurry Colin away, since David was coming, when he flew into a rage and started throwing things about. That was when George decided it was wiser to leave, and ran off. Full stop.'

'There's a big chunk missing from that account.'

'Yes. I don't believe Colin took offence simply at being hurried out the door. And if the encounter had truly been only a routine condolence call, why is George now afraid of Colin?'

'Exactly. And I think I know how we can get George to open up and tell us the whole story.'

Alan looked sceptical. 'I assure you, my dear, the Durham police are well-trained in interrogation techniques.'

'I'm sure. But they're not allowed to terrify a subject. I know someone who can and will.'

Alan's face lit up as we said, in unison, 'His mother!'

TWENTY-NINE

Saturday morning. Instead of being on a train to London, Alan and I were sitting in the Elliot home in Birmingham, along with David and the two Elliots, mother and son. She had flatly refused to come to Durham or Auckland for a conference and was grudging about seeing us in Birmingham, but finally concurred. As I thought about it, I decided that was better anyway. In the house where he had spent his childhood, George might be less inclined to bluster and prevaricate.

Mrs Elliot had also refused to allow police into her home. David and Alan were there on sufferance, because George, who was still in custody as a material witness, had been released to David's care for a couple of days. She had said nothing disparaging about my presence, which surprised me.

The first thing she said when we were settled in her drawing room (that was the only possible name for the elegant chamber) surprised me still more. 'You will see fair play, I trust, Mrs Martin.'

'Um . . . I'll try,' I stammered. Useless to protest that David and Alan would never resort to anything less.

'Very well. George, don't slump. Now. What is it you want to know?'

'Mother, I've already told them—'

'Speak when you're spoken to, George. Mr Tregarth?'

'Thank you, Mrs Elliot. We need to know, in detail, all that transpired from the time Mr Grimsby arrived at your home, Mr Elliot, until you and he left the house.'

Mrs Elliot fixed her son with a gimlet eye. 'In detail, George. All the details.'

George, who seemed to have become smaller, began his recitation. Colin had come to pay his respects, had then flown into a temper and begun throwing things—

'Stop!' said his mother. 'A man does not simply fly into a

temper for no reason. Exactly what did he say at that point? What did you say?'

'He . . . I . . . we were talking about the circumstances of Nathan's death.'

We waited. His mother's toe began to beat a tattoo on the exquisite Persian carpet.

'He told me that he had actually seen Nathan drown, and had tried to rescue him, but failed.'

'Which was a lie, and you knew it was a lie. What did you say to him?'

He coughed and fidgeted.

'Oh, for heaven's sake, George. I suppose you asked him if he'd drowned Nathan. And I suppose you suggested a reason why he might have done. Knowing Nathan, I can guess. Was it blackmail?'

'I – I did mention that I knew he had owed Nathan some money, and—'

'And you told him that the money was now owed to you. Implying, I'm sure, that you would go to the authorities with your suspicions unless he paid. With interest, I'm sure.'

Mrs Elliot stood, brushing imaginary lint from her skirt. I was reminded of Pilate washing his hands. 'I've long suspected you were adopting Nathan's ways. A great pity. You were always the more intelligent of the two, and for a time I thought you might be able to make something of yourself, make an honest living. I see I was wrong. Take him away, Mr Tregarth.'

I could almost find it in my heart to feel sorry for George Elliot. He had no father, no brother, and now no mother. He had deserted his job in Auckland and would certainly face a bit of time in prison for various minor charges.

'And I'll bet,' I murmured to Alan as we rode back to Durham in the back seat of David's car, 'the first thing Mum will do is call her lawyer to write George out of her will.'

'Never understanding that at least part of George's troubles can be laid at her feet. No love . . .'

'At least she has a strong sense of honour.'

'And of discipline. You were quite right to get her involved. George couldn't stand up to that formidable will.'

Eventually we got back to our luxurious hotel. David

dropped us off and then took George back to the police station, where I assumed he would stay while they decided how to deal with him.

I sat down and sighed. 'We should have gone home today. It's too late now, and I'm too tired. Tomorrow will have to do, or Monday. At least our case is now complete, and we can go home with a clear conscience.'

'Oh, no, my dear. We have a lovely set of speculations and a scenario that holds together. Colin kills Nathan. Armstrong sees him and flees to a place where he thinks he will be safe. Colin finds him, kills him, and lets Amanda take the blame, staging another attack to cement the case against her. Thanks to you and your persistence, my love, that case begins to crumble. Colin goes to George – why, by the way?'

'Probably to find out how much George knows, especially if he knows about the money owed to Nathan.'

'Probably. He goes, things do not go well, he loses what little composure he still possesses and wrecks George's house, with the aid of some almost innocent singers. But you're still closing in, you've talked to George, which means it's now time to go after you, first rampaging in the car park and then attacking you directly. For which, incidentally, I owe him something.'

'Yes, dear. But pay it with a withering statement in court.'

'You may be sure I shall. But let me summarize: we have lots of evidence against Colin for many of his offences. But we have not one whit to prove that he did drown Nathan.'

'But – but everything he did later—'

'Conjecture, my dear. Inference. You can't show an inference to a jury.'

I wanted to have a temper tantrum, stamp and scream and rant, but I was too weary and my poor bruised body hurt too much. 'Then I wish Colin Grimsby had an inquisitor for a mother who could get the truth out of him!'

'No such luck, I'm afraid. David told me that his parents are dead and he lives with elderly grandparents. Very strict, very prim and proper, but apparently little backbone. No help there, I fear. Tomorrow is Sunday, love. If you're up to sitting in a pew for a bit, let's take our troubles to the cathedral. Can't hurt, and who knows? Our guardian angels might just come through.'

I felt fairly decent in the morning, but I was certainly not up to a walk to the cathedral, so we took a cab. 'We're spending money like water,' I commented. 'We'll have to go on a bread-and-beans diet when we go home.'

'I've always been partial to beans on toast,' was Alan's unconcerned reply.

The service was as lovely as usual, and as soothing, but we left with no more ideas about Colin and his connection with two murders. As we sat over a light lunch in the Undercroft Restaurant, I worried over the problem like a dog with a bone.

'There's the button,' I offered, without much confidence. 'Colin does have a jacket like that, right?'

'Right. They found it in his flat. Not looking very natty, I'm told.'

'And there's a button missing?'

'Two, actually, according to David. One from the right sleeve, one in front. And two others hanging by a thread. Colin apparently hasn't enough domestic skills to keep his clothes in order.'

'Hmph! Doesn't take much skill to sew on a button.'

'No. I did it during my years as a widower. I'm sure you know the chief reason I married you was to rid myself of that chore.'

'I long suspected your motives. But if the button we found matches the others on the jacket—'

'That's proof he was at George's house. Which we already knew.'

I sighed heavily. 'Alan, what are we going to do?'

'I confess I have no idea. I fear this may turn out to be one of those detestable instances of "we know who dunnit, but can't prove it".'

'No!' People turned to look. I moderated my voice. 'No, we can't let that happen. There would always be some people who believed it was Aunt Amanda, and that's simply not acceptable.'

'She wouldn't know, my dear. And in any case, "always" may not be a very long time for her.'

'Doesn't matter. She wouldn't know why people gave her funny looks, or stopped speaking to her, but she would know something was wrong, and she would be unhappy, and I don't care if it's only for a few more months, she's an old dear, and I won't have it!'

My voice had risen again. The couple at the next table decided they'd finished and left hastily.

Alan said nothing, but his look told me I was making a spectacle of myself, one of the cardinal sins of English society. I finished my cottage pie in silence.

'Can you walk as far as Tesco, do you think?' he asked as we left the cathedral. 'I'd like to find a newspaper. Or I could leave you here whilst I fetch it.'

'No, I'll come. It's a lovely day. We can pick up some naproxen. It helps a bit, and I'm all out. And then I can find a place to sit before we climb back up the hill.'

'I thought I might call David to see if he could pick us up. It's Sunday – no congestion charge.'

Slowly, leaning heavily on the walker, I hobbled down the hill to the Market Square, all the time hating the picture I presented of a helpless old lady. One more debt owed by Colin Grimsby, I thought crossly. I really, really wanted that young man to get what was coming to him.

Vengeance is mine, saith the Lord. The thought merely added guilt to my anger.

We made our purchases and went back to the Square, where the few benches were occupied. When we approached, though, a young couple stood and offered us their place.

I couldn't make up my mind whether to be grateful or insulted. Alan, however, said and did exactly the right things and shamed me into thanking them.

'You're a better man than I am, Gunga Din,' I muttered when they had gone.

'You're just tired. Here's your pill, and a bottle of water, and when you've dealt with that, I bought this.' He showed me a large bar of dark chocolate.

'You spoil me. And I'm an old grouch, and I'm sorry.'

He just patted my hand and got out his phone to call David. 'He'll be here in a few minutes, and you can settle down, love, to your nap.'

'I don't know how I can sleep, with Colin Grimsby tramping through my head,' I retorted, but Alan was already absorbed in the *Sunday Times*. I took the features section away from him and was trying to work the simple crossword (I can't manage the cryptic one) when Alan jogged my elbow. 'Look at this, Dorothy!'

I wondered what international disaster was making news now. They come so frequently they've almost lost their power to shock.

'It's about the chap who's been diving in the Wear. You remember we saw him the other day.'

'Well, not to say *saw*. He was under water at the time.'

'Yes, yes, but there are pictures of his latest finds. One shows a net full of miscellany, with some ancient coins among other detritus. It's remarkably clear for a newspaper photo, and unless I've lost my eyesight completely, here is' – he pointed a finger – 'a button. Quite a familiar button, wouldn't you say?'

The picture was in black and white, but had it been in colour, that button would have been identical to the one we found.

'It's bigger,' said Alan. 'Not a sleeve button. Perhaps off the front of a jacket?'

'Alan! How old is the picture?'

'The article is dated today, but the picture has no date. Could have been snapped almost any time.'

'What do you think the diver does with the stuff that's of no importance?'

'Straight into the bin, I'd think.'

'We've got to stop him!' I stood in a hurry, hardly noticing the pain. 'Alan, this could be it!'

THIRTY

David drove up just then and I almost ran to the car, ignoring my infirmities. 'David, we have to go to the police station, quick! They might be able to stop this guy before he throws everything away!'

David blinked. 'Excuse me?'

Alan explained carefully, while I fidgeted impatiently. 'Alan, that's enough! David understands. And we need to move fast!' Alan and I were in the car by that time, and David had turned it in what I assumed was the direction to the station.

He and Alan exchanged looks, and Alan pulled out his phone. 'Ask for DI Harris,' David said, giving him a phone number. I remembered that the inspector was the one who had appeared at the Milton Home to talk with Eileen.

'Is he also in charge of the Grimsby tangle?' Alan asked. 'I've been moving on the periphery, you know.'

'No, but since we think it's all one, might as well begin with him.'

Alan's end of the conversation was not enlightening, but by the time it ended David was trying to find a place to park near the police station. I'd soon know how Harris responded.

The man at the front desk was not eager to let me in. David was all right; he was almost one of them. Alan, as a very senior officer, though retired, was treated with respect. I was a hanger-on, and the young constable knew how hangers-on were to be treated. Every courtesy, no concessions.

Alan smiled at him. 'Well done, constable. However, this lady is my wife, and an integral part of the investigation. Shall we all go through, or wait for the inspector?'

The young man swallowed nervously, his Adam's apple bobbing. 'Well, sir, you see . . . ah! Here *is* the inspector!'

Harris looked less than overjoyed to see us all, but he showed us to an interview room. 'I understand,' he said to David, 'that you believe some material evidence has been turned up by the chap digging in the river.' He paused. That didn't sound quite right. 'Er . . . diving for artefacts.' That, too, sounded peculiar. He let it go. 'I don't quite understand.'

Alan shot me a stern glance, and I closed my mouth. Okay, let him handle it. This was familiar territory to him, after all.

He handed Harris the newspaper, folded to the picture. 'You can see quite clearly that there is a button amidst the other materials found in the river. Certainly it's the ancient coins that are of interest to the archaeologist, but the button is of great interest to us, because it appears to match the one left by Colin Grimsby at the home of George Elliot – the home Colin damaged. If it is indeed a match, and did come from Colin's jacket, it places Colin in or near the river, at the place where Nathan Elliot was drowned. It seems imperative that the button not be discarded along with other unwanted material, don't you agree?'

Harris pondered, and then sighed. 'It would indeed be pleasant to have a bit of concrete evidence to shore up the elaborate web of conjecture and inference that we've spun. A button is as good as a bullet if it can get the job done.' He sighed again. 'You do realize that the lot may have been pitched already?'

I couldn't keep silent any longer. 'That's why we got here as fast as we could, the moment we saw that picture!'

Harris's smile was wintry. 'Yes, well done. Now if you'll excuse me?' He pulled out his phone, and we were dismissed.

David dropped us at our hotel for our usual Sunday afternoon nap, though a little late. I'd thought I would be too steeped in anxiety to sleep, but I dropped off the moment I lay down and woke only when my stomach began to complain of being unfed. It was well past supper time, and we'd had no tea. I sat up and yawned. 'What do you think, Alan? A big expensive meal downstairs, or something simpler? Only I still can't walk very far.'

'We could have a bar meal. It being Sunday night, I'm not sure what our other options might be.'

For some reason, Sunday night in many English cities, even cathedral cities, is pretty much a food desert. I suppose it goes

back to the days when Sunday was a day of rest and work
was frowned upon. It's a philosophy I actually find refreshing,
but it's certainly inconvenient for travellers. 'I suppose there
might be a pizza place open. We could order takeaway.'

None of the options sounded attractive, but my stomach
was beginning to rumble rather loudly.

Alan's phone rang. 'Ah, David. What news?' He turned on
the speaker.

'They have the button and have matched it to Colin's
jacket. Now it's time to confront Colin with it and ask for
an explanation.'

'His solicitor will be there, of course,' said Alan.

'Of course, and Harris thinks that may mean Colin will say
nothing at all.'

'It's a pity Colin doesn't have a mother like Mrs Elliot to
bully him into talking,' I said tartly.

On the other end of the line, David cleared his throat. 'That's
one reason I'm calling, Dorothy. It seems various officials
involved in the investigation were impressed with your success
in getting George Elliot to talk. They think you might have
some influence with Colin. Would you be willing to come to
headquarters and have a go?'

Would I be willing! Willing to confront the nasty little thug
who had caused me such pain, and who, I was sure, had killed
two people and threatened who knew how many others?

'David, give us time to pick up a sandwich or something
from the bar, and I'm all yours!'

A jail cell is not a congenial place for a chat. I would have
preferred to meet with young Colin there, welcoming any
psychological stress that might put him at a disadvantage.
However, police procedure dictated that the discussion take
place in an interrogation room. His lawyer would, in any
case, have insisted on the least threatening environment
possible, and I didn't actually mind greatly. I had, in my
teaching days, known how to be intimidating in the cosy
confines of a fourth-grade classroom. I'd manage.

'You can't actually threaten him, you know,' said Alan
quietly as we walked to the room. 'Judge's rules.'

'I do know the rules, Alan, having read every English mystery written in the past hundred years or so. I'll be careful.'

He took a deep breath and raised his eyes heavenward, but said nothing more.

The room wasn't all that much more hospitable than a jail cell. The walls were painted in that dispiriting pea-soup green that law enforcement agencies all over the world must have bought years ago by the tanker-load. The furnishings consisted of a table and straight chairs of some dark wood. There was one small window, uncurtained and barred. I noticed a video camera high on one wall.

The four of us – David, Alan, a policeman I didn't know, and I – entered and sat down. I noted that the table was slightly sticky to the touch with varnish that had never dried properly. I hoped I wouldn't stick to the chair, which was, even in the first few seconds, proving to be every bit as uncomfortable as it looked.

The policeman introduced himself as Detective Chief Inspector Drendall, in charge of the complex case. I was delighted to know that someone of high rank had been handed the unwelcome job of trying to put all the pieces together. 'As it is somewhat irregular to have members of the public present for an interrogation, Mrs Martin, I have taken the liberty of deputizing you. For this occasion only, I might add.' There was a welcome twinkle in his eye. 'Mr Nesbitt and Mr Tregarth are, of course, sworn officers, a status which does not lapse upon retirement. I have informed Mr Grimsby's solicitor about the arrangements.'

'I don't imagine he's happy,' I commented.

'Not entirely, no, and he will certainly be vigilant in making sure his client's rights are not violated.'

Two men, one young, one older, came into the room just then, and for the first time, I met Colin Grimsby.

I said nothing as everyone was introduced, but my mind was busy. How was I to approach this young man? A mere boy, he seemed to me, with the truculent look of a cowardly bully, sullen and insolent. Oh, I'd met his type dozens of times, and I knew how to deal with them. This wasn't going to be at all hard.

I hoped.

Mr Drendall opened the session with the customary date, time, and names of those present, for the sake of the recording. With no equipment on the table, I assumed the video cam was equipped for sound. The attorney made a brief statement, also for the record, that he objected to the presence of non-police personnel, especially as one of them could be assumed to have an attitude prejudicial to his client. Alan kicked me unobtrusively before I could object to the objection.

The inspector spoke. 'Now, Mr Grimsby. You have confessed to several crimes, and your confession is on record. You have been accused of other very serious crimes and have refused to answer questions about them. We now have evidence to connect you with one of them. Have you anything to say?'

'My client prefers to remain silent,' said the attorney swiftly.

Colin smirked.

Inspector Drendall looked at me.

I pulled a button out of my pocket, set it on the table, and looked steadily, silently, at Colin.

The smirk disappeared. He looked at his lawyer, looked at the floor, looked at the video cam.

I pushed the button forward an inch, still looking at Colin, still silent.

It didn't take long for him to break. 'That . . . where did you get that? What are you trying to prove? I thought the police didn't allow evidence out of their hands. That doesn't mean anything! You could have got it anywhere. Anyway, I never saw it before.'

His attorney tried to shut him up. 'My client will not answer any more questions.'

'Your client has not been asked any more questions, sir,' said Alan gently.

I let him stew for a little longer and then said, 'It's always easier in the end to tell the truth. It's very hard to tell a long, consistent lie.' I decided it was time to risk it. I sat back, trying to seem at ease in that inquisitorial chair. 'Tell us, why did you kill Nathan Elliot?'

'I didn't mean to! It was an accident! He slipped off the

bank. I tried to catch him. That's how the button came off. Damn cheap jacket, shedding buttons all over the shop!'

'You were talking about the money you owed him?'

'You think you know everything, don't you? I told him I'd pay him back, but he wanted it right that minute, and I didn't have it. He said he'd go to my grandparents and—'

'Mr Grimsby is upset! I demand that this interview be terminated!' The lawyer was shouting, but Colin paid no attention.

'They're too old! They don't understand that a man needs some fun, and some money in his pocket. It wasn't my fault the bloody horse fell down! Just my damn bad luck!'

He was raving, but the inspector could sort it all out later. 'And your bad luck that Dr Armstrong saw the whole thing with Nathan.' I said it very quietly.

'Stupid old git! He was sick anyway. I just helped him along. Did him a favour, really.'

The attorney stood and roared 'This interview is over!'

The inspector looked at the camera. 'Interview terminated.' He glanced at his watch and spoke the time. He opened the door, and a constable came in to take Colin away.

THIRTY-ONE

'The solicitor will claim intimidation, threats, coercion, what have you.'

We were halfway to London, comfortably seated in a first-class carriage, courtesy of David. 'Of course he will,' I replied. 'But the video is perfectly clear, and perfectly damning. All the police did later was clarify bits of that wild statement, what he said about his grandparents and about his betting on the horses. Do you think his insistence that Nathan's death was an accident will stick?'

'Don't know. Doesn't matter. He admitted to murdering Armstrong, in front of witnesses and on tape. He's not going to be endangering the public for a very long time.'

I watched the sheep in the passing meadow. Not quite full grown, but no longer frisky lambs, they nibbled grass in their stupid, placid way, paying no attention to the monster speeding past them. I wondered what their future held? Were they doomed to appear on someone's dinner table before too long, or would they provide scarves and sweaters for many years?

'Alan, do you think prisoners can really become rehabilitated?'

'Some do. The ones who want to change, who fell into crime because they had no other way to live.'

'Colin isn't like that. He's just a surly, selfish boy who thinks the world owes him a living. You know who I feel sorry for?'

Alan smiled and patted my hand. 'The grandparents, of course. You always have to find someone to feel sorry for. What do you want to bet they're thoroughly nasty, stern, judgemental people, just as unpleasant in their own way as Mrs Elliot?'

The drinks cart came up the aisle. Alan got us each a bottle of wine, poured it, and raised his glass. 'Here's to someone worthy of your sympathy: Aunt Amanda, now free to live out her days in peace!'

'Aunt Amanda!' I echoed. 'And I'll throw in David, settled in a home of his own with a terrific lodger, and Tim's lawyer, who thinks he can prove undue influence and get Tim's inheritance back. *And*, with great love: to home!'